SEARCHING FOR SOMETHING SPECIAL

CAROLYN MERS

CAROLYN MERS

Copyright © 2017 Carolyn Mers

All rights reserved. No part of this publication may be reproduced, stored in a retrieval system or transmitted in any form by any means, electronic, mechanical, photocopying, recording or otherwise without the author's express written permission, except for brief quotations or citations for literary critiques or reviews as provided by USA copyright law.

Written and published in the USA by Carolyn A. Mers

ISBN- 10:1542449006

ISBN-13:978-1542449007

DEDICATION

This story is dedicated to the memory of my grandparents and the little country church where they worshipped in Orchardville, Illinois.

Julias Linza Manring

November 18, 1903 – January 13, 1984

Married October 26, 1926

May Sons Manring

February 10, 1906 – August 13, 1970

DISCLAIMER
The towns mentioned in this story are real communities within the southern region of Illinois, however, the story is a work of fiction. Any reference to an event, place, or person, living or deceased, is coincidental, fictitious or used with permission. The author acknowledges the reference of various products that are protected by trademark rights. These references were used fictitiously and without permission. They were not authorized nor sponsored by the trademark owners.

ACKNOWLEDGMENTS

With heartfelt gratitude, I want to thank Gary and Andrea Dahmer for allowing me to use their names as well as The Davie School Inn as a starting point for this novel. Though their names are real, their identities and life stories have been fictionalized (and aged) for the purpose of this book. A story about overcoming grief, rebirth and moving forward.

The Davie School Inn is a prime example of rebirth and repurposed use of a 1910 school building in Anna, IL. A unique transformation of a historic school building into an awesome and unique B&B that should be on everyone's list of places to stay while visiting Southern Illinois. It was a weekend stay at The Davie School Inn in 2015 that inspired the author to begin writing her first novel.

www.davieschoolinn.com

Like Davie School Inn on Facebook

I want to thank everyone who encouraged and supported the effort to bring this novel to print, especially my dear friends and proofreaders:
Patricia Bethea
Debbi Clover
Rose Marie Fitzgerald

Editor:
Cindy K. Manjounes, EdD, PhD

Cover photo provided by:
Elizabeth Crocker
Rainbows 'n' Frogs Photography
Houston, TX

Follow her on Facebook at: Rainbows 'n' Frogs
or
www.thewayiseeitthroughmylens.blogspot.com

INTRODUCTION

Monday afternoon, with all the mundane chores completed, DK relaxed in the olive-green wing back chair near the oversized, picture window. A cup of hot tea on the table next to her had turned cold. The small plate of cookies was untouched. Bandit, the calico cat, slept contently on the hearth of the fireplace with the afternoon sun streaming in on her. Tea and cookies had always been a comforting quiet time in her day before she set about to prepare dinner for her and David. Now, the afternoon routine, only served as a reminder that she was alone and didn't need to plan a dinner after all.

DK held the morning paper in her hand, attempting to read the news. However, her mind kept wandering away from the printed page. Nothing particular on her mind, she was just unable to concentrate on any of the written words. DK stared out the window at the summer flowers growing in the perfectly manicured flower beds that David had helped her build over the past thirty-eight years. The field of Day Lilies created a beautiful rainbow of color, from creamy white to deep burgundy red, and neon orange.

Then, suddenly, she spotted them; the Surprise Lilies! Her Grandma Bridges called them Naked Ladies, due to their bare stems without leaves. The bare stalks seemed to just pop up in full bloom out of the ground overnight without any preview of their coming, no tell-tale buds waiting to open, which is why they are often called Surprise Lilies. DK always took delight in the first sighting of the pink trumpet shaped flowers and shouting to David,

"The Naked Ladies have arrived!" The first year they popped up in her garden, David charged from his home office to the living room window to see what in the world she could be looking at. When he learned, it was only a simple flower with no leaves, he half scowled, half laughed, shook his head, then retreated to his office to work on a new client's quarterly taxes. Spreadsheets and numbers were his world. He just didn't understand her excitement over that silly looking flower. As the years went by, he continued to play along in her little ritual, just to make her smile. He always ran with exaggerated wonder to the window, then faking disappointment that there weren't real naked women dancing around on his front lawn, he would retreat to his own personal sanctuary.

Today, she stops herself just short of shouting for David to come see the naked ladies. He won't be coming to do his usual laugh and feigned disappointment, but she knows most certainly he is watching her smile from his place in heaven.

For the first time in her life, the sight of those flowers brings tears to her eyes, instead of the usual excitement associated with the surprise. Her once cherished memory becomes the reality that she is now all alone.

CHAPTER ONE

DK awoke with a pounding headache. The bed, a disheveled mess from tossing and turning, barely an hour of good sleep all night. She staggered her way to the kitchen, put on a pot of coffee, made her way to the family room couch to wait for the coffee to brew, then promptly fell into a deep sleep.

Sometime later, Bandit was sitting on DK's chest, nuzzling against her face and meowing loudly. Her continuous purr sounded like a motorboat. She was tired of waiting for her breakfast and was determined to not be kept waiting any longer.

DK awoke a bit more refreshed this time around. She fed Bandit, grabbed a yogurt for herself, and realized just how long she had been asleep when she reached for the coffee pot. The coffee pot timer automatically shuts the pot off after one hour and the pot was quite cold. She looked closely at the clock and calculated she had been sleeping for over three hours. With that; she grabbed a glass, added a heavy pour of milk, a few spoons of sugar, then filled the glass with ice and added the cold coffee. Iced coffee it would be today.

After she showered and was fully functioning, she paced around the room and tried to figure out what to do with her day. She was feeling completely alone, unneeded and lost. She felt caged and confined, almost like a prisoner in her own home. She grabbed her cell phone and quickly searched for Liz's phone number. When Liz answered the phone, DK asked if she was available to keep an eye on Bandit, that she had a sudden urge to get out of town for a while.

Liz responded, "Of course, I can. When do you want me to start?" DK told her she had fed Bandit this morning and that the litter box had been cleaned, but if Liz could come by this evening and feed the cat, then start the normal schedule tomorrow, she would pay her for the whole day today. DK told her she would be gone about a week and would call her if her plans changed. Liz had a key to the house, knew the routine and had contact numbers in case of an emergency, as she had been Bandit's caretaker for over three years.

The next phone call was to Gary at the Davie School Inn in Anna, Illinois. "Gary, it's DK. Do you have any open rooms this week? I must get away from here for a while. I want to come down later today if possible."

"Hey Sweetheart! You know there is always room for you anytime," Gary replied. "Come on down. I'll have a room ready for you."

DK hung up the phone, grabbed a small suitcase and started throwing in jeans and tee shirts, and at the last minute threw in a sundress…just in case. You never know what you're going to need when you don't know exactly where you are going or what you will be doing. She quickly grabbed another small suitcase for shoes. She threw in tennis shoes for walking, her hiking boots, flip flops, casual flats. Might as well throw in a pair of sandals too, to go with the sundress… just in case. She grabbed the makeup bag, camera case, and turned on the radio so Bandit would not feel all alone. She was out the door and in the car.

Two hours later, wheeled suitcases in tow, DK rang the buzzer on the front door of the Davie School Inn. Gary, opened the door and wrapped her in a big old bear hug, welcoming her in, saying how glad he was to see her again. As always, he was wearing his maroon SIU baseball cap. When they were at the reception desk, Gary said, "Andrea and I have been worried and was wondering how you are doing. We knew you were busy with details and loose ends after David died. You know you are practically family to us, but we wanted to give you space and time. Andrea was very excited when I told her you were coming down, she can't wait to see you. You know she is going to want some special girl time with you, right?"

As DK looked into the short, scruffy bearded face of David's best friend, the tears welled up in her eyes, she fought to compose herself and keep them from spilling down her cheeks. It was to no avail. She stuttered and stammered. As the tears fell, she quivered, and through the tears she sobbed, "I'm so tired of trying to be strong for the kids. I don't want them worrying about me. Yes, they have seen me cry and they have felt my frustration over so many of the things that I cannot do for myself, but I do not let them catch me with my guard down. They each have their own lives and I do not want to burden them with my insecurities." She broke down in uncontrollable sobs. Thank goodness there weren't any other guests checking in at that moment. Gary came around the counter and wrapped his arms around her. He held her and let her cry. Andrea and their two grandchildren came in. The kids looked puzzled as she nudged them off towards the family space downstairs. She came over to give DK a hug and said that she would take her to her room. The two ladies walked arm in arm down the hallway. Gary followed behind with DK's suitcases.

As Gary unlocked the door to the Blue Room he said, "I thought you might prefer being in here for this trip instead of your usual Gold Room. I'm sorry for upsetting you out there." DK assured him that her breakdown was not his fault. She had never openly shared the feelings that she was dealing with since David's death with anyone. And it was beginning to take its toll on her. She told him she would be fine with a couple of nights of good undisturbed sleep, some fresh Shawnee Forest air, and the freedom to cry.

After Andrea and Gary left the room, DK stretched across the bed and promptly fell into a deep peaceful sleep.

Around six o'clock that evening, the ringing cell phone woke DK from her nap. It was Andrea asking about dinner. She said all the guests had checked in and the grandkids had gone home. She asked DK, if she would put on a pot of coffee, she and Gary would like to bring dinner and visit with her. DK agreed that was a lovely idea and said she would look forward to them visiting.

Gary and Andrea arrived with chicken and dumplings, salad and apple pie. Andrea said, "Of course we brought wine too." Laughing while she raised two bottles, one in each hand, for DK to see. As Gary set the food on the table, Andrea informed DK that the food was a gift from the Main Street Diner. "They sent their condolences and insisted on sending the entire meal over. Like most of the folks around here, they have appreciated yours and David's continued support over the years and this was the least they could do for you."

Gary and Andrea tried to keep the conversation light, by filling DK in on the latest events going on around town, and their own latest business expansion plans. After a while, DK was feeling comfortable and relaxed enough to share her story with them. She again apologized to Gary for breaking down in his reception area. She said this was the first time she had experienced such a meltdown in public. She credited Gary and Andrea for being like family, to which they both acknowledged that is exactly how they felt about her and David too. They all agreed that friends who had been together for nearly forty years were closer than some blood relatives.

Trying to not talk ill of her deceased husband and Gary's best friend, she told them how difficult it had been trying to figure out the finances and the bills that needed to be paid and when. While David had been a great provider, he had not kept her as informed as she would have liked. Not that he was ever trying to hide or keep anything from her. He always told her that he didn't want to bother her with such detail; that he would take care of the finances and she would take care of the house. She admitted that she was partly at fault, for never trying to hone her computer skills and since he kept everything on the computer, she was at a loss. She had a huge fear of messing something up or deleting important files, so she preferred to not touch his computer.

Andrea interjected, "Sweetie, you and I both know that

while he said he was protecting you and keeping you from worrying, it was also that whole male ego thing of still maintaining a level of control. I'm sure in his own mind he didn't think he was controlling, but come on, men are men!"

"I do know on some level that is true, but I have always maintained my own checking account for the household and personal expenses. I also had a check book and debit card to access our joint account, which I could at any time with no questions asked, ever! David did not make me accountable for any of my spending, I guess because he knew I didn't abuse our money," DK responded.

Gary broke into the girls' conversation. "Speaking as the only man here, I know that David was not controlling. He sincerely did think he was taking care of his family and he did not want DK burdened with the boring day to day aspects of running a home. He wanted DK to be comfortable in having the home of her dreams and he also wanted to make sure that she would be well provided for - with or without him around. Trust me. He was always looking out for your best interest, DK."

DK went on to tell her friends that in the last few months she had been relying a lot on her son Randy for help with David's computer. He was so much like his father and he understood his dad's way of thinking and organizing the computer files. Randy first helped her with all the insurance papers and then figured out when the utilities were due and what was on auto payment plans. Though she would have preferred to sit down with a desk calendar and a real check book and pay the bills like she used to, Randy took the time to teach her how to do them on the computer. He convinced her that in time all bills and payments would be paperless, and she should know how to do it this way. He showed her how to set up a calendar with pop-up reminders of appointments and due dates for bills. Randy also changed all the passwords to ones that she could remember. He also suggested she write them down in a secure place where she could refer to them, if she ever forgot one.

DK lamented, "It has not been easy adjusting to being a widow and it is so much more than just being lonely. I don't know whether I am angry that he left me alone or angry that he didn't teach me what I needed to know. It took me months to feel comfortable enough to pay a water bill all on my own or to balance the checkbook, without Randy sitting right there by me. And he was right. I have been able to do it and I am quite proud, if I say so myself! Why couldn't David have taught me? I pleaded with him so many times, always asking, '*What-if?*' David would always say, 'Nothing's going to happen.' He was always so damn invincible!"

Andrea reached out for DK's hand, looked her square in the eye, and said, "Deborah, dear! It has ONLY been six months since David died. You and David have been together since you were teenagers! Six months is not that long for grieving. Even a year is not too long to mourn such a loss. You have to give yourself time to heal."

Gary agreed with her that David was always the caregiver in any situation. He said, "David was like a big brother to me in college. We were more than just football teammates. When Andrea and I started dating and you two girls were roommates, we were like the Four Musketeers. We did everything together and even though our careers have taken us in different directions and many miles apart, we have always stayed in touch. You two have been here numerous times since we opened in 2002. No one has been more loyal to us than you and David!"

DK reached over to touch Gary's arm. "I knew this is where I needed to be right now. I realize I have been in shock since the day David had his heart attack. I guess I have been in much deeper than I knew, until just now. I think some of the numbness is beginning to wear off and that is why I am feeling so restless and lost, not to mention...afraid. The paperwork and details of his death and funeral are over, at least I think they are! I think being here in Southern Illinois is going to help a lot."

She took a deep breath before speaking. "As you know, David had been in his office at the house, working on a client's income tax. I was in the family room drafting out a new quilt design to work on. I heard him call out my name. He sounded desperate. I jumped from my chair and ran down the hall to his office. As soon as I walked in, I knew. I knew… I… I… knew… he was already gone. I called 911, but they seemed to take forever to get there. While I waited for the ambulance to arrive, I knelt by his chair, cradled his head to my chest, and begged him to wake up. When the paramedics arrived, they confirmed what I already knew. I can't believe it has been six months that I have been living in this fog. The one thing that haunts me the most is that we never got to say good-bye. We were living a normal ho-hum day and the next thing you know, he was gone. No good-bye kiss, nothing! He hadn't been sick. There was no preparation, just gone! I did not know how to live in such grief, I still don't. I have just tried to go on day to day, not wanting to bother anyone else. Not wanting to be a burden. Not wanting to worry the kids. I have tried to be strong for them. Of course, we have shared many memories and tears and they know I often cry myself to sleep at night. I just don't burden them with the depth of my grief. Mothers always try to protect their children from the hardships in life and try to educate them at the same time. Andrea, I'm sure that as a mother, you understand what I am saying. I want them to know that it is perfectly normal to feel pain and loss. It is okay to cry. I just don't want them to know how deeply it hurts, even though I know they do. They have the same feelings themselves and they are trying to protect me as well." Andrea squeezed her hand and nodded her head in agreement.

"Besides the dread of eating or going out alone, I feel like I am extra baggage when I join friends. I know I am not the same fun person I used to be. I think my girlfriends look at me differently now, like I am going to go after their husbands. I also think, they feel uncomfortable around me. They do not know what to say or even what not to say so I am not included in a lot of invitations, especially ones that include the husbands. I think the worst part is that I do not feel David's presence near me." DK said, her voice breaking. "I hear others talking at my grief support group how they feel their loved ones near them. Some even say that they have seen them standing nearby, or how a song comes on the radio that keeps them connected. I haven't had any of that. Even though I sleep every night snuggling David's old robe, because it smells like him, I do not 'feel' him. I think I should start to move on but I am not ready yet to move on. Actually, what does that mean? Move on? I know I should be giving some thought to what I am going to do with myself. I should start planning what to do with my life. I cannot 'just exist,' which is what I have been doing - just existing. I do the day to day stuff that must be done and nothing more."

Gary placed his free hand on top of hers, and said, "DK, don't 'should on yourself!' You know in your heart that David would want you to move on. He would not want you to be stuck in this grief! You two had dreams and hopes for so many things that you wanted to do together, and in time, you will do something special with your life. It may or may not be in the next few months, but I believe it will happen"

DK acknowledged that he was right, let out a little laugh and said, "Oh yes, we had dreams all right. A new one every week!" She pulled her hands free from her friends and wiped away the tears that had drenched her face. "Let's see," she said as she sniffled. "Over the years, it has been: open a gift and flower shop, a quilt store, a bar, an antique shop, a café, or move to Hawaii and just be beach bums."

Laughing, Andrea interjected, "Don't forget, you were also going to open your own B&B and give us some competition!"

DK laughed and said, "Yes, we did say that, didn't we? Well, you should take that as a compliment! You have set an example of what a great B&B should be. You know very well, before you opened this place, David and I had stayed at numerous B&Bs all over the state. Once you opened the Davie School Inn, nothing else could compare. Don't worry, my dear friend, I am not about to tackle running a B&B all by myself! You won't get any competition from me!"

Gary said, "DK, you have a strong will, a variety of experiences and a creative talent. You can do anything you put your mind to! You can take any one of those dreams that you and David shared and turn them into a reality, when you are ready. Why, you could even open a B&B in Hawaii if you wish, and Andrea and I can come stay with you! Spiritually, you know David will be by your side, leading you and guiding you."

Gary further elaborated that it was because of David's wisdom that he was able to purchase this building that is named for the town's founder, Winstead Davie. and turn the B&B into what they have today. It is no coincidence that the building and my best friend have the same name. I believe it was Divine intervention that brought David and I together in college and kept us together all these years. David will always be a part of this adventure that Andrea and I are on and he will always be a part of whatever path you end up taking. Just do it for yourself and no one else. We all know with what David knew about money; he no doubt has left you well provided for and most likely enough for investing in a business of your own."

Gary said that he and Andrea needed to leave and let DK get to bed. 5:00 a.m. would come very early and he needed to get to bed and get some sleep so he would be alert enough to cook breakfast for the guests. As he and Andrea stood to leave, DK asked Andrea if she could stay a while longer. They still had another bottle of wine to open and she could certainly use some girl talk. Gary and Andrea exchanged looks. He nodded and told Andrea to take her time.

The two women cleared the table. DK washed the dishes

while Andrea dried and put them away. This was just one of the unique things that DK liked about staying at the Davie School Inn. Each room was a complete suite: private bathrooms, a divided sleeping and sitting area, a complete kitchenette stocked with nice dishes and glassware, a microwave and a refrigerator, just no stove. Conveniences you don't find in most B&Bs. David used to say it was like the Hilton of the B&Bs.

After the dishes were put away, they opened the remaining bottle of wine and proceeded to the sitting area. Andrea sat on one end of the couch, DK plopped on the floor leaning in to face Andrea so they could talk.

They reminisced about the very early days of their friendship and the double dates that were usually bowling or movies. A lot of weekends were spent at either Gary's or Andrea's parents or grandparents' houses since they lived so close to campus. They were more than happy to provide home cooked meals for the kids. They truly all, became the best of friends. Nearly inseparable.

Andrea asked DK how the kids were doing since David's death.

"Each one is handling things in their own way, coping as best as they can. Davey and Maria were divorced last year, and he is sharing a bachelor pad with another divorced friend until he can figure out where he wants to settle. Maria couldn't handle him being gone all the time with his advertising job. Maria and I keep in touch, and she was around to help Davey through those first tough weeks after David died, but I think she has backed off now.

Annie and her husband Bob bought a new home in Waterloo near the new elementary school where they both teach. The twins, Jeremy and Jacob, are a handful to say the least! Annie did ask me to consider moving to Waterloo to be closer to them and, I did think about it, for about a half a minute. Seriously, why would I sell my beautiful home in Belleville just to move 30 minutes away? I know Annie wouldn't intend for it, but one of two things would happen if I did that: one, I would become the unofficial babysitter on call; or two, I would be included and expected to attend everything that they do, whether I wanted to or not. Their feelings would be hurt if I didn't go along with something they wanted to do. They have their routines and schedules working for them just fine, and so do I. I can go down there and attend what I want, when I want. Moving there is not an option for me right now. Maybe when I am old and need a caretaker myself!"

"As for Randy," DK continued, "he is managing the office pretty well on his own. David taught him everything he knows. He has been bringing in new clients on a pretty regular basis. I worry though that he is taking on too much too quickly. I hope he will be looking for another partner soon to help ease some of the work load. Besides, he is young and single. He needs to find a girl to build a life together with. I do not want him falling into the same work trap that his father and grandfather did. It took me throwing screaming and crying fits in order to get David to take some time off and see the outside world once in a while!"

"Don't get me wrong, David was an excellent provider for us and he was a good father and husband. He made sure the family went to Sunday Mass and breakfast together and he made sure he was home every night for dinner. After dinner, if he wasn't working in his home office, he was zoned out in front of the TV, oblivious to anyone else around. In the meantime, I went to school plays, ball games, scouting events, and whatever else the kids were involved in."

"I hope Randy will remember those times and will be more involved in his family, whenever that happens to be. There is a new young secretary, cute as a button. Her name is Chelsea. I think she could be the one for Randy. I have seen the way that he looks at her. He doesn't know it yet, but he's in love."

"Now, it's your turn. Tell me about your grandkids. I have monopolized the entire conversation. But first, let me get us some more wine."

When DK returned with the refilled glasses, Andrea was now sitting on the floor as well.

"Charlotte is in the third grade, makes very good grades, and is on the girls' soccer team. She enjoys spending time with her Grandad here at the inn and is quite the little helper. Gary likes having his little shadow close by, too. As for Dalton, he is a typical six-year-old boy; loves being outside, digging in the dirt, and going fishing with Grandad. He gets by in school, but far from the top of the class. Now, if they would move his desk outside, he would do a whole lot better! He is such a dreamer, and doesn't care about the book learning."

DK laughed and said, "I can hear my mother with that statement! Deborah, you are such a dreamer! You need to focus on something. You try to do anything and everything. Honey, when are you going to learn, you can't do it all?"

"That was the one thing that we did not agree on my whole life. I always wanted to learn more, do more, to try anything that came my way. After all, how would I ever know what I wanted to do, if I haven't figured out what my options were? Mom was of a different generation; a homemaker and mother were what was expected of her, and it was what she did. I always knew I wanted to do more. The fact is, I still don't know what I want to do when I grow up."

Andrea stood up and said, "With that dear, I need to go. We both need to get to bed. Besides, you are not going to figure out tonight, what you are going to be when you grow up! Call me if you need anything."

They shared a hug before Andrea walked out the door. DK pressed her back against the closed door and felt at peace…for the first time in a long time. Coming here was definitely the right thing to do.

CHAPTER TWO

DK struggled to get her bearings as she heard a gentle knocking on the door. She was in such a deep sleep, she couldn't quite figure out where she was. With the second knock on the door, DK realized that she was at the Davie School Inn and that it was Gary with her breakfast. Another reason she loved this place: breakfast served in your room every morning. No need to get up and dress presentably enough for going to a dining room with other guests. She grabbed the terry cloth robe lying on the bed and tried to clear the fog from her head as she made her way to the door.

As Gary entered the room with the breakfast tray, he greeted DK with his warm and cheery deep voice. "Good morning, Sunshine! How are you doing today? Although, I doubt if you know the answer to that just yet."

DK yawned and replied groggily, "I do know one thing; I slept better last night than I have in quite a long time. It was like coming home after a very long absence. Can I just move in here?" she said with a laugh as she padded towards the table in her bare feet.

Gary chuckled, "Sure, you can move in. I can always use some help, but I must warn you it does get kind of crazy sometimes. Umm.... could that good night's sleep have anything to do with the two bottles of wine last night?" Then with raised eyebrows he asked, "Is that David's robe you are wearing? That thing is so big on you that it is dragging the floor! What keeps you from tripping as you walk? And those sleeves! They are twice as long as your short, little arms! Not to mention it looks a bit worn out. How old is that thing anyway?"

DK tugged the lapels of the robe a bit tighter towards her face and sniffed them as she said, "I don't care if I look like an old worn out brown bear. It brings me comfort. It smells like David's musk after shave. Besides, most days I feel like I want to hibernate like an old bear!"

Gary set the tray on the table, "I hope my special French toast and fresh fruit are okay. I know it is one of your favorites."

DK shook her head in agreement, as she had already popped a piece of melon in her mouth. Gary bent down and kissed her forehead, telling her to be sure and enjoy the day as he headed for the door.

After she ate her breakfast and showered, DK threw on a pair of jeans and t-shirt and slipped on a pair of casual flats for easy walking. Though she had no plan of where she was going or what she would do all day, she wanted to be comfortable. She hated the confinement of wearing socks and tennis shoes or hiking boots. Her feet couldn't breathe and she felt trapped - all tied in and confined. Barefoot would have been her preference, but being out and about, shoes are required…. like it or not.

As she headed out the door, she told Gary at the front desk she would be back sometime later, that she needed to go riding around the hills and unwind.

She rolled all the windows down and opened the sun roof of the white Toyota Highlander. She tuned the satellite radio to a station that played music from the 70's and cranked the volume up a few notches. As she headed north on Highway 127 into the Shawnee National Forest, the tunes played and the warm breeze blew through her hair. She could feel the stress easing from her body. She became fully aware of just how tense she had been as she felt her shoulders relaxing and dropping from their stiff, drawn up position. She rotated her head in circles to allow her neck muscles to ease. No destination in mind, no time schedule to keep, no commitments to anyone or anything. She just drove… and sang along to the songs of her youth. The songs that reminded her of the early days with David.

After a while, she realized that she was in Carbondale, on the grounds of her alma mater. She parked the car in the visitor's parking lot and got out of the car. As she slowly walked across the grounds, she reminisced about the days when she went to classes here and the days when she first met David. She walked past her old dorm building. The building itself hadn't changed at all; except it was now an office building – not a dormitory. She walked to the campus bookstore. Here, the changes were quite evident. Electronic accessories and battery chargers were in abundance. Note cards, pencils and pads of paper took up much less space than they did forty years ago. In fact, it was quite noticeable that there were even fewer books than before. The digital age had certainly changed a lot of businesses and lifestyles. With almost every book now available on a laptop or tablet device, how does a shy guy initiate a conversation with a girl? He certainly can't ask to carry her books for her anymore. She doesn't have any to carry!

  DK wasn't completely out of touch with the electronic age. She could get around on a computer as much as she truly needed to, but oh, how she missed the simpler days. She still preferred to keep a paper calendar on her desk and a smaller one in her purse. She preferred to write her appointments with a pen and not with a stylus on a screen. With computers and smart phones, everything needed a password and she had such a hard time remembering which password was for what. It was always a vicious cycle of trying to open a program and getting locked out of her own device and then having passwords reset. Maybe she should check into an adult computer class. Of course, it would need to be much closer to home. SIUC was over two hours away. That would just not be a feasible commute.

  Next, DK made her way over to the stadium. This is not the same place where a young girl had gotten an education in football by watching and falling in love with the team captain! The original McAndrew Stadium was where DK and David met their future in-laws for the very first time. No one knew then that the homecoming weekend of 1970 would be the first of many years of celebrating autumn days with football and family togetherness for all of them. McAndrew Stadium was gone now, replaced by Saluki Stadium. It wasn't the same, but it was still the home of the

Saluki's where the football spirit and memories prevailed!

David's parents and grandparents had arrived early on Wednesday morning before the big game. They always stayed at the Ridgewood Motor Lodge, because it had little kitchenettes that allowed the women to cook a few meals in their own rooms. Both women always came armed with loads of home baked and home canned treasures for their boy. This year, especially, since David and a couple of his buddies had rented a small house off campus, the two women went overboard to stock the pantry for them. David's dad and grandfather teased the women about how much they were bringing, that there was barely room in the car for them to sit. Grandma Kingston had two of her famous Sour Cream cakes that she had cut into large chunks and had frozen into individual bags for ease of long term storage. Plus, there was one whole uncut cake for eating right away. Grandma also had a supply of homemade deer jerky, one of David's favorite treats from Grandma. His mother had a Tupperware container of her special recipe of powdered hot chocolate mix, enough to last the whole winter season. There were boxes filled with jars of homemade chili and spaghetti sauce, in addition to the obligatory chocolate chip cookies and the oatmeal peanut butter bars. David's roommates knew that for a few months after Homecoming, they would all be eating well.

Deborah was quite nervous at the thought of meeting David's parents. Though her relationship with David was new and no talk of commitments between them, she knew that his parents would be studying her very closely to see what kind of a girl she was. She also wanted to know just "who" they were and what they were like. David had not talked much about any of his family, so she had no preconceived opinions about them.

David, on the other hand, was unconcerned about meeting Deborah's parents. As far as he was concerned this was no big deal. He had not given any thought to the idea that they could be his future in-laws, someone that he should try to impress or win over.

※ ※

As she headed back towards her car, the memories of David walking with her across these very sidewalks made her slow her pace and savor the memory of their early days together on this campus. She could smell the familiar scent of the musk scented aftershave that he always wore. She could feel his presence with her. This was the first time in six months she had felt David's presence. She slowed her pace even more, not wanting to lose this feeling, fearing that if she got in her car, he would disappear. She spotted a bench and sat for a few moments, drinking in the hot but breezy July air, and especially, the musk! She watched young people darting around and going from building to building, trying not to be late for various summer classes. She noticed that no one was really communicating even if they were walking side by side. Everyone looked the same from the back, wearing their black backpacks with dangling water bottles. Most kids were plugged into one kind of electronic device or another. White cords dangled from their ears as they listened to music, while others talked on cell phones. Some walked with their heads bent down texting, not watching where they were going, while other people moved out of their way. She wondered to her herself, why does everyone hurry so? Life is too short to always be rushing.

Did she and David rush around like that when they were students? She tried to remember. No, she didn't think so. She could only remember the long, slow walks between classes, holding hands and stopping to look into each other's eyes as they talked about life and what the future would hold for them. She remembered David carrying her books for her and lingering over late night coffee while they studied together. She remembered packing picnic baskets for Sunday afternoons in the park, where they fed the ducks on the pond. She wondered if the tree where David carved their initials was still there. She remembered the day very well. She had made lemonade and packed ham sandwiches along with potato chips and Brownies that she had picked up from the Bake Shop on campus. They sat in the shade of a Mulberry tree talking about their future. That was when he first mentioned the idea of marriage. Oh, they had talked many times in the past about 'someday' and 'what-if,' 'what do you think about kids?' But on this one particular Sunday he said to her, "So when do you think we should set the wedding date?"

"Wedding date? Well David Kingston, I don't know that you have properly proposed to me!"

"You mean, like down on one knee with a ring and everything?"

"Yes, that is exactly what I mean."

"I don't have a ring with me today, but I can give you something even more permanent than a piece of jewelry."

David stood up and reached into his right pants pocket and pulled out a pocket knife. He made Deborah stand on the other side of the tree so she could not see what he was doing until he was finished. He warned her not to peek. He started deeply carving initials into the bark of the tree. After what seemed to take forever, he finally told her she could come see what he had done.

There on the tree were the initials "DK + DK forever"

"David, my initials are DB. Why did you put DK?" She asked.

"Because once we are married, your initials and mine will be the same and that's what they will be forever. Now I ask you Deborah Suzanne Bridges will you marry me and be my DK forever?

Deborah shouted, "Oh, yes! Yes! Yes!" she cried as she jumped into his arms and he twirled her around and held her tightly.

SEARCHING FOR SOMETHING SPECIAL

Once again, DK was in her car and out on the open road. After a short time, she found herself in Jonesboro at the little antique shop where she and David first met. Was going there intentional or just a happy accident? She didn't recall planning to head south just yet.

Inside the antique store, she walked around the familiar little place. Not many changes here. The old furniture and bookshelves holding what used to be sacred treasures from previous generations, now waiting for someone to relive old memories or to start new ones for generations yet to come. The treasures ranged from priceless ornate furniture to kitschy salt and pepper shakers. There were cut crystal, depression, and milk glass items, old Christmas ornaments and other decorations, jewelry and decorative tins that once held cookies and crackers. There were quilts, aprons, doilies, and fabrics ready to become new treasures. One could only imagine the stories that each piece could tell.

The memories of previous generations are what initially brought Deborah and David together. When they accidently bumped into each other that fateful day almost forty years ago, they were both attempting to search out memories of their own, something that would soothe the homesickness they were both experiencing.

Deborah enjoyed looking at all of it. Everything reminded her of someone in her family. Though she had been raised in a small Midwest Illinois town, she had spent a great deal of time with both sets of grandparents. Their lifestyles were very different from her own, but she treasured what they had taught her and the stories they could tell about the "old days." Her Grandma Range, lived near enough that little Deborah could walk to her house on her own. Grandma Range was her mother's mother. She taught Deborah how to sew by hand with a needle and thread: and eventually, how to use the old black portable Singer sewing machine. Deborah vividly remembered Grandma Range taking the thread out of the machine and handing Deborah a piece of lined notebook paper and telling her to sew along the lines. The needle would punch holes on the paper wherever she was "sewing." Grandma Range took another piece of paper and drew circles of different sizes and told Debora to sew along the circles. The lesson here was that when she could control the needle following the lines of the paper or the round circles without a bunch of squiggles, she would be ready for the thread and real fabric. But she had to learn how to control the speed and maneuver the paper around first. In due time, she made doll clothes, pillows, aprons and even little summer dresses for herself. Grandma Range taught her to take great pride in being able to make her own clothes and accessories. One of the lessons she had to learn, was that ripping out stitches and starting over, was just as important to a quality finished product as the actual stitching. Grandma Range insisted that if she wasn't willing to rip out what didn't work right the first time, she shouldn't be sewing at all.

The day she and David first met in the antique shop, Deborah held a small zip lock sandwich bag stuffed tightly with lady's handkerchiefs. Some had fine lace edging, others with delicate cotton crochet all around the edge. There was a rainbow of colors and designs, from pink and purple flowers on one, to Christmas designs on another. When she spotted this collection of hankies, she remembered her grandma's pocketbook, which always had a hankie in it. Deborah decided that this great find of the day would not take up any space in her dorm room and would go home with her on her next trip to be safely tucked away in the cedar chest at the foot of her bed. Maybe someday she could use them on a quilt top or something. At five dollars for the whole bag, she felt she had found a bargain.

When she turned the corner of the aisle and literally bumped right into David; he was holding a cast iron skillet in his hands. She was lucky that he didn't drop it on her head when she collided into him. She smiled as she remembered how shocked he had been to have been caught in an antique store. His face turned red and he stuttered and stammered as he tried to explain why he was there. Eventually he said, "This old skillet makes me think of the biscuits and gravy that my grandma used to fix for me on game days. Of course, her skillet would never have all the rust on it like this one does. She took care of her cookware. This pan is a disgrace, rusted all over. Who would ever buy anything like this piece of junk?" He went on to say, "Look, I don't know you, but I would certainly appreciate it if this could kind of stay between us. No one else needs to know that I was hanging out at an antique store."

Deborah laughed, "Sure thing, but personally, I don't know what the big deal is. You can find some great bargains in here if you are looking for tools or something to furnish an apartment, along with a free trip down memory lane."

David said, "Yeah, well, that's the part that the guys just wouldn't get ... uh ... that trip down memory lane part. We all put on this big macho façade, but we each have our own game day ritual. Some we talk about, some we don't. This is my ritual that I don't talk about. I come in here and look at the cast iron pans, and think of my grandma."

He put the skillet back on the shelf and mumbled again about the nasty, rusty old thing and how his grandma took better care of her pots and pans. He said he was going next door to the café to get a bite to eat. "You're welcome to join me if you like. I'll buy."

Deborah reached over and gave his arm a friendly little punch with her fist and said, "What you really mean is; you're buying so I won't tell. It's more of a bribe. Sure, I'll join you, but you don't have to buy me off. I can pay for my own."

Deborah stopped at the register and paid for her hankies and told the lady she didn't need a bag. She shoved her treasure into her crocheted crossover handbag that hung from her right shoulder. Together, she and David walked next door to the café.

As they ate their lunch of scrambled eggs with biscuits and gravy, they talked like they had known each other for years. Not like two people who had just officially met. They talked about the classes they were taking and what their crazy schedules were like. They talked about life back home. Deborah learned that David grew up in a suburb of Chicago, but wasn't a real city boy. His grandparents owned a farm in Long Grove, just on the other side of the covered bridge in town. He spent lots of time with them on the farm. He helped his grandfather in the garden and he learned not only how to plant and harvest crops, but also how to repair the equipment to keep things running smoothly. He talked about the great meals that his grandma cooked in her cast iron skillet and how she always rubbed it down with oil and reheated it every time she used it, so it wouldn't rust. He said one of her favorite things to do on his game days was to fix a big pan of biscuits and gravy with scrambled eggs.

Deborah interrupted with a gleam in her eye and said, "Ah, that is why you were next door holding the cast iron skillet, and why we are eating biscuits and gravy now. There is a game later today, isn't there?"

With a sheepish smile he replied, "Yeah, you got me."

He went on to tell Deborah how his grandparents encouraged him from an early age to play football. They said it would help him to become a big strong man and it would help him to go far in school. "Of course, they were right," he said. "I was the quarterback in high school and was offered a full scholarship to come here and play. It's a long way from home, so my parents come down several times a season to see a game, but my grandparents only get to come down about once a year, usually for Homecoming weekend or Thanksgiving weekend, unlike high school where they attended every game. Here, it is more like a job that I do. I go to work out on the football field, but there is no one here rooting for me, David Kingston. They are rooting for the quarterback to win the game for the school."

Deborah said, "I know what you mean. College life is very different from high school. I feel like I am a little fish in a great big pond. I was not prepared for all the changes and how different things would be. I had wanted to stay close to home and go to the local community college and live at home; or go to cosmetology school and become a hairdresser. But my grandma convinced me to come here for at least a year, spread my wings and experience the outside world. My parents weren't too happy with her for doing that. Even when she offered to pay for the first year's tuition, they wanted me stay at home. But here I am! Grandma said that if I didn't like it after the first year, I could always go back home."

David asked her what she thought so far. "Well, since I am barely into my first semester, it is a bit too soon to really know. I think I'll need a little more time to figure that out."

"Oh, so you are just a freshman! I assumed you were at least a sophomore or junior."

"Do you have a problem with that?" she asked.

"Well, no, what I meant was…oh, never mind. I'm sorry, I need to run. I have to get back and get ready for the game. Lunch is on me. See you around sometime. It was nice meeting you." He said as he scrambled to his feet and headed towards the cash register near the door.

"Yeah, well, uh…. I guess… Bye. See ya." She stammered, as he hurried away. She wasn't sure if he even heard her as he rushed towards the door..

Deborah sat there several more minutes while she finished drinking her iced tea and processing the events and conversation of the past hour.

Before getting into her car to leave, she went back to the antique store, picked up the rusty iron skillet David had been holding earlier. She studied it closely and saw that it wasn't really as bad as David thought. She looked at the price tag and nodded. She took the skillet to the checkout register and then put her new purchase in the trunk of her car before heading back to school.

Later that afternoon, she found herself sitting in the bleachers of her first college football game looking for the quarterback. What is a quarterback, she wondered, and what makes them so special? She knew nothing at all about football. But, she did know that she was there to root for the guy with "Kingston" written across the back of his jersey.

When she had finished her shopping, and reminiscing about her early days with David, DK stopped at a diner close by the Inn, picked up a burger and a salad to take back to her room. While she ate, she watched the evening news, then poured a glass of wine to take outside to sip while she sat on the porch swing. DK was glad to find Andrea already out there watching the grandkids play in the yard with some of their friends.

DK sat down on the swing next to Andrea. She told her that she felt at peace. Yes, she had spent a lot of time thinking about David and the early days of their courtship. DK told Andrea about going over to the campus and walking around there and the odd but comforting feeling that David was there with her. She said, "You won't believe this, but I actually smelled his after shave. It happened a couple of times. The first time was on campus, while I was walking along the sidewalk, and then again this afternoon at the antique shop. I was in the aisle where the old cast iron cookware is located. I picked up a piece and thought back to our very first meeting over a cast iron skillet and the scent of his aftershave just seemed to waft through the air, right then and there."

"I think of David a lot when I am at home, but I haven't felt his presence like I have here today. I think it is kind of odd, that I haven't had any of these same thoughts and feelings in the home we shared for over thirty years. And yet, here in just one day, I feel more at peace than I have felt in the last six months since David died. DK smiled and touched Andrea's arm. "In fact, I think I will sleep very well tonight, without needing two bottles of wine like last night!"

CHAPTER THREE

DK was up, showered and dressed. She was already enjoying her first cup of coffee when Gary arrived with her breakfast of a spinach, mushroom, and tomato omelet, rye toast, and of course, the fresh fruit and pitcher of orange juice.

"Well, good morning, Sunshine! It looks like a good morning indeed! I see that you have on your hiking boots and the camera bag is sitting on the table. Where are you headed today?" Gary asked.

DK replied, "I'm thinking I might go to the Garden of the Gods, climb a few hills, cherish a few good memories and soak up some of the beautiful scenery there. It was one of David's favorite places to be."

Gary smiled and said, "It is good to see you becoming your old self again. I think it is the fresh forest air that we have around here. David would be pleased to see the pink back in your cheeks."

As usual, DK was already into the dish of fruit.

Gary reminded her that it was late July and the temperatures were quite warm, even with nice breezes blowing. "Be sure to wear some sunscreen!" he warned. "Actually, if I was any kind of a friend, I would insist that you take someone with you. You know very well, you shouldn't go hiking around there alone. But I have also known you long enough to know that once you get an idea in your head, there is no talking you out of it. I wish Andrea was free to go with you, but she has some appointments today that she can't change. Any chance of you, uh, maybe going tomorrow instead of today?" He questioned rather sheepishly.

DK shook her head no, then asked, "So, tell me. How is your sister Connie doing, since she and Ed bought your grandfather's old farm?"

"They are doing very well, thank you. Okay, I get it! No more questions about where you are going and what you are doing.

Like I said, once you get an idea in your head, you dive in, regardless of anyone's warnings. I always did tell David he had his hands full with you."

DK laughed. "Yes, I know you told him that lots of times and I also know it is a true statement. It's what makes me...me! Right?"

Gary shrugged, laughed, then said, "I can call Connie and see about going out to the farm. You will be surprised to see what all they have done to the old place.

DK thanked Gary for his concerns and promised she would be careful. Besides, she wasn't going hiking; just for a pleasant walk in the woods and was looking forward to the beautiful vistas, flora and fauna that she could capture with her camera. She promised she would do nothing dangerous.

Choosing to cruise the back roads all the way, DK was wishing she had brought David's Mustang convertible instead of the Highlander. She would have liked even more wind blowing in her hair than what the moon roof offered. She did not realize when she left home just a few days ago that she would already feel such freedom.

DK was standing on a cliff, overlooking the depths of the valleys below her. She was absorbing the vast array of colors among the numerous rock formations, along with inhaling the fresh air and drinking in the amazing beauty before her eyes. She felt empowered standing high on the cliff and looking over the vastness before her, and yet very small knowing that only God could create such a masterpiece of work. She was in awe. She sat on the ground cross-legged with her eyes closed. She said a prayer of thanks to God for leading her to this place and bringing comfort, at long last, to her troubled self. The trees behind her rustled in the slight breeze and then with a startle, she opened her eyes. That smell! She looked around. No one had joined her on the cliff and yet the scent of musk was there. She smiled.

"Hello, David, I know you are here with me, and I am glad

to know that you approve of what I am doing and you know I am at long last finding me again."

At that very moment, DK's cell phone rang. She looked and saw that it was Annie. She hesitated. She thought about ignoring the call, but knew Annie well enough to know, that she would not be ignored. Annie would just keep calling, so she might as well answer the phone now and get it over with.

"Hello sweetheart, how are you?"

"Mother, where in the heck are you and what in the world is going on? I am at your house and Liz is here. She said you left town with the intention of being gone about a week! What's up? Why didn't you let me know? What if something happened to you? We wouldn't even know that you weren't home! BESIDES!!! We were supposed to go school shopping with the boys today. We are at your house to pick you up!" cried Annie. She sounded frantic with worry, but also very dramatic, which Annie was quite capable of doing most anytime.

"Oh, Annie, I am so sorry, I forgot all about our shopping trip. I have been in such a fog lately, and I suddenly felt the urge to get some fresh air, and hopefully, a new perspective on things. When I decided to get away, I just packed a bag and hit the road. I will make up the shopping trip when I get back, sweetheart. I promise." Said DK.

"But Mother, WHERE in the world are you?" demanded Annie.

"Well, actually dear, at this very moment, I am on top of the world, and enjoying every breathtaking moment of it. I am in Southern Illinois at Garden of the Gods. I am sitting on a ledge overlooking the valley and it is just beautiful. Remember when we would bring you kids here and you wanted to know if you could go sit on the Camel Back Rock? I feel more alive than I have in months. I know you are going to think I am crazy, but your dad is here with me and we have been having a very nice visit. You know, he loved it up here." DK told her daughter.

"So, when are you planning on coming home?" asked Annie.

"To be honest honey, I don't know. I feel so at peace here. There is a part of me that never wants to leave, but the reality is, I guess I will be home in a couple of days. I just needed some time to myself away from the house. I needed time to think about my future and what I am going to do with it."

"Mother!" Annie said in a more condescending tone. "I understand your sense of loss. We all do, and we understand your need to get away and think, but seriously!! You are standing on top of a cliff all by yourself and no one knows where you are! Do you remember how many times you told each of us kids that we always had to be with someone? To never go anywhere alone, just in case something happened, there would always be someone who could go get help. Mother, what happened to your always preaching about the buddy system? Who is going to help you if you slip and fall, or sprain an ankle? What about the rattlesnakes that are up there?"

DK could not resist the urge to let out a chuckle. "Yes, daughter dear, I did say those things, and they are true. You are right. I should have let you know where I was going, but I didn't know myself until I got here. I guess I taught you well. Look who is acting like the mother now! I'll be leaving here soon. I just want to take a few more pictures. I promise I'll call you later this evening."

When they ended their conversation, DK smiled with pride at the daughter she had raised and knew that she would be a good mother to the twins. She realized, she would always be able to count on her daughter if she ever needed her help with anything. And yet, she knew she did not want to be a burden and have Annie always having to worry about her. The mother – daughter bond had come full circle and now Annie was acting more like the mother, rather than the daughter. Where did that little girl go? And when did she change into a clone of DK? And why must she be so dramatic over everything? The girl should have been an actress!

※ ※

Chelsea answered the phone on the second ring, "Kingston Financial Services, how I may help you?"

Annie replied in a short tart response, "Chelsea, I need to speak to my brother, right now!"

Chelsea put Annie on hold for a moment while she transferred the call to Randy's office.

Randy pressed the button with the blinking red light, "Hey, Sis, what's up?"

Annie began rambling. In fact, she was talking so fast and practically shouting into the phone that Randy could not understand a word she was saying. Randy had to ask her to take a breath and slow down.

Annie slowed down her words, but her agitation came through loud and clear to Randy. "Did you know that Mom left town and is now standing on top of a cliff talking to Dad? Have you noticed anything about her lately that would indicate that she needs help? Have you been paying any attention to her at all, or are you too busy with your calculator to know what is going on around you?"

Randy interrupted Annie, "Whoa, Sis! Calm down, take a breath! What are you talking about? Mom has been just fine around here. Of course, she is lost without Dad, but she pops into the office a couple of times a week to check on things and we go to lunch together. We talk about looking for a new business partner for the firm and me finding a nice girl to spend my life with. She thinks it is time for me to settle down and start a family, but I have not noticed anything to really be concerned about with her."

Annie continued to voice her frustration. "Well, Brother, Dear!! We were supposed to go school shopping today for the boys. It was supposed to be a full fun day together getting the boys ready for first grade. I went to the house to pick her up and I found Liz there taking care of Bandit. She said Mom had left town for the week. She didn't call and cancel the shopping trip. She didn't tell me she was going out of town or that she felt the need to get away. Did she tell you that she was leaving town? She went to Shawnee and, right this very minute, she is at the Garden of the Gods, on a cliff talking to Dad!"

Randy responded, "No, she didn't tell me she was going out of town. Their friend Gary from the B&B called me a couple of days ago, and said that Mom was there. Said she was very depressed when she arrived, but he and Andrea are keeping a close eye on her and she is doing much better." Randy resisted the urge to ask Annie if she was more upset about Mom skipping out on the shopping trip, or taking time out for herself. He did not want to get her any more riled up than she already was.

"WHAT!!! You KNEW she was out of town and you didn't let me know?" She screamed into the phone. How could you?

"Annie! Annie! please calm down! Mom is a responsible woman. She has friends who are watching out for her. She needed some time to herself to think about her new life. She misses Dad, and she alone must figure out what she is going to do now. She has a cell phone if she needs help." Randy was trying hard to calm his over-reacting sister.

"Well, a lot of good that cell phone is going to do her, when she falls down and drops it off the cliff!" Randy heard the phone click as Annie hung up without saying good-bye.

In the meantime, Annie took the boys to the mall and treated them to lunch in the food court and time to play in the arcade area for a while. They did a little bit of shopping and then it was ice cream before heading home. She had explained to them earlier that Grandma had to suddenly go out of town and she would take them shopping when she returned. Of course, they were disappointed, but those feelings disappeared as soon as they were in the arcades playing video games.

                                             ❧ ☙

Randy looked up to see Chelsea standing in the doorway. He ran his hands through his dark wavy hair and shook his head. He leaned back in the chair and uttered, "Oh, that girl! She thinks the whole word should revolve around her. She cannot see that Mom is really okay, and just taking a vacation from reality. Mom will come home refreshed, renewed and ready to start living her life again. You wait and see, she will be running an ad in the paper looking for a business partner and, then she'll be looking for a wife for me. How about some lunch, Chelsea? You pick the place, my treat."

Chelsea and Randy went to a sports bar around the corner from their office. Chelsea didn't often splurge on burgers and fries, but, occasionally, she craved sweet potato fries and this place had the very best. Cooked to perfection, they were crispy on the outside and soft and chewy on the inside then sprinkled with a little bit of cinnamon, and served with honey. It was like eating dessert and calling it healthy! After all, it was a sweet potato, right?

Taking a sip from her iced tea, Chelsea said to Randy, "So, Annie really gets to you, doesn't she? Your whole demeanor changes whenever she calls, especially today."

Randy lamented, "Yeah, well, I don't know who she thinks she is sometimes. It is like she thinks she is an only child and everyone must consult her before they do anything or that she must be included in everything. God forbid someone should go spend time on their own without her. I can understand her being upset that Mom skipped out on the shopping trip, but gee whiz, it is not the end of the world! There will be other shopping trips! The bottom line is, she wasn't consulted first, and I knew where mom was and didn't think it was important enough to tell her. Seriously, if Gary had indicated to me that he thought Mom was suicidal or anything, I would have been there myself. Gary and Andrea have known Mom and Dad since they were all teenagers, long before any of us was born. She is in very capable hands."

Chelsea said in a consoling tone, "Randy, I kind of know where Annie is coming from with her concerns. I remember when my mother died, my dad just turned inward and didn't want anyone fussing about him, yet he was lonely and couldn't express what he needed. For that matter, I'm not sure if he even knew himself, what he needed. He has always been a man of few words. My sister and I tried to watch over him and take care of him, but it was no use. We felt helpless, and in time, we all settled into our own lives and we moved on, just letting him be. He has become a recluse. He has no hobbies, does not socialize with friends. He doesn't even attend school functions for my two nieces. To this day, I wish I could have done more to help him. I know we thought he would just get over it, but it has been five years and he has retreated further and further into his own lonely world. I think that is what Annie is feeling right now, that she is not doing enough for your mom."

Randy replied, "Yeah, maybe so, but if I know Annie, she has her own agenda with this, too. She wants everyone else to know that she is the one who cares more than anyone else. She wants to be sure that if anything goes wrong, she can always say, "I told you so." She wants to be in charge and take all the credit for everything, but deep down she doesn't want any of the responsibility. All her life, she has relished being the only girl, living like she was a little princess."

He continued, "Like I said earlier, Mom is going to be home in couple of days and she is going to be her old self again." He glanced at his watch and said they needed to head back to the office. He had a conference call in about 30 minutes and he needed to gather his notes for the meeting.

Chelsea reached across the table and took Randy's hand.

"Just keep in mind, you know your sister quite well, and spoiled as she is, she is hurting too. The little girl in her lost her daddy, and her mommy is going through something that she can't fix. Her world is just as upset as your mother's. Maybe more so."

Randy looked down at her hand on top of his and said, "Wow, I never thought about it quite like that. I only saw the drama queen not getting her way. I will try to be more understanding of her. Thanks for helping me to see things from her point of view. You're the best."

As they strolled down the sidewalk, Randy reached down and took Chelsea's hand and thanked her for being a good listener and helping him to get over his confrontation with his sister. He didn't let go of her hand, until they reached the office and he held the door open for her.

※ ※

DK was completely absorbed at looking through the lens of her digital 35mm camera. David had given it to her when Annie was expecting the twins so she could capture every moment of the pregnancy and their birth. She had loved the results of playing with the different settings and lenses, especially taking pictures of scenery like this. Taking pictures of the twins was always fun and unpredictable, but beautiful scenery was like taking pictures of heaven. God had created such wonders, and capturing them on film was breathtaking. Seeing the rays of bright light stretching down through the clouds was like seeing God's arms reaching down, to offer a helping hand. The bright-rimmed edges around the clouds reminded her of halos; as if the angels were playing a game of peek-a-boo behind the clouds. There were the sights of the rock formations and their many layers of color. A tranquil painting that only God could create, one she could only hope to copy through the lens of her camera.

She reminisced about the first time that David had brought

her here. He told her he loved the way the sunlight changed the color of her hair. Much of her dark auburn locks looked more like the color of a shiny new copper penny. Her olive complexion blushed from his compliments. She had never been courted before and she was not sure how to act or what she should say. She tilted her head and shyly said, "Thank you."

She giggled to herself, that now her auburn and copper streaked hair was the result of her talented hairdresser.

∼ ∽

No one had prepared her for the deep depression that had engulfed her these last six months. Nor, had she truly recognized what she was feeling, or not feeling. She had not really understood grief before, at least not like this. She previously thought grief was supposed to knock you flat on your back; you are supposed to be curled up in bed, ignoring the ringing phone, constantly crying your eyes out and hoping that no one would come knocking on the door.

In the months since David died, she had merely gone through the motions of living, she kept her home in order, cooked healthy meals for herself, and spent time with the kids and grandkids. She continued her activities at church and always maintained the mask of everything being all right in her world. But at home alone, she felt guilty for going on with her life as usual. She felt she was betraying David's memory. She felt guilty for living a life without him. She knew in her heart he would not want her crying for months on end, but the mind can be stubborn when facing reality. Her mind would not let go of the fact that she was living and he was not. She realized by being here away from her normal day to day life, that she had been depressed and deep in the grips of grief; she just had not admitted it to herself. Here, as she was beginning to thaw, she knew she had to go on, and create a life of her own. She could not just exist like she had been doing.

It was time to truly think about what her options for moving forward would be. Does one calculate and plan the next phase in life, or does it just happen and flow before you? Starting here and now, she would look at life as an opportunity for growth and for becoming her own woman.

As DK made her way back down the trail, she took various pictures of the plants and wildflowers along the way. Butterflies and bees caught her attention as they flittered about, doing their own thing in God's world.

Though it was late summer, to DK, it suddenly felt like spring, with a renewed awakening.

~ ~

Realizing it was lunchtime and she was suddenly very hungry, DK decided to stop at one of the wineries she would be passing on her way back to the Davie School Inn. She stopped at one she and David had never been to before. A very nice outdoor wrap around deck with panoramic views all around her. While waiting for her House Salad topped with grilled chicken, DK snapped pictures of the scenery, as well as the birds that she enticed to sit on the railing with bits of the warm fresh baked bread. The salad was delicious and she savored every bite, then asked for the dessert special.

As she lingered over her coffee and dessert, she tried to call Annie. However, the call went straight to voice mail, so she left a message. "Sweetie, I am so sorry for not letting you know that I needed to get away. The thought suddenly came to me and I went with it. Totally forgetting about our shopping trip. I promise, I will make it up to you and the boys. I am having a very pleasant time all by myself, embracing nature and all the beauty that God has put before me here. I truly needed this. Love you, dear. I'll be home soon and we will catch up."

Later that afternoon when she returned to the inn, both Gary and Andrea were sitting on the porch swing, they said they were waiting on one more guest to check in and then they were free to go to dinner. Gary said he had called Connie and, Ed would throw some pork steaks on the grill, if DK wanted to go out to the ranch. DK said that with a quick shower and change of clothes she would be ready to go.

As Gary turned his pick-up truck into the lane that led to the big white farm house, DK immediately took notice of the wrought iron archway that hung high above the lane. The metal sign read; "CJ's Stables." DK commented to Gary and Andrea that she loved the awesome sign and, knew of course, the C was for Connie and the J was for Jackson, their grandfather's last name. Gary told her she would be really impressed later when they leave and she sees the spotlights on it. He also told her that he and Ed had dug up every one of the stones that created the support pillars for the sign. He said they had dug them out of the planned walking trails. It took them months to get enough rocks for the size pillars that Ed had wanted.

As they drove up closer to the house, Connie ran out to meet them. She hadn't changed much over the years. Her thick, long single braid still hung down the middle of her back touching the waistband of her denim jeans. However, it lacked the once youthful shine, now, mottled with mostly gray, dull hair. Connie was a no make-up, no fuss kind of girl, which complemented Ed's easy going, no frills, laid back personality. Ed's short beard and mustache were more gray than the deep reddish brown hair of his younger days.

As soon as she was out of the truck, DK complemented Connie on the sign and said it was very impressive and she knew right away the meaning behind the name. Connie told her that, Mr. Curtiss, the blacksmith in town, had created it for her as a tribute to her grandfather and his long time best friend. Mr. Curtiss knew that his friend Jack would be very proud of what Connie was doing with the place. With the back of his property connecting to theirs, he was more than willing to help them to improve the old farm and allowed them to bring some of the trail up through his own property.

Connie was anxious to show DK all the updates they had done so far to the place. Ed waved from his post at the gas grill. He shouted that he would show her his space after they ate.

The main barn had been reinforced and turned into stalls that were leased out to people in town to board their horses. Connie had also bought a few horses that were used to take people on trail rides.

Inside the house, she had stripped off the big English floral wall paper and painted the walls white. Leaving the stained wood casings around the doors and windows, gave the house a fresh updated look in a traditional farm house. The women all agreed that Grandma Rosalie would approve of the new look, even without her beloved pink floral wallpaper; especially since her hand-made Austrian Lace curtains still hung in the floor to ceiling windows.

Many years ago, when Grandpa Jack brought his war bride home to the wooded Cobden farm, she vowed to keep her English heritage alive inside the home. Connie made sure that Grandma Rosalie's spirit remained inside with the updated décor, just as Grandpa Jack's spirit lived on outside in the barn and the fields around them.

There was another spirit that Connie made sure remained alive in the old farm house. That was the spirit of her and Ed's deceased daughter Chrissy. Chrissy was killed in a car accident when she was sixteen. A deer ran into the path of the car that she and several friends were riding in following a high school football game. Three teenagers tragically died that night. Even though Chrissy had never lived in the home that her parents now owned, Connie recreated every detail of Chrissy's previous bedroom into the farm house. The Alan Jackson and George Strait posters were hung on the walls. The dried homecoming corsage was clipped to the mirror of the dresser. Her makeup bottles and jars scattered just as if she had left in a hurry that very morning.

&

When the pork steaks were ready, they sat inside the screened in porch with the ceiling fans circulating the warm air. Andrea had brought along potato salad and deviled eggs to go along with the barbecued pork steaks. Connie opened a jar of her home grown green beans; there was fresh corn on the cob and sliced ruby red tomatoes. Dinner was wonderful. Even though she was enjoying this evening with her long-time friends, her heart ached for the man missing from the table. Suddenly, and without warning, she felt like the odd person out, like a fifth wheel, in the group. She hoped no one would notice how hard she was fighting to maintain control of her emotions and to not cry. She hoped the ear of corn at her mouth would help control her quivering lips.

Ed interrupted her thoughts, when he asked if she was ready to see his little office. They walked across the yard towards one of the buildings that did not look familiar to her. Ed explained that it had been one of the old tool sheds, but he had fixed it up a little bit.

His 'little bit' involved having installed large windows with window boxes on the white upper half of the building. The lower half of the building had a stone façade attached. It looked like a miniature version of the main house. When Ed opened the front door, DK was pleasantly surprised. It was a beautiful office. Insulated and dry-walled; painted a soft blue gray color. Besides the usual desk, bookcases and other furniture that one usually finds in an office, there was a nice comfortable sofa and a matching recliner. A small oak dining table with four matching chairs and a small kitchenette in the corner.

DK exclaimed with a bit of a chuckle, "This is quite a nice little man cave you have here for yourself, sir."

Ed thanked her for the compliment and then went on to tell her that this office is for the next phase of his life. He said, "You know, to really live, we must all keep evolving and changing. If we don't change, we don't grow, and even at our ages, we should continue to grow. We don't want to become stagnate, do we?"

He went on to tell her that following his recent retirement as editor of the newspaper he knew he still wanted to be involved with writing. His degree in journalism from SIU Carbondale had allowed him to meet people and live an interesting and comfortable life. Now he wanted to write about that life. Not only that, but he wanted to help other people to share their own stories, too. He said that he had already had several books and short stories published and was now ready to move on to the next phase by creating his own publishing company. With the entire world being so computerized, he could reach out to small local authors, both near and far, and help them to realize their dreams and become published authors as well. He said that by being here at the farm, he was also available to help Connie if she needed it. Ed went on to tell her that he would continue to teach a couple of classes at the college on publishing. He was certain that retirement was going to be fun and productive for both of them.

అ ఞ

Once they were on the road heading for home, DK brought up the subject of seeing Chrissy's bedroom, "I was not prepared to see the shrine to Chrissy."

Gary replied, "Sorry, we forgot to warn you about that. We've gotten used to it and don't think anything of it."

Andrea added, "Yes, it was very hard at first when Connie insisted that they set up Chrissy's room just as she left it that day, even though Chrissy had never lived in that house. We tried to tell her she was only making it harder on herself to get over Chrissy's death. She said she was never going to get over it anyway, so what did it matter. She said at least by having Chrissy's room as it was, she could go in there and visit with her and smell her presence in the clothes and her perfume and to be able to feel her presence when she held her collection of teddy bears.

"I cannot imagine losing any one of my children, but to lose your only child is just unthinkable! Of course, she would want to hang on to something. When we were in Chrissy's room, Connie told me that everyone tried to talk her out of setting up the room. Even Ed told her it would be too hard to always look into the room and know she wasn't coming home," DK said.

Gary added, "Yeah, that is about the only thing those two do not agree on. Ed will not go in that room, and Connie goes in there daily. I think she could use some professional help, myself."

DK said, "Wow, I know grief is hard and different for everyone, I can't judge her for what makes her feel comfortable. I am not ready to face the task yet to get rid of all of David's things, but I do believe the day will come when I will get rid of most of his stuff. Some charity will certainly benefit from all his good suits and clothes."

"Let's change the subject," interrupted Andrea. "If you don't have any plans for tomorrow, let's have a girl's day together. Maybe go to Paducah and do some fabric shopping and go to the quilt museum too. I know you can never pass up the opportunity to go fabric shopping! I can leave right after we finish up the breakfast service in the morning. We only have a couple of rooms tonight, so it won't take long. We can probably be on the road by ten, if that works for you."

DK was thrilled with the idea. She said, "I'll skip breakfast. That will save you one meal to fix! I'll get up and go to early Mass, next door, at St. Mary's and then meet you at the café. You can drive."

CHAPTER FOUR

DK dressed in the bright floral dress and sandals that she had thrown into her suitcase as an afterthought on the day she made her escape from her depressed reality. Today she would attend Mass next door at St. Mary's Catholic Church where she would thank God for her supportive family and friends. She would thank Him for bringing her to this beautiful place where she had a sense of healing. She would ask for forgiveness of her anger that she had let take over her senses at her loss of David.

Following Mass, she walked over one block to have a light breakfast at the Main Street Café while she waited for Andrea to join her.

Andrea arrived around nine-thirty, saying that Gary had everything under control and had told her to go on and enjoy the day. The girls were off for a day of girl bonding like they had not shared in quite some time. They were as excited and giddy as two teenage girls skipping out of school for the day.

The hour-long drive allowed the two friends time to catch up on a friendship that had begun so many years ago. They talked and shared the little things of their day to day lives. Just small talk, nothing that mattered for the most part, but also realizing that their friendship had not been changed by time and distance. Through the years of becoming mothers and grandmothers, they had always stayed connected. While their families were their first priorities, they always scheduled girl time together at least two or three times a year. They both valued their friendship and their 'roomie weekends' were always special events for them. David and Gary understood their bond and encouraged their special weekends.

Andrea reminisced about their first meeting in college. She told of their very first day of becoming roommates, the uncertainty of the person that they would be sharing their life with, day in and day out. Would they get along? Would one love loud, blasting rock and roll music and the other prefer country? Would one be a night-owl party person, while the other preferred to study quietly? Andrea reminded DK at how quickly they bonded and how much alike they were then, even coming from two entirely different backgrounds.

DK reminisced about the football games they attended together, watching the guys that they were both falling in love with. They talked about the nights that they danced until dawn and then went out for breakfast before going to bed.

Andrea said, "I especially remember when the guys moved out of the dorm and into that dingy little apartment. You told them we would be over on Saturday morning to cook them breakfast and you arrived with that shiny black iron skillet. David's jaw dropped when you told him it was the same one he nearly dropped on your head the day you two first met. He couldn't believe you had made it look like new again. I think that is the day he truly fell in love with you. Not to mention your awesome biscuits and gravy!"

DK replied, "You know what they always say, the way to a man's heart is through his stomach, and in our case, I think that was true!"

Andrea asked, "Do you remember the very first time we attended a party at their apartment? There were so many people there, we could barely move around the room."

DK responded, "I certainly do. I was terrified. I had never been to a party like that before and I just knew that my daddy was going to come rushing through the door and drag me out of there! I knew I would be in really big trouble if he found out." Andrea agreed that she too had been worried about being at her first unsupervised party.

DK went on to say, "However, I really thought our relationship was over during that whole anti-war riot back in 1970. As soon as it all started and was making the TV news, Daddy said he was coming to get me and take me home. I held him off as long as I could, but when the fire at Old Main broke out and they shut the college down, he was there with a rented truck and trailer and hauled me home. He said that was "it" for me. No more college away from home."

She continued on with her story, "You know, I went to work at Miss Lola's Beauty Shop, working as shampoo girl and appointment scheduler, while going to cosmetology school. I didn't think David would come looking for me. He was going to graduate college with a degree in accounting, what would he want with a college drop-out who cut hair for a living?"

Andrea said, "Yes, and I remember when he showed up at your parent's house with a bouquet of roses and said, "I get free haircuts for life, don't I?"

They both laughed.

They reminisced about the various times that DK would come back to visit the campus and attend special events, like homecoming and concerts. They both agreed that when the Carpenters came to the campus, was the very best concert ever, and they were both still big fans of their music. Even though Karen Carpenter had died several years earlier, her music still lived on.

Andrea asked DK if she had anything special she would be looking for at the quilt shops. Any special projects in mind? Andrea said that she herself was thinking ahead to Christmas and hoping to get teacher gifts made early this year.

DK hesitated with her response. Dreading the thought of her first Christmas without David, she replied, "No, nothing special, aside from escaping reality. At one time, I had big plans for this coming Christmas. In fact, on the day that David had his heart attack, I was drafting a gingerbread wall hanging. I had plans to create an entire gingerbread theme for the kitchen and dining room. I thought the boys would be old enough to enjoy making gingerbread houses this year. Now, I don't even care if Christmas is celebrated or not."

"Oh honey, I am so sorry. I didn't mean to bring you down," said Andrea.

Silence filled the air. Both ladies unsure of how to pick up the pieces of their shattered conversation.

※ ※

The girls arrived at the quilt museum, looking for fresh ideas for upcoming projects. They were always amazed at the intricate patterns and the talent shared by so many people from all across the country. They spent about an hour going through the museum and then more time in the gift shop looking at books and patterns. DK spotted a book titled, "A Merry Ginger Christmas." She quickly flipped through it and with a tear in her eye promptly put it back on the shelf and abruptly walked to the other side of the room.

Both ladies paid for their purchases in the gift shop and then walked down the old brick paved sidewalk to a little café for lunch. The café was housed in a refurbished wood frame building from 1915. It had large plate glass windows where they could watch other shoppers walking by and tourists taking rides in the horse drawn carriage. They chatted about the different quilts they had seen and sketched pictures from memory, since picture taking was not allowed in the museum. Then, it was off to start hitting the various fabric shops, looking for the perfect pieces of fabric for creating memories and treasures, or as all quilters know, building a good stash!

※ ※

When they arrived back at the inn. Andrea seemed anxious to be on her way. She quickly dropped DK at the door and asked, "Will you join us at our place for dinner tonight, around seven? I'll cook."

DK agreed.

That night after dinner, Andrea brought out a box wrapped in pretty Christmas paper with a big red bow on top. DK looked at

SEARCHING FOR SOMETHING SPECIAL

her very puzzled. When she opened the box, there on top was the book, with various gingerbread designs scattered around the title, "A Merry Ginger Christmas." DK looked at her friend with tears in her eyes and started to speak, "How did you? When did you?" Andrea said, "I watched you in the gift shop. I saw you quickly put it back and I knew you really needed that book."

Below the book were stacks of red, green and white fabrics. One was striped like peppermint candy, another was a tiny red checked. There was also a mottled brown and tan, perfect for making gingerbread men. Tiny gingerbread boy shaped buttons and even a bag of gingerbread potpourri. Tears came to DK's eyes and rolled down her face as she sifted through the box.

Andrea wrapped her arms around her friend and said, "I know this Christmas is going to be hard on everyone, even for those two little boys. You need to try to make this the most memorable Christmas you can for them. I wanted to help you get started making new memories."

DK hugged her friend and sobbed into her shoulder. She shook her head in agreement. Their friendship had lasted a lifetime, and words were not needed to express the love they had for each other.

CHAPTER FIVE

With a renewed energy as well as a sense of confidence, DK packed the suitcases into her car and said goodbye to her dear friends. She told them she was not going straight home, she would head up I-57, and then zig-zag her way through the back-country roads to get to Orchardville. She had not been there since her Aunt Dorothy died six years earlier. She felt the time was right to go back to the old homestead.

Her great, great grandfather had been given the farm as separation pay after the Civil War. One hundred acres had been in the family for four generations. She had treasured memories as a child visiting the farm and, for most of her life, had dreamed of one day being the next generation to hold the deed to the farm. That dream died when somehow DK's cousin, Marsha, ended up with the farm. DK had been so heartbroken over the whole deal that she didn't even go back to the house to visit with the rest of the family after Aunt Dorothy's funeral.

Cruising along through the back roads, seemingly alone, her satellite radio tuned to a classic country station. DK sang along with Dwight Yoakam as he crooned about being one thousand miles from nowhere with heartaches in his pocket and echoes in his head. Jo Dee Messina with her U-Haul van searching for the Promised Land, and Kenny Chesney touting a sexy tractor and his farmer's tan. Of course, she had to laugh out loud as Teri Clark belted out about being an emotional girl laughing and crying at the same time. The Good Lord knows; DK had done that on numerous occasions. All the songs were perfect background music to accompany her own personal feelings; along with the unique beautiful sights all around her.

Then, suddenly out of nowhere, she was passed by a

SEARCHING FOR SOMETHING SPECIAL

speeding car as if she were sitting still. She realized that even out here in the country, life moves much too quickly. Why must everyone be in such a hurry?

The wide-open fields displayed a beautiful God made quilt of various hues of green from the tall, dull, stalks of corn, to the short bright soy beans and various other crops in between. The large farms were dotted with an assortment of homes, barns, and grain elevators. Some appeared to be new, others showed their age. Even the lonely dilapidated, almost ghostly, deserted barns held their own form of beauty, telling long ago stories of their own. Occasionally, an old truck sitting out in a pasture rusting away could be seen. All this acreage was separated, yet knitted together by deliberately planted hedges of cedar, catalpa, and hickory nut trees. Clumps of bright yellow wild sunflowers occasionally accented the sides of the road. A clear blue sky dotted with perfect fluffs of white seemed to say that everything was and would continue to be right with the world.

The four-way stop in Orchardville had certainly changed in the last few years. She was not expecting to see a Dollar General Store and Subway sandwich shop on the corner where a family farm had once stood. She missed her turn, but realizing that the house across the road belonged to her Aunt Patsy, she made a quick U-turn in order to get back to the road she needed.

Orchardville seemed to have changed a lot, yet still remained the same. The firehouse was now a large metal building with three oversized garage doors, instead of the white barn that used to house a single firetruck. The former wooden clapboard school house was a new brick building. However, the general store still stood just as she had remembered. It had been meticulously cared for and stood as a tribute to a long-ago era.

DK pulled onto the gravel area in front of the building and just sat for a few minutes soaking up the sight of so many memories of her youth. Realizing too, that this building held the memories of many generations long before her. The oversized windows on either side of the double screen door were no doubt designed to let in natural light long before there was electricity in the town. The wooden benches on the porch under the windows had provided many years of visiting with neighbors while taking a break from their daily chores. The wooden awning offered shade from the late afternoon sun. For over a hundred years this building stood at the crossroads of town, offering more than the necessary food staples in life. It was the social center of town, where people shared their daily news and friendship, and offered help to those in need.

    DK slowly emerged from her car, taking a deep breath of the country air before going in to get a bottle of soda. Yes, she was thirsty and could use a cold drink, but the truth was, she wanted to see how much the inside had changed.

    As DK opened the screen door, a bell jingled overhead to announce her arrival. The proprietor who was in the back of the store slicing meat for another customer, hollered over the counter, "I'll be right with you ma'am."

    DK told him to take his time. She wasn't in any hurry; she wanted to look around. (She wanted to relish in once again being the little girl of six years old, exploring the old store as it once was.) The place was neat and clean, and yet she noticed immediately the musty old wood smell. Of course, wood that was over a hundred years old, would have a certain odor to it. The smell made her feel at home even though there were obvious changes. Upon closer inspection, she was surprised to see how much was still the same. That white glass front meat counter looked like the exact same one that she and her grandma used to order their bologna and cheese from. She knew it couldn't be the same counter after all these years, or could it? Country folks had a way of taking care of and repairing things. Maybe, just maybe, it is the same old meat counter.

    The old shiny, red metal Coke chest was gone. In its place stood a modern-day glass front case that held the usual plastic bottles that can be found in any convenience store. DK treasured the memory of the old chest where, when the shiny aluminum lid was opened, it revealed a treasure of brightly colored bottle caps of red, purple, orange and brown peeking out of their bed of finely crushed ice. On the front of the chest was the bottle opener that popped those collectible caps off the little glass bottles and caught them in a small metal trough. Deborah would always gather up all the caps that were there and take them back to the farm. Grandpa would use an ice pick to poke a hole in the center. Grandma would give her a ribbon to string them to make a necklace. The boys pushed the caps between the spokes on the wheels of their bikes. Oh, how those bottle caps were fun for everyone.

She remembered back to the days when her parents had not allowed soda at home, so what a treat it had always been to come to town to choose one of the sweet bottled drinks from the red chest. Each time she chose a different one, in order to be able to taste them all. Thinking back, she could still taste the crisp freshness of the Orange Crush, the yummy Grape Nehi, or Root Beer, and the very distinct fruity flavor of Dr. Pepper and its logo printed on the bottle that said 10, 2 and 4. It took her years to figure out that it meant you should have a Dr. Pepper at 10, 2 and 4. Even now, Dr. Pepper remains her favorite.

The simple, wooden benches that used to line the side walls in front of the shelves were gone. It's where she'd sat and waited for her grandma to finish shopping, and it was where all the old folks sat to catch up on the town gossip. The bench also offered a little girl the opportunity to reach items on a higher shelf. The benches had been replaced by several sets of wooden tables and chairs, placed back by the meat counter, where customers could now sit and have a cup of coffee with a sandwich while catching up on the current gossip.

She could remember sitting on the old wood floor and using a cotton rag to play tug of war with Uncle Clete's dog, Blackie. All four paws spread out, flat on his belly, his furry little body being swished back and forth like a dust mop on the wood floor. No matter how hard the struggle, Blackie never gave up his end of the old rag.

Strange that the place still smelled of the same old wood from long ago, even though it had been painted over more than a time or two. Some scents just never seem to go away.

The owner of the store, a short round man, with a chubby round baby face to match, approached the front counter. He was wiping his hands across the front of his white butcher's apron, before reaching out to shake hands with the stranger who had entered his store. He looked over the top rim of his black framed glasses, as he asked her if she was just passing through. "My name is Charlie King, I own the place. Don't think I have ever seen you here before." DK sensed a mixture of pride and country hospitality mixed in with a bit of reservation on his part.

She explained that she had deep family roots in this town and that it had been several years since she had been around. Of course, he wanted to know all about her, who she was related to and if there were any family left in town.

Before she could give him any answers to his questions, she thought back to the old people who used to sit on the bench listening and waiting for gossip. Though the benches were gone, she knew the people sitting at the tables drinking coffee were from the same lot. They were all ears, waiting to hear who the stranger in the store was and where was she going.

"Most of my immediate family are all gone," She hesitantly replied, "I have an aunt and a cousin along with her family here, probably more than a few distant relatives still around somewhere. Not real sure where to find some of them. But if you have been around for any length of time, I'm sure you knew of the Bridges, Cunninghams, Porters, and Martins. They are all related in one way or another.

"Well, I'll be," he said. "Sure enough, I know all those names. Right over there in the red plaid shirt is Sam Cunningham.

Sam! Get over here! You need to meet this lady. She's one of your kin."

It was obvious that the tall, rugged, broad shouldered man had been listening and was already slowly working his way over to the counter. When he was close enough to talk, he asked DK what their connection might be.

"I don't know the whole family tree all that well without looking at my grandpa's Bible," she said, "but my dad's family was one of the Bridges family. Somewhere along the way, I know one of the Cunninghams married one of the Bridges."

"Their farm was right up that road a piece and to the left," Sam said.

"Yes, it was. I spent many weekends and parts of every summer there on the farm when I was a kid. Lots of fun memories. Oh, by the way, my name is DK, uh...sorry...not DK. I mean Deborah... Deborah Kingston now. It used to be Deborah Bridges," I am trying to drop that old DK nickname I used to go by. Forget that I said that. Time for me to be just Deborah again. Deborah replied as she shook hands with both men. She could not take her eyes off the tall broad shouldered man with the deep gravelly voice. He reminded her of Sam Elliot, the actor, even down to his graying, well-trimmed, horseshoe mustache.

Charlie said, "Miss Marsha lives there now. Has a couple of little grandkids that she takes care of most days. Guess'n she must be your cousin? She got the farm from her Aunt Dorothy."

"Yes, Marsha is my cousin. We haven't seen each other in years," answered Deborah. It still stung that Marsha had ended up with the farm with never an explanation from Aunt Dorothy or Uncle John as to why.

Charlie began to fill her in on his own connection to her family. He said, "I married Cletus' granddaughter, Gloria. You remember Cletus. He owned this store when you were a kid. Cletus had three sons: Tony, Thomas and James. Tony had two girls: Gloria and Marianne. I married Gloria. We live in the same house that Cletus did. We fixed it up a bit, but it is still the same house. It only made sense to keep the house in the family too, especially since I bought the store from Tony after Cletus and Carol Anne died. Gloria is a school teacher, so we both walk to work. Makes it convenient for both of us."

DK proclaimed that it indeed was a small world and, even after all these years she was still related to most of the town in one way or another. She paid for her Dr. Pepper and bag of pretzels, then turned for the door.

Charlie shouted out, "You going by the farm now?"

Deborah hesitated, but said, yes, she wanted to see the old place again. She stepped out onto the time worn wooden porch and surveyed the area around her. The store sat at the T-intersection where the county road led in and out of town. She knew from this point, if she went left on the hardtop road, it would take her in the direction of the little white church and cemetery that she had often visited with her grandparents and where they were both buried. If she went straight down the gravel road facing her, she would be headed towards any one of the five family farms. She wasn't sure who owned them all now, except that Marsha had the farm that she had always wanted. If she went right on the county hardtop, it would take her back out of town, the same direction that she had come from. For a short moment, she thought about doing just that: heading for the comfort of home. She was uneasy about going forward to the farm.

She stepped off the porch and looked up to the front of the store. The sign above still said, "Clete's Grocery." Not everything changes, she thought to herself. She got into her car and closed the sunroof to keep the dust out as she proceeded down the gravel road.

She turned left at the first road and was surprised at how well maintained the trees and brush were. The last time she had been on this road, it was completely overgrown and tree branches had slapped the sides of her car as she tried to make her way down the road to go visit Aunt Dorothy and Uncle John. It was the last time she had tried to make her pitch for buying the farm and keeping it in the family. Uncle John was no longer physically able to keep up with all the fields and take care of Aunt Dorothy, too. The farm had looked extremely neglected during that disappointing visit. It still hurt as she thought about that day, so long ago.

~ ~

She slowly drove past the farm, taking a long look as she drove by. Trying to see if anyone was home or not, and debating if she should stop and knock on the door. She went on down the road towards what at one time had been her great uncle Willie's place. The house and barn were long gone, but she could turn around on the old gravel lane.

She crept ever so slowly up the road towards the farm again, wanting to see all that she could, but trying not to be seen. It's kind of hard to go un-noticed in a town like this, where everyone knows the look and sound of every car that belongs there, and pays special attention to the sounds of a stranger's car. She knew that if Marsha was home she would be looking out the window to see who was driving by.

Deborah rolled to a stop just short of the driveway, still somewhat shielded by the edge of the cornfield. She could see the house and hoped she was hidden from Marsha's window. She remembered the "new" house the whole family worked together to build for her Grandpa and Grandma Bridges. It had three bedrooms and a real bathroom with a tub and running water! A living room and large eat in kitchen, and electric lights. No longer would they be using oil lamps and going to bed as soon as the sun went down. Best of all...no more trips to the outhouse...or emptying the chamber pot in the mornings!!

Beyond the barn, Deborah caught a glimpse of the old brown-shingled original house, built by her great, great grandfather, Alvin. Aunt Dorothy had long ago turned the old house into a storage building filled with family treasures and keepsakes. Deborah remembered being a little girl fascinated by the hand pump in the old kitchen that pumped water directly from the outside well into the kitchen for easy access when cooking. A country version of running water. Her memory flashed back to the wooden bucket that sat on the counter with the long-handled dipper for drinking. Everyone drank out of the same bucket, from the same dipper, and never gave a thought to spreading germs.

The sounds of laughing children and a banging screen door brought Deborah back to reality. She looked toward the yard and saw two little girls with long braided blonde pigtails and a toddler boy with chubby little legs running behind them. All of them were headed towards the swing-set over in the side yard of the main house. The girls were about the same ages as her own grandchildren, Jeremy and Jacob, but the little guy was a new addition that she had never met.

As much as she wanted to, she could not bring herself to go talk to Marsha, not yet. She put the car into drive and ever so slowly edged away from the protection of the corn field, hoping that Marsha would be at the kitchen sink facing the back of the house.

As she pulled forward, her attention was drawn to the empty field on her right. The oil rig pumping in the field caught her eye. She had completely forgotten that there was a working oil pump there. The last time she was here the place was so overgrown, the pump could not even be seen. With her gaze fixed on the oil rig, she missed noticing Marsha come out the back door with a glass of iced tea and giving a neighborly wave. Marsha, of course, had no idea who the stranger in the white Highlander was.

As Deborah gave a final glance in her rearview mirror, she saw Marsha placing the chubby little boy into the toddler swing.

                                                          ❧ ☙

Deborah drove straight to the church and cemetery. She knew she wouldn't have to face anyone who might want to ask a lot of questions about why she was suddenly in town. No one there would be doing any talking.

She turned left onto the familiar road, but the first sign that things were not the same as she remembered, was that there were no signs on the road to indicate that there was a church in the area. The trees and brush were so overgrown that the little white building could not even be seen from the road. As she turned up the long gravel lane leading to the church, her eyes fell upon the aging building. The once pristine white clapboard was now dirty and spotted with green mold. It held an aura of lonely sadness. Her heart sank as she pictured the old preacher standing at the top of the stairs, greeting church members as they arrived for Sunday services. Everyone carrying their own worn bibles in their arms; pages dog-eared and wrinkled, definite signs of being read often. What would those dedicated worshipers think about this now?

Even though she had been here six years earlier for Aunt Dorothy's funeral, it was the memories of her youth that enveloped her as she looked around. The gravel parking area had never been paved over. She could still visualize her grandpa's old truck slowly rolling onto the gravel and stopping exactly where she had just parked herself. To her right sat the new parsonage. Funny that everyone still called it the new parsonage, since it was new back in 1971. (The original parsonage had been in the basement of the church.) The new brick ranch style house with large picture windows faced the church. There was a two car, side load detached garage that was connected to the house by a breezeway. She had never been in it and only imagined what the inside looked like. She chuckled as she pondered the idea that it probably still had green shag carpet that was so popular at the time.

Deborah knew the sun would be setting soon and her time here was limited, but she wanted to take a quick look around and maybe take a few pictures with the setting sun in the background before she headed for home.

As Deborah walked towards the cemetery, passing across the front of the church, she couldn't help but notice the Surprise Lilies blooming on either side of the steps. It was as if they were there to welcome her back to the old place. Delighted at their sight, she couldn't help but laugh out loud and mumble, "Look, David, even the church has Naked Ladies!" She had to pause and take a few pictures.

The sound of a gas-powered weed-eater, could be heard coming from the cemetery side of the church grounds. As DK walked around the side of the church building heading towards the cemetery, she saw a man dressed in jeans and a bright yellow safety vest over a long- sleeved, lime green tee shirt. It was obvious that he was taking great pride in his work of trimming around the headstones with his large commercial sized weed-eater. He used both hands holding onto the handlebar like grips of the machine and, with a steady back and forth rhythm, he moved from stone to stone and row to row. She wondered if he was listening to music while he worked or were the headphones simply ear protection. Concentrating on his work, he had no idea that she was there.

Not wanting to scare him, she made a wide berth to get around him and headed towards the graves of her grandparents, but the groundskeeper spotted her movement and turned off the gas of the weed-eater. He turned to acknowledge her presence and walked towards her. As he got closer he removed his safety goggles, they both gave a little laugh.

"Well, hello there! We meet again. It's Ms. Deborah,

SEARCHING FOR SOMETHING SPECIAL

isn't it?" It was Sam, whom she had met at the store earlier.

"Yes, it is. This is a surprise! I wasn't expecting to see you here," she replied.

"I'm the groundskeeper and security guard. I live over there in what used to be the parsonage," Sam told her, as he pointed over towards the modest brick house.

"You said, "Used to be parsonage?" The preacher doesn't live there anymore?" Deborah asked.

"Oh, no ma'am. We haven't had a preacher around here for a few years. Not many people getting married here, or baptizing babies. When one of the old-timers dies, the preacher from Wayne City comes here for that. Most folks now go into Wayne City or Salem on Sunday mornings so they can eat at a restaurant and then go shopping. The town hired me to take care of the place and keep the kids from partying here at night. There was a lot of that going on since the church grounds are hidden behind, that tree line that runs along the road. It's pretty quiet and peaceful around here now. Just what I needed when I came here to Orchardville. Can I help you find some names here? You said earlier that you were related to half the town."

"Yes, I did want to at least visit with my grandparents and Aunt Dorothy and Uncle John. The rest will have to wait for another time. It's getting late. The sun is almost set and I need to get something to eat before I hit the road. How late is that Subway on the corner open?" she asked.

In his deep gravelly voice, Sam said, "Honey, you are in the country. Everything shuts down and locks up by seven. Earlier if they haven't had any customers in a while, and they feel like going home. If you'd like, I can call Charlie and see if he has any meatloaf left. That was his dinner special today. He makes a really good one. Usually sells out pretty quick. I can tell him to hold a plate for you."

With a grateful voice, Deborah said, "That would be very kind of you" she replied, "But I don't want to interrupt your work here, which I guess I already did. I'm sorry."

"No bother at all. It will soon be too dark to see anyway. Let me put this thing away while you look around a bit. I'll go call Charlie," Sam said as he turned and headed for the storage shed next to the parsonage.

Deborah walked around the familiar cemetery. She had to ramble around a bit to find the names she was looking for. The trees that had at one time been her markers were either, dead and gone or had grown and didn't seem to be where she thought they were. But she quickly found her grandparents and her aunt and uncle. She said a little prayer and asked for their help in guiding her in this new phase in her life. She did direct a sincere act of apology to her Aunt Dorothy. She was sorry for not keeping in closer touch during her last couple of years. She said she was so hurt that Dorothy would never discuss with her the desire that burned in her heart to own even just one small piece of the family farm. Why had it always been such a closed discussion? With most of the relatives gone, she would probably never know the answer to that question.

Even now, with hardly any family left here in Orchardville and the strain that she felt towards Marsha, she felt more at home here than she could have imagined. Something about this day felt right. She kissed the palm of her hand and touched the top of Aunt Dorothy's headstone and whispered, "I'm sorry."

As Deborah turned to walk away, the scent of musk was suddenly there with her. Tears immediately stung her face. "Oh, David, of course, you would approve of my apologizing. You always tried to encourage me to visit with her more, but I was stubborn. My whole life I wanted to live here and she ignored me, and in the end, I chose to ignore her. I know it was wrong and I hope she knows I didn't mean to be so selfish." The musk seemed to swirl in the wind and then evaporate.

Sam met Deborah at the side of her car and said Charlie would be keeping a plate warm for her. Sam gave her a puzzled look as she tried to hide her tear stained face. With her head bowed down, she mumbled a thank you to him and got into her car.

※ ※

Charlie told Deborah to have a seat at the table and he would bring her a plate. The table had already been set with the silverware and a glass of tea. He told her he could get her something else to drink if she didn't want sweet tea. She assured him that the tea would be fine.

When Charlie brought the plate to her, he sat in the chair across from her. Said he didn't like to see anyone eating all alone.

He asked about her visit with her cousin Marsha. Said he had noticed her car go by not long after she had left the store. Maybe Marsha hadn't been home?

Deborah hesitated, not wanting to get all into the family business and her hurt feelings, but it also came to her mind that in this small town, Charlie already knew all of that and was most likely fishing for details.

She said, "I am kind of in a hurry to get back home, and really did not want to feel obligated to have a long visit with Marsha. I just wanted to see the old place and relive some memories. Maybe next time I am in town, I'll have more time to spend with her. I do intend to stop in and say hi to my Aunt Patsy on my way out of town."

Charlie told her, "I can tell you she is not home. This is Bunco night. All the ladies are over at June Collier's house. I can give you directions. Do you play Bunco? I know they were looking for a sub. Ms. Fern Abernathy is under the weather and couldn't play tonight."

"I'll pass on the Bunco. I need to head home. I've been away for a few days. Been exploring all around the Shawnee Forest area, rejuvenating the soul," she said.

"This whole southern region is good for that," Charlie said. "Lots of peace and quiet all around these parts. Sometimes too much quiet. Hard to keep good folks living around here. The young ones all want to go to the city and the old folks are all dying off. Needin' some new blood around here really bad. The town board is hoping that if we can sell off the old church, something new will spark some life back here. But we don't want to advertise it yet with a realtor or on one of them internet sales sites. We don't want a bunch of high and mighty city folks coming in and making big changes. Just a little spark of life is all we want."

Deborah choked as she swallowed the bite of food in her mouth. "Sell the church? You can do that? What about Sam? Where will he go, and what will he do? Besides, who wants to buy a cemetery?"

"Those are questions we have all been askin' ourselves. We are hoping to find a semi-retired preacher who could live on a small salary. You know; one who isn't young and trying to raise a family on what we could pay." "As for Sam, he's a really good guy. He was a God-send to us when we needed it and I guess it's safe to say, we were for him, too. He was in a bad way; a real mess after his time in Iraq. We hope if we get a preacher, he will keep Sam as the grounds keeper. Between the parsonage and the small apartment in the basement of the church, there would be room for both."

Deborah stood to leave and wished Charlie good luck on finding a part time preacher. She said she would check with some of her friends in Belleville. Maybe there was a retired Air Force Chaplain or other retired preacher she could refer to him. She told him to not give up hope.

Charlie responded, "Yes ma'am. God will provide when the time is right."

CHAPTER SIX

Deborah was glad to wake up in her own bed, feeling refreshed and content with a happy cat snuggled against her side. She knew the trip had been exactly what she needed, but now it was time to focus on moving forward and trying to figure out what her new life would bring and where it would take her.

The first order of business was to call Liz and let her know that she was home and not needed today. Then she called Annie to see if they could meet for lunch.

Deborah was barely out of the shower, wrapped in David's old brown robe, when her phone rang. The sharp voice on the other end was that of a very un-happy woman. "Deborah Suzanne Kingston! What is this I hear about you being in Orchardville yesterday and not even stopping to say hello? I went out to get some bread and milk this morning, Charlie and Sam said they met you yesterday afternoon!" She was indeed one feisty little lady, when she wanted to be.

"Hello, to you too, Aunt Patsy!" Chuckled Deborah. "I did intend to stop and was told that you were gone for the evening playing Bunco."

"Well, why didn't you let me know you were coming earlier? You haven't been here in years and then you drove all the way from Belleville, without calling first! We could have made plans."

"I'm sorry, Aunt Patsy. It was a spur of the moment thing, I didn't know I was going to be there, until I arrived. Besides, I didn't come from Belleville. I had been spending the week with my friends in Anna. You remember Gary and Andrea, don't you? Mine and David's friends from college. I stayed at the Inn that they run, and Andrea and I went to Paducah to do some quilt shopping. When I left there, on a whim, I just decided to go to Orchardville. I had an interesting time meeting Sam and Charlie. They were both very nice."

Barely taking a breath, Patsy went on to say, "Charlie also told me that you went by the farm and that you didn't even stop and talk to Marsha either! Sounds to me, like you didn't want to talk to nobody! Why did you even bother driving through here?"

Deborah grinned, shook her head and rolled her eyes. Grateful that her dear aunt could not see her face right now. "I guess you are right. I didn't want to talk to anyone. It has been six years since I was in town and I kind of wanted to look around without getting into anything with anyone. I have missed being around there, but not quite ready to talk. I wanted to get a 'feel' for the old place again."

"Girl, are you still sore about Marsha getting the old farm? You can't blame her for what Dorothy did for her and didn't do for you! My sister must have had her reasons for leaving the farm to Marsha, and we will never know why she chose her over all the other kids, but it's done and no amount of wishing it were different ain't gonna change a thing! Now, when are you comin' back for a proper visit?"

"I don't know for sure when I will be back, but I am feeling much better these days and I do plan to do more outings for myself. I promise I will see you one day real soon, and I will take you to lunch in Wayne City if you would like."

Aunt Patsy thought that was a mighty fine idea and said she would look forward to Deborah coming to visit. Maybe she could come to next month's Bunco night. Patsy said she would be hosting and knew they would need a sub since Fern Abernathy was scheduled for surgery that week. Patsy suggested that Deborah should just plan on spending the night since Bunco would run late. Deborah agreed, unable to tell her aunt, "No."

❧ ☙

Before heading to meet Annie for lunch, Deborah stopped at Randy's office to check on things there. Randy told her he had

SEARCHING FOR SOMETHING SPECIAL

talked to someone about joining the firm and the man seemed to be exactly what they were looking for. Randy said he was waiting for her to return so they could schedule a time for everyone to meet.

Chelsea called Douglas Schaeffer and had him on speaker phone so they could all compare their calendars. It appeared that this very evening was open for all parties involved. Chelsea made reservations for dinner at seven at the Japanese Steak House.

∽ ∾

Annie arrived at the stylish little tea room in a chipper mood, and appeared genuinely interested in her mother's recent trip, as she looked at the photo's that Deborah showed her while they lunched on the house quiche and salad.

Deborah filled Annie in on her morning phone conversation with her Aunt Patsy. Deborah suggested that sometime before school starts that they take the boys to Orchardville, and show them around the old homestead, and maybe take them fishing. Aunt Patsy would certainly enjoy seeing the boys again. They could also take a side trip down to Metropolis and see the large Superman statue. Annie agreed that it sounded like a fun idea and, of course, the boys would love it.

Deborah went on to tell Annie about meeting and talking with Sam and Charlie at the store. She told her about the Grace Bible Church and grounds being up for sale and how they were hoping to find a part-time preacher, but no prospects were coming forth.

Annie asked, "So, why don't you buy it?"

Deborah looked quizzical, with furrowed brow, she wondered, "What would I do with a church? I have been looking for something, but a church?"

Annie said, "I don't know, you could do lots of things. Live in it? Create a photography studio or gift shop? I don't know. You're creative enough, you could come up with something."

Deborah laughed and said, "I guess I could, but right now we need to set up a make-up date for school shopping with the boys. How about one day next week?"

❦ ❧

Deborah arrived for dinner at the steakhouse, dressed in a stylish olive green summer suit with a cool, sleeveless, free-flowing breezy top. Randy and Chelsea were already waiting at the bar. Deborah noticed that Randy's arm was casually draped across the back of Chelsea's bar stool and they were leaning into each other talking. Deborah smiled, knowing that she had been right about those two. When she approached the bar, she did not let on that she had noticed the closeness between them.

Moments later, Mr. Douglas Schaeffer arrived and introductions were made while they waited to be seated. Douglas seemed to be about ten years older than Randy, which was good. It meant he was old enough to have a little bit more experience in the business than Randy and wasn't thinking of retiring any time soon, yet close enough in age that they could be friends. Not a father figure for Randy, but a mentor.

Over dinner, they discussed the needs of the office as well as what Douglas hoped to achieve by coming on board. They all seemed to be on the same page as to what each of them wanted and where they saw the company heading in the next ten years. All in all, it was a very productive dinner. Randy said he would call Douglas soon and let him know his decision.

Randy walked his mother to her car, and then he and Chelsea proceeded to walk over to Randy's car. Deborah was even more certain of their relationship when she saw them exchange a kiss as Randy held the car door open for Chelsea.

SEARCHING FOR SOMETHING SPECIAL

❧ ☙

Deborah had been sleeping peacefully but must have been dreaming, before she jumped out of bed, scooped Bandit up in her arms shouting, "YES! That is, it! I know what I am going to do!"

Deborah ran to the desktop computer that was set up in David's home office. She plopped Bandit on the desk, logged into the investment file and found the account with the inheritance money that her Aunt Dorothy had left Deborah in her will.

When Deborah received the one hundred and fifty thousand dollars, David had insisted that they invest the money for some future use. He told her that someday, she would find a true need for the money. With having it well invested for six years, it had grown quite nicely, and yes, this should certainly be enough to buy the little white church. She searched around on the website and found that she could transfer one hundred thousand dollars to her personal checking account on-line, anything more than that required an office visit with a signed form and forty-eight hour waiting period before any more money could be released.

Deborah successfully transferred one hundred thousand dollars to her personal checking account. Quite pleased with herself, and grateful that Randy had the patience to teach her the computer skills to be able to do it. She wanted to call him and shout for joy at what she had accomplished, but knew he would not appreciate a phone call at three in the morning!

She went back to bed with numerous thoughts of what all she could do with her little church house. The ideas flowed through her mind kept her reeling, tossing and turning, as she tried effortlessly to sleep.

❧ ☙

First thing the next morning Deborah quickly showered, and fed Bandit. She then went to the computer one more time to make sure that the money was still there and that her newly found computer skills had not screwed anything up.

She poured her coffee into a thermal travel mug and was out the door, headed towards Highway 161. She figured she would be at Clete's General Store around nine thirty or ten.

Just as she had expected when she arrived, Sam was sitting at one of the little tables drinking coffee and talking with a couple of other folks from town.

"Well, what have we here?" Asked Charlie. "Didn't expect to see you back this quick. Miss Patsy said you would be coming back next month to play Bunco. Did she know you were coming today?"

"No. I didn't take the time to call her yet." Deborah looked around the store and realizing she didn't know any of those folks, nor who knew what, she wasn't sure she wanted to say anything more in front of them. She thought for a moment, then said, "I have a surprise I want to give her later today at lunch, so I am asking if everyone could please not tell her that you saw me here today. She is going to be so surprised when I tell her my news! Please help me to keep this secret! Okay?"

They all agreed that they wouldn't say anything.

Stalling for more time and hoping to ward off any thoughts of suspicion from anyone, she asked Sam if he could unlock the church so she could take some pictures of the inside. She added that the pictures were part of her surprise.

Sam said that he was finished with his coffee and he would be happy to meet her over there. As she headed to the door, she turned and reminded everyone again that this visit was a secret. Then wondered to herself, "I wonder if I am talking to the woodworks here. Do these people know how to keep a secret, or who had already started calling Aunt Patsy?" Deborah was well aware of how quickly news of any kind spread around town.

SEARCHING FOR SOMETHING SPECIAL

The church still had the same old smoky wood smell from the wood burning stove that Grandpa used to get stoked before the rest of the congregation arrived. She especially remembered being there on Father's Day every year. Grandpa was always acknowledged for having the most family members present on that day and the church Elders gave him a white carnation boutonniere. He was proud as a peacock of his large family who showed their love and support.

Trying to keep her cool, she took pictures of the hand hewed wood support beams across the ceiling. Pictures of the large casement windows on the side walls of the building. There were long views of the pews as well as close -ups of the hand-carved end caps. She took pictures from all different angles: front and back and side to side. She used the fish-eye lens, took wide angle shots and close-ups as well.

Sam watched her work quietly for a while and then finally asked, "Ms. Kingston, you sure seem to know what you are doing with that fancy camera there. Why are you taking all these pictures? Are you going to put them in a magazine or something?"

Still not sure who she wanted to tell just yet, but knowing also she had to start somewhere. She said, "Sam, this really has to be kept a secret for now. I hope I can trust you, I think I may know someone who would like to buy the church, but umm, the buyer has requested more information."

"Oh Wow! Ms. Kingston! That would be the answer to this town's prayers if we got a part time preacher."

"Well, I'm not so sure about the part time preacher part just yet, but maybe in time. Do you know how much they are asking for the church and how much land besides the cemetery comes with it? Who is in charge of the sale; since you don't have it listed with a realtor and are not advertising? Deborah had hoped by rambling off a lot of questions that Sam would forget that a preacher was not in the deal right now.

"I guess, you would say it is sort of by committee now. Which would include Norm Johnson, since he is the town trustee. Your Aunt Patsy, since she is the oldest member of the congregation. Charlie and myself. We would have to meet with the buyer and discuss their plans and make sure they are what we want in our town. Like we said before, we don't want someone coming in here and tearing down or disrespecting the history of our church. We all have a lot of memories here."

"Sam, I would like to walk around and look at the grounds real close. I cannot tell you yet who the buyer might be, but I can tell you what plans they would like to do here. I promise you, the plans will respect the history as well as make many new and happy memories. Can you arrange a meeting today, maybe over lunch? Is there somewhere private where the committee can talk freely and uninterrupted? I will speak on behalf of the potential buyer. I am going to take some more pictures outside…you know… so the potential buyer can see what all they might be getting."

Sam told her that he would go into the house and make some phone calls and see what he could arrange on such short notice, and she should feel free to walk around and take all the pictures she wanted.

"By the way, Sam, can you please not mention my name to Aunt Patsy? I want to surprise her."

After she finished taking pictures and looking around, getting even more ideas in her head of what could become of the little church, she took out her cell phone to call Aunt Patsy. "Hi, Aunt Patsy. It is Deborah, I was thinking of being in town later today and was wondering if you would like to go to lunch?"

"Well, I am glad you called first! I just made lunch plans with the church committee, it seems that the Good Lord has sent someone who might be buying our church. I can't miss this meeting, so you will have to come on another day, Deborah dear, sorry." With that she hung up the phone without giving Deborah a chance to say goodbye.

Smiling at the excitement in her aunt's voice and knowing what a surprise she was going to get at lunch, Deborah simply said, "Well, OK. I will see you later" to the dead air on the other end of the line.

Now she had to figure out where she could hide out until lunch time. She couldn't go back to the store where someone may come in and see her. She couldn't go by the farm and visit with Marsha, who would for sure call Aunt Patsy. While she was contemplating what her options might be, Sam came outside to tell her that the phone calls had been made and everyone will be meeting here at the parsonage. Charlie would bring lunch for everyone. Sam offered Deborah to go on into the house and make herself comfortable while she waited for everyone to arrive. He said he had a few things he needed to attend to. Deborah told Sam she wanted to move her car to the far side of the church, so it wouldn't be the first thing that Aunt Patsy saw when she arrived.

Sam said, "I can do you one better than that. My garage is empty, and I will be going over to pick up Patsy, so you just pull your car into the garage. She won't know you are here. Sam showed her into the dining room and offered her some sweet tea, told her he would be back in about an hour or so, and to make herself comfortable.

Deborah settled in at the table with a sketch pad and the pictures she had taken on her last visit. The ideas she had were multiplying quicker than her own brain could keep up with. With each new idea, she got more and more excited about the possibilities, not giving any thought to any pending obstacles.

Charlie arrived first, carrying a large brown paper bag with all the fixings for sandwiches, along with a few homegrown tomatoes and fresh leaf lettuce. Deborah helped him set out the food on the breakfast bar between the kitchen and dining room. Just as they were finishing up, both Norm Johnson and Sam pulled into the driveway. Sam came around the side of his pickup to open the door for Patsy, but the spry little lady was already out and quickly stepping towards the breezeway door that connected the garage to the main house. For a lady, just a few months' shy of turning ninety-five, she could certainly move quickly. The determination in her steps toward the door, were definitely those of a lady on a mission.

Deborah watched from the kitchen window and had a sudden moment of panic, wondering what her aunt would say when they came face to face. Of course, the elder woman would have lots of questions. Deborah could only hope she could get through them without blowing her cover just yet. The door swung open and in charged a very excited woman. Dressed in a small floral print, cotton, shirt waist dress. A thin white belt cinched to show off her tiny frame. An appropriate dress for a business meeting or Sunday service.

"Where is this man that is going to buy our church? I want to know what his plans are. I'm an old woman and I don't have a lot of time to play around now!"

Deborah stepped out from the kitchen and said, "Hi, Aunt Patsy! It is so good to see you!" As she moved to give her aunt a hug.

Patsy accepted the hug, but then took a step back, "Deborah, what on earth are you doing here? I don't understand. I told you just barely an hour ago that I had a meeting…wait! Are you here for the meeting? Are you buying the church?" she asked rather puzzled.

Deborah had wished that Aunt Patsy had not been so direct with that last question. She didn't want to lie to her aunt, but also didn't want to commit herself to say that she did indeed have intentions of buying the church.

"All I can say at this time, is that I am representing an interested party who has some unique ideas that you may or may not be responsive to. The buyer would rather remain anonymous for the time being, until after you hear the proposal. I hope all of you will understand and appreciate their wishes." explained Deborah.

Deborah was introduced to Norm Johnson, a tall lanky man, who appeared to be in his late eighties, dressed in blue jeans and a plaid cotton shirt, with his white hair, flat-top cut. Deborah assumed it was probably the only hair style the man had ever worn.

Everyone fixed their sandwiches and gathered around the table. Deborah began to explain the tentative plans. "First of all, I have to tell you what wonderful memories I have had in this church, and I very much understand your wanting to preserve everything that it stands for. The grounds are quite lovely and very well maintained. The entire piece of land is a hidden gem, and any potential buyer would be honored to own it. I must say, I was surprised when I found that there is a small pond beyond the first tree line behind the church."

Everyone started to talk at once. Finally, Norm Johnson, the town trustee, became the designated speaker for the group. He said, "We had to dig that lake about ten or twelve years ago. The insurance company insisted there had to be water close by, in case of a fire, especially since we added on the new fellowship hall across the back of the church."

Deborah asked, "Is it possible to clear out some of that tree line, so the lake, as you call it, can be seen from the church yard? I think the buyer would like to see it as a decorative asset to the property instead of just a functional watering hole in case of fire."

Eagerly, they all agreed, that could be taken care of with no problem. Sam added that it was mostly overgrown brush and he would be more than happy to start cutting it away.

Deborah went on with her pitch, "The other day, I was told by Charlie that you have been looking for a part time preacher for quite some time, to no avail. I asked around with some of my connections at my own church in Belleville, and sadly, no one knows of anyone who would be suitable for your needs at this time. However, an idea was presented to me by someone and I think if you hear me out, you will agree that even without a preacher, this church and grounds could become something special."

"It was suggested that this church and its grounds would make a beautiful setting for a photography studio. Oh, but not just any ordinary photography studio; it would specialize in wedding pictures and portraits."

In unison, the group resounded, "What?? A photography studio??"

Deborah quickly added, "I know that is not what you expected, but please look at these pictures that I took the other day when I was here and imagine with me, if you will. All along the side of the church are beautiful flower beds, picture a bride in her dress standing in front of them. And here, this one of the front steps, visualize the groomsmen standing on each of the steps and the groom at the top by the door. And when the lake is cleaned up, just picture a bride standing in front of it, or a family getting their portrait made there. Even the cemetery can offer a unique backdrop for some family portraits. Generations pictured together; the living and the deceased, together for eternity. I've seen it magazines."

Norm seemed aggravated when he replied, "Young lady, I don't know who your buyer is, or where they came up with such a crazy notion. Some crazy city fella, no doubt! First of all, ain't no one in these parts going to come here to have some pictures made when we ain't got a preacher, and they have to go somewhere else to get married! That is just downright silly thinking, if you ask me."

"Please sir, if I may finish," Deborah pleaded. "Here are some sketches that were done this morning before I came here. Picture a white wrought iron arched sign over the drive way. On top is the outline of a large bell. Below that it reads, *The Wedding Belle*, Family Life Chapel and Photography Studio.' Now, I mean no disrespect, but today's brides will drive and fly for hours for the right place, just to take the pictures besides going someplace unique to make her day special. In many of your neighboring towns all around here are wineries that are always booked for weddings and they don't have what is sitting right here. Doing this can bring revenue to your town without losing the history or dignity that this church and hallowed grounds so richly deserve."

"You are forgettin' one thing; you can't have a wedding without a preacher," replied Norm Johnson.

Deborah was feeling totally deflated, but not yet ready to give up her idea.

"I'm sorry sir, but yes, you can. Anyone of us sitting at this table can go on line and get a certificate that gives us the right to marry people. Granted it is not an ordained minister, but the weddings are legal. Sam, you could even be the one to officiate at the weddings. I think you would look pretty good in a tuxedo or an old time, long-tailed preacher's coat! With your horseshoe mustache, you would look like a dapper preacher from years gone by. Who knows, maybe in time God will send a minister here, when there is a reason for being here. Right now, you have no real draw to entice a preacher to move here, but I think this wedding chapel could be your answer. You also have the fellowship hall for receptions, and other special events. You are already paying a groundskeeper and security guard. Let him be the preacher, too!"

Sam looked at her in total shock. What was this crazy woman thinking?

Deborah told the group she would take a walk outside so

they could talk freely among themselves, and if they could see some of the vision that the potential buyer has, they could then discuss money and terms.

∽ ∾

About thirty minutes later, Sam called Deborah back into the house.

Aunt Patsy fired off several questions in quick succession. "When do we get to meet the potential buyer? Where does he intend to live? Will Sam have to move? Why doesn't the buyer get the marrying certificate himself? How quickly would he be ready to start working here and building up the business? How are we supposed to advertise and get people to come here?"

These were all very good questions in her favor. At least they didn't tell her no. Deborah took a deep cleansing breath. "Aunt Patsy, those are all very good questions and I believe I can answer most of them on behalf of the buyer. The buyer does not want to preside over the ceremony, since they will be managing and coordinating the event. Sam will not have to move out of the house. The basement under the church has a suitable apartment where the first preachers lived until the parsonage was built. The lower level of the fellowship hall can be used as an office. My oldest son David works for an advertising firm in St Louis and I think he could be persuaded to help draft some advertising literature to get things started."

"I know we have not talked money yet, but if you are willing to go along with this plan I am authorized to give you a deposit of one hundred thousand dollars today."

Everyone's eyes lit up and they all seemed to nod, as if in agreement that this idea might not be so bad after all, until Norm Johnson spoke up. "Young Lady, we have been discussing the idea and some of it does have some merit and we might be able to come to terms, but I have to know why you are doing this, and what is in it for you?"

Deborah choked on her tea that she had been sipping. Her palms started sweating, and she suddenly felt flush. She took a deep breath as she searched for just the right words. "Mr. Johnson, I may not have physically lived here my whole life like some of you sitting here, but this town and this church mean as much to me, as if I had been born and raised here. I'm sure you know how deep my family roots are. I have been lost and lonely since my husband suddenly died six months ago and I have been searching for a new purpose in my life. When I was here the other day and heard from several people about the dilemma of the church and the hardship of keeping it up, well, I just thought I could do something worthwhile. I did some research on the internet and found someone who had enough money to invest in a very worthwhile project. They decided that it was a call from God to do all they could to preserve this bit of history for future generations." Deborah chuckled as another thought popped into her head. "Besides, if this works out, I think the owner might hire me to be the photographer."

Deborah was worried as she looked around the table. Had she said enough to convince them it was a worthy business plan? Aunt Patsy did not make eye contact with Deborah, but nodded yes to Norm. Sam sat back in his chair, with his arms crossed over his chest. A glint in his eyes and a smile beneath his graying mustache. Almost as if he had figured it all out. He too, nodded yes, to Norm before giving a wink towards Deborah. Charlie nodded to the others that he was on board with the rest of the members. Norm Johnson was the last vote. He looked around the table and shrugged his shoulders before saying, "Sure, what have we got to lose? The church has been sitting empty for a couple of years now, and this young lady has presented some fresh ideas that none of us here could have come up with."

Norm added, "Before we make this official, I have to be certain that the cemetery will always be respected as the final resting place of our loved ones. I don't want to see a bunch of kids running all around like it is a playground or anything."

Deborah quickly responded, "We can put up a short decorative iron fence all around it with a pretty entrance gate. Would that work?"

Everyone agreed and the asking price had been negotiated to a firm two hundred and fifty thousand dollars, and the paperwork would be ready at the lawyer's office in Wayne City on Monday afternoon.

Deborah added, "Another thing to think about, as everything falls into place, is that there will be jobs for other people in town as well. We will need a florist close by, as well as someone who can bake wedding cakes and an organist or other musicians.

Aunt Patsy was bursting at the seams with excitement! "Marsha is the baker around here; nobody celebrates anything without getting a cake made by Marsha. And Fern Abernathy's husband, Steven is a fabulous organist. He used to play here every Sunday morning, until we quit having services. Now he teaches music at the high school, and plays for weddings and funerals where ever he can get the job. I know he would play here again whenever we have a wedding! Oh, Deborah, I am liking this idea better and better every minute!"

Deborah shook hands with everyone as they started to leave and thanked them for their time and confidence in this new idea. She told Mr. Johnson to be sure and get her the name and address of the attorney so she could give it to the buyer for Monday afternoon. Deborah offered to give Aunt Patsy a ride home.

As they started to leave the church yard, Deborah took a long look around the grounds and smiled at the accomplishment she had made this afternoon. She swelled with pride, knowing she had developed an idea all on her own with good prospects ahead.

Before they reached the hardtop road, Aunt Patsy asked Deborah to go by Marsha's house so she could tell her the news.

As they pulled into Marsha's driveway, Deborah did not even have the engine turned off yet when Aunt Patsy was already out the door. Running across the yard with both arms flailing in the air, her little white pocketbook swinging in the crook of her arm, screaming; "MAR-R-SHA!!, MAR-R-SHA!! We sold the church! We sold the church!"

For a nearly ninety-five year old woman, she was running around like a spring chicken!

CHAPTER SEVEN

After visiting with Marsha and filling her in on the details of the afternoon church committee meeting, DK dropped Aunt Patsy off at her house and headed home to Belleville. Driving home, recounting the events of the day, she relished what she had accomplished with the church committee. She looked forward to creating something new and special out of her childhood memory. Even more so, she was grateful that Aunt Patsy had paved the way to bridge the relationship between herself and Marsha. They had once been very close cousins, sharing childhood antics as well as teenage thoughts, dreams, and secrets. Deborah hoped that maybe one day in the future they could be close again. She had missed Marsha, her cousin, and very first best friend.

Deborah called Andrea to tell her what she had done, and of her plans for the Grace Bible Church property. Andrea was very excited for her dear friend and offered to help in any way that she and Gary could.

Once at home, Deborah spent the evening surfing the internet for ideas and unique photography suggestions. She made a list of questions for Randy on insurance needs and licenses that would be required. She checked one more time her investment account to verify what kind of money she had to work with. She called each of the kids to make sure that they would be at her usual Sunday afternoon dinner. She wanted to be certain that no one had made other plans, so she could tell them her news all at one time.

The next day while grocery shopping for Sunday's dinner, she picked up every bridal magazine in the newsstand as well as magazines on landscaping and photography. Several pieces of poster board were added to her cart, for creating a visual aid of her ideas. She felt like a kid working on a much-anticipated school assignment.

On Sunday, the family arrived right on schedule at noon, like they had done on so many previous Sundays. Randy brought along Chelsea, which was fine with everyone. They had all sensed she would be family soon enough. Deborah was anxious to share her ideas but didn't want to rush into it. She wanted to wait for the right moment. That moment came when Davey asked about her recent trip to Southern Illinois.

She recapped her week with excitement and showed some of the pictures she had taken. She turned to Randy and Chelsea and said, "I will need to come into the office tomorrow to take care of some personal business, Chelsea, if you can have some paperwork ready for me first thing in the morning, I would appreciate it, I have a three o'clock appointment in Wayne City and I would like to have this taken care of before I go.

Chelsea said she would be happy to take care of it, but she needed to know what papers to have ready.

Randy asked, "What is this all about? What is going on in Wayne City?"

Deborah looked at Annie and said, "I did it, Annie. I took your suggestion, I bought the church!"

Annie screeched! "What? A church? My suggestion? What on earth are you talking about, Mother?"

Deborah followed with, "When we were at lunch the other day and talking, I told you about the church in Orchardville, needing a preacher. You told me I should buy it and turn it into a photography studio. That's what I am going to do!"

Annie was dumbfounded. "Mother, I didn't mean it literally! It was just an off the wall comment. It was a joke. Never did I think you would actually do it! At least you haven't done it yet. It is just talk, a wild and crazy fantasy. Right? Randy, you cannot let her do this!"

Deborah responded that the deal has already been started

and the deposit paid. She informed them that she has an appointment on Monday afternoon to sign the final papers and pay the balance due. She explained how she accessed her investment account from the inheritance Aunt Dorothy had left her, in order to make the deposit. She thanked Randy for his computer coaching skills. Then she asked Davey for his help in creating advertising literature and a website.

Annie exploded and started yelling at Randy. "This is all your fault! You taught her how to access her bank accounts and she is going to spend it all recklessly! She does not know what she is doing! You cannot allow her to go through with this. This is her grief ruling her common sense."

Both brothers ignored Annie's rant. They seemed happy for Deborah and said they would be glad to help. Randy even said he would arrange his schedule to go with her to Wayne City. Reminding her the funds would not be ready for access for forty-eight hours.

She told him she was fine with using her personal account to pay off the church and the investment account would be to reimburse herself as soon as the funds were available.

Annie interrupted, "Now wait, just a minute, all of you! Mother, what are you thinking? You cannot go off a couple of hundred miles all by yourself and run a business with a bunch of strangers! Besides, you are needed here! We do not want you that far away! Right, guys? Mom, you are not thinking clearly!"

"Oh Annie, dear, I am thinking more clearly than I have in a very long time. This is the ideal opportunity at just the right time for me ... to be me... as I have never been before. I wish you could be happy for me. I have thought long and hard and prayed even harder for guidance with this. This is right. Besides, other than just saying no, you have not given me a real reason why I shouldn't do it. What reasons are there?"

"First, of all Mom, that is too far away. We need you here, closer to us. The boys need you. What if you get sick or hurt?

Who will take care of you? You have never done anything like this before. I would worry about you."

"Yes, you are right, Annie. I have never done anything like this before, which is precisely why I should do it. I am approaching sixty years old and not getting any younger. I am in good health physically and mentally. If I don't do this now, I never will. God willing, I could run this business for a good ten maybe, even twenty years. I would have a true purpose for getting up every day. If I stay here in this house, what will I do with myself? Continually work at cleaning a clean house? Piddle around the office with Randy? Chelsea has that very well under control. They do not need me at the office attempting to look and feel busy and needed. Annie dear, Orchardville is only two hours from your driveway. Even round-trip is still a good Sunday afternoon adventure for the boys, and we can always meet half way for lunch. The boys could come for long weekends or spend time in the summer fishing and playing. I do wish you could see things from my point of view. You know how long I have wanted to own something and live out on the farm. I have loved that place as long as I can remember and I was so disappointed every time Aunt Dorothy brushed off any of my ideas for living there. It was like she didn't want me out there for some reason. But in the end, she did me a favor. By leaving me that money in her will, she gave me the opportunity to own the heart and soul of the community. I know this has been the work of the Lord, to make everything fall into place as it has, and I know your dad approves of what I am doing. I feel him with me out there, I smell his cologne, and I sense his nearness, which I do not feel here. I am supposed to be there. I wish you could be happy for me."

Annie pouted and shed real tears. "Oh, Mother! I wish you could see my side. I feel like you are running away from your home and all of us here. Daddy built this house for the two of you and your family to be, now you want to just walk away from our home. We need you here. I'm sorry, this whole idea just does not make any sense to me. I cannot go along with this idea."

"Annie, yes, your father built this house for us, and I'm sorry but there is no more "us." It is time for me to find "me" replied Deborah

"Come on boys! Let's go home! I can't stay here and listen to any more of this nonsense! I am going to call Aunt Lucy. Maybe your sister can talk some sense into you!" Annie shouted as she darted for the front door.

※ ※

Randy and Deborah were on the road headed to Orchardville by nine am. Randy wanted to go early enough to look around for himself and see what Deborah's insurance needs might be, as well as get a personal feel for what she was planning on doing. Deborah reminded Randy to not blow her cover yet as to the fact she was the buyer. She wanted no one to know until it was time to sign the papers. She didn't want anyone to "hand" her anything because of who she was, nor did she want anyone to tell her that she couldn't do this. She wanted this to be a real business deal that she had earned on her own.

They went directly to the church. Sam was out mowing around the lake. He had already cleared out all the brush and the lake was completely visible and much larger than Deborah had originally thought. She was very pleased. Sam dismounted from his zero-turn mower and came to greet them.

Deborah quickly started telling Sam what a great job he had done with the work and that he must have been working around the clock since her last visit to get all the brush cleared out. She was very impressed. It was going to be a beautiful background for pictures. She asked if she could show Randy the inside of the church and the fellowship hall. Sam unclipped the keyring from his belt loop and handed them to Randy, "Here you are, sir, I don't see any problem of you looking around on your own. After all, those keys will be belonging to you in just a couple of hours. Go look around all you want. Feel free to go on into the house, too." It was obvious that Sam thought he was talking to the new owner of Grace Bible Church.

Randy said it would not be necessary to go into the house, Sam had no need to worry about that. It was his home, and it was going to stay that way. Randy said he had an inspector on his way to check all the buildings including the house for any structural problems, but he did not need to personally inspect the house.

While exploring the church and the hall, Deborah rambled on about all her plans. What needed to stay to preserve the history and uniqueness of the little church; and what was needed in the fellowship hall to dress it up and make it something special and yet understated. Nothing over the top.

Randy turned to his Mother and said, "Mom, you are glowing as you describe your vision. I see what this place does for you. You are alive and bubbling, talking about your plans. You have a spark that I have not seen in a very long time. I do need to take my own pictures and take measurements so I can get the insurance papers written up. I want to be sure you have adequate coverage for your plans.

As they walked around the grounds with Randy taking measurements with his laser beam and pictures with his own digital camera, Deborah noticed Sam sitting on his mower watching them. She also noticed he was talking on his cell phone. Apparently, the community hot line was already at work. By now everyone in town knew that she was there with a young man who was checking the place out.

When Randy was finished, they made the obligatory stop at Clete's grocery store and were not a bit surprised to find both Aunt Patsy and Norm Johnson there drinking coffee. Deborah made the introductions to Mr. Johnson and to Charlie. Randy bent down to give Patsy a kiss on the check. "Hello, Aunt Patsy, it has been a long time since I've seen you. You must be doing well; you look as lovely as ever."

Mr. Johnson and Charlie studied the young man with Deborah. Mr. Johnson quickly asked, "So, Randy, may I call you Randy? Tell me just what is it that you do for a living?"

"Sir, I am an investment broker which also includes property and life insurance. I am here to make sure that this is a sound business investment for everyone involved and to make sure the buyer will have adequate insurance coverage. The bottom line is, if the investment is worthwhile for the buyer, it is a good investment for the community, and from what I have seen here today, this is a win-win proposition for all involved. I do believe you can rest assured that the buyer has your best interest at heart and it will be a very good thing for Orchardville. Now, if you will excuse us, we need to head to Wayne City and have the buyer sign those papers so everyone can move forward and get this business going. Nice to have met everyone."

Norm Johnson shook Randy's hand and said, "I am heading to Wayne City, myself to sign the sale papers. Thank you, sir, for putting us at ease with this. You sound like a wise young man, even if you are still a bit wet behind the ears! We all thought for sure you were the buyer, and we wondered what such a young whippersnapper would want with our town."

"No, sir. I am not the buyer. Just watching out for the buyer's interest as well as yours."

Deborah paid for their two bottles of Dr. Pepper. When Charlie gave her the change, he proclaimed, "Well lookey here, will ya! It must be your lucky day! You got one of those new state quarters. It has an image of the Camel Rock from Garden of the Gods. Peoples' been a fighten' over them. I don't know how I missed seeing that earlier, or it would have been in my own pocket! But, I guess this one belongs to you."

Deborah studied the coin in her hand, looked up to towards the ceiling and smiled. Mentally thanking the guardian angel who had just made her day. She closed her hand tightly around the quarter. "Thanks, Charlie! Yes, indeed, this is my lucky day! Thanks, for the special quarter. It means more than you know! Let's go Randy, we have an appointment we need get to. See you later, Mr. Johnson!"

∽ ∾

At the attorney's office, Randy and Deborah were ushered into a conference room upon their arrival. They were told that Mr. Johnson was in another room and had already signed his paperwork. Randy read over the papers and told his mother that everything seemed to be in order. It was a simple, straight forward sale, since she was paying cash. Deborah signed everywhere as indicated. She wrote the check for the remaining balance and handed it to the attorney. He left the room to have his secretary make copies of the signed contracts and to let Mr. Johnson know they were completed. Deborah waited nervously. The rest of her life was about to be changed in ways she could never imagine. "Randy, how is it possible to have such fear and calmness at the same time? I honestly do not know if I should laugh or cry! I am so excited and yet scared to death."

Randy smiled at his mother, seeing how much she had grown in the past few weeks. She seemed secure in her decisions, not at all a woman acting irrationally. "Mom, I am proud of the strength and determination you have shown through all of this. I believe you are doing the right thing for you, at this time in your life. Everything is going to be fine." He leaned over and gave her a kiss on the cheek. "I love you, Mom!"

The attorney came back with the envelope of signed papers and handed Deborah a set of keys. "Congratulations, Mrs. Kingston, you are now the proud owner of Grace Bible Church of Orchardville. Mr. Johnson would like to come in and meet you.

When Norm Johnson walked into the room and saw only Deborah and Randy, he looked puzzled. He crossed his arms across his chest and in a gruff voice started to speak, "What is going..."

Deborah quickly came to stand by him. "Mr. Johnson, please forgive me for being secretive about all of this." She gingerly placed her hands on his crossed arms. "I only wanted to be sure that I was getting the church on the merits of my ideas and plans, not for who I am and who I am related to. I know you have been friends with my family for many years and I did not want the church handed to me. On the same note, I have wanted to live here my whole life and my Aunt Dorothy put up obstacles and excuses every time I discussed the idea. I did not want to take any chances that Aunt Patsy would do the same, which is why I did not even tell her that I was the one wanting to buy the church. Please try to understand, I wasn't trying to be deceitful. I wanted it all done fair and square for all of us."

"Young lady, it is a good thing I like you! I could have half a mind to cancel this whole thing right here and now, but I do like the ideas you presented and I believe you honestly think it will work, and your boy here seems to think it will benefit us nicely. I trust that the good Lord knew what He was doing when He sent you here."

Deborah hugged the old man and thanked him for trusting her and God on this. Handshakes and hugs were shared throughout the room. As they headed out to their cars, Mr. Johnson told her she better hurry up and call her Aunt Patsy and be the one to tell her the news. "It won't take long before it is all over town. She'll want to hear it from you."

Deborah quickly pulled out her cell phone and dialed Aunt Patsy's number. "Hi, there! It's Deborah, I have some news for you. The paperwork on the church is completed and I am the new owner. I will be moving here very soon and opening my studio."

"My, oh my! I knew it!! Deborah, I knew it was you! That day of our meeting, I could see it in your eyes, child. You had a hunger and determination to sell the committee on your ideas.

Way more than someone speaking for some other interested party! I did not want to give you up to the rest of the group, but I planted them with a lot of questions just to try to show your hand and you never did. I am proud of you, girl! I hope I live long enough to see your dreams come true. You better get things going quickly!"

&

Upon arriving home and feeding Bandit, Deborah called Annie and told her she was home and the paperwork was completed. She told Annie that she would like to go out to her house and talk. She wanted to be sure that Annie was not harboring any ill feelings.

&

Annie's husband, Bob, had taken the boys out for ice cream so the women could talk privately. They went out to sit on the patio with a glass of wine.

Deborah took a deep breath, "Annie, I really want you to be okay with this decision. It is the first one I have made on my own without any advice from a husband or a father. I have put a lot of thought into what I am doing. It has been a dream come true for me on so many levels. It has also been strengthened by my belief in the after-life and understanding how our loved ones can reach out to us from beyond. No one has ever prepared me for these feelings. In fact, no one had ever prepared me on how to handle grief! It was never talked about…it was something I witnessed from a distance on many occasions. You know, it is cliché to say that everyone handles grief differently, but it is very true. We have talked about it many times in my support group, but I never put all the pieces together until now."

"Annie, dear, looking back at both of your grandmothers and the deaths of loved ones that they endured, and how they handled grief was something that I did not understand, nor was I mature enough to question them about it. My mother handled grief completely in solitude. She never talked about it at all. In fact, she never talked about her brother, Bob, my grandparents, or my dad. It seems once they were gone, they were gone. She never talked about memories of them or shared stories from the past. I do not know what she thought or felt when she was alone. She kept it bottled up inside her." Deborah paused to let Annie process what she had said, then continued.

"You know, your Grandma Kingston was a very strong willed woman. She was the head of the household, no matter what Grandpa Kingston might have thought. When he died, she became a very bitter, hard edged, bossy, needy woman. She constantly needed your dad or I to do something for her, take her places, fix things, or just talk on the phone for hours at a time. She couldn't or wouldn't do anything on her own. She became very negative. She argued with everyone about everything including, whether or not it was a cloudy day or a sunny one. There was just no making her happy. I do not want to be that woman. That is why I would never consider living here in Waterloo with you. I would not want to become dependent on you and Bob. Nor do I want you to be dependent on me. You are a grown woman with your own family. You don't need me to worry about, too. I want to visit with you and the boys and I want all of us to enjoy our times together and not resent them."

Deborah continued on, "Also, after Grandpa Kingston died, no one else could compare to him. No one could cook anything like he did. No other man danced as well as he did. No other man was as attentive to her as he had been. She lived only in his memory and could not imagine even a friendship with another man. I know you are not ready to hear this, dear, but I do hope to find someone to share my life with someday. Your dad and I were very happy for a very long time and I do not want to spend the rest of my life alone. Nor would he want me to. He would want me to have someone to feel safe and secure with, and you know that is true. I am not saying it is going to be right away, but someday. Whoever that person turns out to be, he will not take your father's place. He will be a part of my new life and hopefully, you will let him be a part of yours, too."

Annie had tears running down her face. She shook her head and said, "I know, but I cannot imagine someone taking my daddy's place in your life."

"Oh honey! No one could ever take his place!" Deborah responded. "I have made a decision about something else, too. I want to discourage people from calling me DK. That is what your dad called me. It was his term of endearment, I would rather not hear it from anyone one else now. It hurts too much, to know I will never hear him say it again."

"Oh, Mom, I get it. I don't like hearing other people call you DK either," replied Annie.

CHAPTER EIGHT

Deborah spent the next couple of days making lists of things to be done and phone calls to be made. She scoured the house, packing boxes of items she would need to take with her on her first trip to Orchardville. There were cleaning supplies packed in one box. Sketch pads and drawing pencils, books and magazines in another box. Her sewing machine and the treasured set of luggage that went with it. The hard leather, peacock blue suitcases had belonged to her Grandma Range. Years ago, Deborah had turned them into her sewing supply cases. The small square makeup case now held her boxes of pins and needles, the rotary cutters, scissors, tape measurer and other small items. Even though it had been many years since her grandma had used the makeup case for its intended purpose, it still had a smell that reminded Deborah of her grandma's floral scented dusting powder. She closed her eyes and inhaled deeply to gather in as much of the memory as she could. One of the larger cases was filled with lace and other remnants from the bridal factory where her grandma used to work. She would certainly be able to use those treasures in her new adventure.

Deborah dug through her mother's cedar chest and found a bag of old costume jewelry that had belonged to both of her grandmothers. There were several pairs of white dress gloves, consisting of wrist length to elbow length, with decorative buttons. These would make some pretty wall hangings. She also pulled out the old wedding pictures of grandparents from both her and David's families. She was beginning to think she should take David's truck instead of her car for her first trip. So many things to think about and so much stuff to take, just to get started.

She packed one box with food staples to set up in her new basement apartment. There was a box with a few cooking essentials and dishes. She knew she didn't need everything right away, especially since she would be residing in two places for quite some time. On her grocery list, among other things, she added a new litter box so Bandit could easily travel back and forth with her between their two homes.

By Thursday, she had everything that she felt she would need to get started. Her laptop and Bandit were the last two things to go into the car. Randy had told her he would bring the desktop computer and set it up for her when she was ready for it.

~ ~

When she pulled into the lane of Grace Bible Church, she was overcome with emotion. She could not believe that this was truly hers. She stepped out of the car with Bandit in her arms. Happy tears escaping from her eyes; she felt relieved, overwhelmed and in awe. She took a long draw of the air and knew that this was right. She at long last felt like she was home. She reached into the right front pocket of her denim shorts and pulled out her special quarter. Looking at the image from the Garden of the Gods, she felt elated. She flipped the coin in the air and caught it again, pleased with the path that she was being guided, by some other power than just her own.

Sam came out of the church's basement door and said, "I thought that would be your car I heard pulling in. I was just straightening up a few things down in the apartment, Ms. Kingston."

"Well, that is very nice of you Sam, but let's get something straight right now. Call me Deborah please, not Ms. Kingston."

"Since you will be my boss, I thought it only proper that I show you respect with Ms. Kingston." Sam responded.

Deborah laughed, "As for Ms. Kingston, I appreciate the respect and yes, I will be your boss, as you say, but I would like to think of this as more of a partnership. You gave this place lots of love and care for several years and I know you are about as emotionally attached as I am. I would like to think we are more like partners in this adventure. And, this is Bandit. She will rule the place, once she gets comfortable here."

Sam laughed, "OK, Deborah, we are going to do this. Tell me what goes where and I'll get that car unloaded for you. Oh, by the way...partner...I made a decision before you got here. I moved my personal stuff over to the basement apartment. I want you to have the house. You will need more room than the apartment offers. You have your kids and grandkids who will be coming to visit and you need an office space for clients. It just makes more sense. OK?

"You didn't need to do that. I did not intend to displace you from your home," she said.

Sam replied, "No ma'am, I insist. You will need more space than me. The only reason I stayed in the house was to show that someone lived here. You know, with lights on and what not. It is your home now."

When Deborah opened the refrigerator to put away the perishables she had picked up in town on her way in, there was a surprise waiting for her. A six pack of Dr. Pepper had a bow tied to it, along with a note that read; "Welcome to your new home."

She turned to see Sam standing in the doorway with a grin on his face. He said, "I knew I couldn't go wrong with the Dr. Pepper. Thought I could earn a couple of gold stars right from the start."

Deborah thanked him and told him they were going to get along just fine.

With all the boxes carried in and Bandit's litter box set up in the utility room, Deborah asked Sam if he had time to walk around the property with her and go over some plans.

He said, "Now that you're here, you're the boss. I will do whatever you tell me needs to be done."

With that, she dug through a box and pulled out two clipboards that each had a pad of paper attached. Pens, pencils, a folder of sketches and magazine pictures, a traditional tape measurer as well as David's laser beam measuring device.

"All right. Let's get to work," she said. "I want to show you some of my ideas and I need to know if you have suggestions of whom I should call upon for professional services as we go along."

Once outside, she walked towards the end of the lane. She said, "Let's start here, at the entrance. I know exactly what I want. I saw it at a friend's ranch in Cobden and I know who can make it for me. A stone pillar on each side of the lane, supporting a white wrought iron archway. It will say, *The Wedding Belle* Family Photography Studio.

Sam looked at her, amazed and puzzled. "I like the name, and the idea, but that is a lot of words for one archway. A lot of work for the sculptor as well as difficult to read. It needs to be something simpler. Like, maybe just, *The Wedding Belle*. That is the name of the place. The rest is a secondary.

"Okay, that makes sense. I'll have Mr. Curtiss over in Cobden get working on some design ideas."

They moved over towards the lake which looked so much better now that it could actually be seen. Deborah thanked Sam for the hard work he had put into clearing all the brush. She pondered the idea of making the lake a little bit bigger. She showed him a sketch as she explained, she didn't mean, bigger, but more shaped. One end swooping longer, like with a tail and at the crook of the swoop, they could build a footbridge to get to the other side. The bridge could also serve as a photo spot. Once the bridal party was on the other side of the lake, she could take pictures from this side, with the lake in the foreground. She could also take the camera to the other side of the lake, take pictures of people with the church in the background, and still have the lake in the foreground as well. So many photo options to consider. Then, over on the larger main part of the lake, a deck with a pergola attached could extend over the water. Weddings could take place there if a bride would choose an outdoor setting instead of inside the church.

Dashing over to a huge oak tree that stood between the lane and her proposed extension of the lake, she said, "In this tree, I want an old-fashioned rope swing with a large wooden seat, like my grandparents had in their front yard on the farm. Of course, the wood needs to be sealed to not stain or get splinters in a bride's dress, but I want it as natural looking as possible." She bent down and placed her hands forming a square frame with the tree centered within and said. "I do believe, from the right angle, the extended lake will be seen in the background. It will look perfect!"

The entire time that Deborah was rambling on, Sam was quietly writing notes on his pad of paper. He was amazed at her excitement and how thought out her plans were.

Inside the church, there were many more ideas. Keeping the historical charm of the old place, but just freshening it up a bit. She wanted to strip the painted floors, sand them down, and stain them a deep golden honey color. Sand off the years of paint on the pews and give them a paint and stain combination. Stain on the seat and backs that could be polished to a shine, with fresh new white paint on the support posts and end caps. The open ceiling beams needed sanding to remove years of dust, but she liked the raw exposed wood and wanted to keep it that way. Maybe, new light fixtures could be added.

They moved on to the fellowship hall that had been an addition across the back of the church. More ideas flowed from her enthusiastic rambling: strip the floors and make them match the church floors, with the addition of a tile dance floor at the far end and a small stage for bands or DJs. The stage could also be used for the head table or guest speakers at events. The raw beams would remain just like in the church. A couple of chandeliers instead of the current plain glass globes would add elegance. An awesome combination of country and class. Of course, the kitchen would have to be carefully looked at to see what updates would be needed to bring it up to code for catering.

Deborah turned to Sam and asked, "What do you think?"

He took off his baseball cap, scratched his head and said. "Whew! You have really given this a lot of thought! I don't know how or where you came up with all of this, but it sounds pretty good. I know no one else could have envisioned anything like it. Folks around here just expected a preacher to give Sunday services and an occasional wedding or funeral. You have a whole new plan. I like it, but it is also going to take a whole lot of work. Are you sure you are up for the challenge of this project?"

"Absolutely!" she giggled back to him. "This is a dream come true for me. I can do this! What about you?"

He hesitated before answering, not sure if it was his place to ask his next question or not. "You do know, it is going to take a lot of money, don't you? Especially that pond extension and building the bridge and pergola deck. You are talking about a lot of labor here."

Her eyes swept across the lake and the lane, resting a moment on the old Oak tree, and then back at the front door of the church. She had tears in her eyes that she fought to keep from falling. "Sam, I have to do this! I don't know why, but I am meant to be here and revive this church. I am a hard worker and I am not afraid to get down on my hands and knees and sand, paint and stain! I don't know what everything will cost, but I just have to make this happen. Can you estimate some prices for me, so I have a budget to work with? I promise you, I WILL do this!"

He said he would sit down and do some calculating and would have something for her as soon as he could, hopefully tomorrow. He also told her he knew a few people he could call on for some help.

Deborah entered the house through the screened in breezeway that connected the house to the two-car garage. In fact, once she stepped into the kitchen she realized that the kitchen and dining room is as far as she had ever been in the house. She had no idea what was beyond the dining room. She had never considered looking around the house because this is where Sam lived. She had every intention of living in the church basement. Yes, in all reality, she should have looked at the house, but her only concern throughout the process of buying the property was the church. Why hadn't Davey asked her about the house? Why didn't anyone else suggest that she look around the house? Without realizing it, she had bought a house that she had never really seen. Who does that? She felt very uncomfortable right this very moment. She was about to walk around inside a strange house that she now owned. She stopped at the large dining room picture window that faced the church, and noticed that Sam was in his truck and driving away. She paused as she turned away from the window and wondered for the first time, "Oh Deborah! What have you done now? What did you get yourself into? Could Annie have been right about all of this?" She sighed as she turned away from the window to explore her new home.

A comfortable sized living room with a stone fireplace and wood mantel on the end wall, a large picture window facing the church that mirrored the one in the dining room. The hallway led to three bedrooms. The first room, quite plain and barren of decorations or color, had a double bed and two night stands. The second room was much smaller and completely empty. Totally void of any furniture or decorations. Her footsteps echoed as she walked across the wood floor. She made a mental note to get bunk beds for the boys, and a large rug.

The master bedroom was unique in design. Something she had never seen before. She was unsure if she liked it or not, and yet, she was intrigued. At the far end of the room was a recessed alcove area that held a double sink, with a wall-to-wall mirror that filled the entire area above the sinks. She opened the door to the right of the alcove where she found the toilet, tub and shower. The door to the left of the alcove was a huge walk-in closet. She stepped back out of the closet and stood at the open alcove and looked around the bedroom itself. She liked the bay window with the built-in window seat. It reminded her of the window seat David had built in the dining room of their Belleville home. She thought the queen-sized bed and two night stands looked comfortable enough, but the place certainly needed some color. No, she thought, this place needs more than color. It needs a woman's touch. There is nothing here that is warm and welcoming. It is just a house. How long had it been since a woman lived here and made it a home? Had there ever been a woman live here? She turned back to the alcove and gave it another look and decided that if she were sharing the house with someone, the sink here in the bedroom would have its advantages if someone were using the other facilities. It is kind of quirky cute she thought to herself. Definitely a product of the early 1970's.

 Back in the kitchen, she checked into the utility room. It was obvious that Bandit had made herself at home, with her new litter box. It was time to start settling herself in and try to figure out what to do first to turn this new house into a home.

 For now, the dining room table would also serve as her desk, until she could set up an office. While she nibbled on a turkey sandwich for dinner, she worked on notes and sketches. Time passed quickly while she worked, diligently trying to get everything ready for tomorrow's busy day. Her to-do list had grown quite lengthy before she called it night. It was nearly midnight when she decided to turn out the lights and go to bed. She couldn't help but notice that Sam had not returned home yet. It was late afternoon when he had left. She wondered where he had gone. It suddenly dawned on her she really did not know this man who lived on her property. She knew nothing about him. Again, she asked herself, "Oh Deborah! How could you have been so stupid?"

Suddenly she became very anxious. She was in this strange house all alone, with a strange man living just a few feet from her front door. Her mind raced with fear. What if he was a deranged axe murderer? What if he was a sexual predator? Or a drunk who would break in and beat her, thinking she was in his house? After all, it was his house until this very morning. Then she wondered, did he keep a key? As she locked up the house, she made sure she locked the storm door as well as the wooden door. She turned the deadbolt latch as well hooked the security chain. Remembering on TV shows, people always braced a chair up against the doorknob. She drug a dining room chair over to the front door and put it in place. For a little extra measure of emotional security, she dug out the roll of duct tape and pressed a long strip down the length of the door opening. That way if anything did happen to her, it would be obvious someone had broken in. She did the same thing with the kitchen door to the breezeway. Then she grabbed another chair and the duct tape and took them to the bedroom with her, to place on that door.

Once she was safely secured in her room, she called Andrea crying hysterically.

"I am so sorry for waking you up," Deborah cried to her friend. "I am here at the house, all alone and I am scared to death!" She was sobbing and gasping for air. Andrea could barely understand what she was saying. Andrea talked her down enough that Deborah was finally able to make some sort of sense.

Deborah filled Andrea in on the day and how Sam had insisted that she move into the house instead of the church basement. She relayed all her fears to her friend and was doubting her decision on buying the church. She admitted she had acted very hastily. She had not thought the idea through. "Annie was right. I had let grief cloud my thinking. Andrea, what am I going to do?"

They talked for over an hour. Andrea reassuring her friend that things will look better in the daylight. She told her to get a locksmith and have the locks changed on the house and the church and to only give Sam the keys that he needed for the church. She also told Deborah to go to the sheriff's office and have a background check run on Sam.

While they were talking, Deborah noticed that Bandit was pacing the room, meowing loudly and scratching at the door. She suddenly realized Bandit's litter box was in the utility room and they were both barricaded in the bedroom. Deborah asked Andrea to keep talking to her while she went to retrieve the litter box. As she passed the dining room window she spotted Sam's truck parked next to the church and the apartment lights were on. At least she knew he was home. Was that a good thing or not?

Once Deborah was secured again in the bedroom, she thanked Andrea for listening to her ramble. When they hung up. Deborah laid in bed and scolded herself over and over for letting her heart lead her to being here in the middle of nowhere all alone. She cried for David who wasn't here to talk to and guide her anymore. She cried for not listening to Annie, her daughter, much wiser than her mother had given her credit for. She cried for Davey and Randy not objecting to her foolishness. They never even hesitated! They never asked about the house or Sam. Did they not have any real concern for her well-being?

⁂

The morning sun glared brightly through the bay window, shining right into Deborah's face. She battled between opening her eyes to the new day, and shielding them from the bright light. Her swollen eyes burned as she finally gave in and headed to the shower. Stopping to look in the mirror, she could barely see through the tiny open slit between her swollen eyelids. She must have cried all night, even in her sleep.

Deborah pulled her damp hair into a ponytail, pulled on a pair of old denim shorts and a tee shirt suitable for digging in and starting on her project at church. But first she had to remove the homemade security system in her bedroom.

As she prepared a pot of coffee, her eyes still barely functioning, she noticed a strange gentleman standing over by the lake talking to Sam. Then several cars pulled in together and teenage boys and girls started spilling out from the cars. There must have been about a dozen kids.

She grabbed her sunglasses and slipped into the flip flops on the floor under the dining room table and quickly headed over to the breezeway door. Darn it! She had to pull the chair away and then rip off all the tape. She still had trouble opening the door since it was double locked. She was finally free from her self-made prison. She charged across the yard towards Sam, ignoring the kids gathered around their cars.

"Sam! What in the world is going on here this morning? Who is this man? What are all of those kids doing here?" she asked.

"Good morning, Deborah!" Said Sam quite cheerily. "This here is Jim Henderson. He is a county inspector. Yesterday afternoon, I was telling him about your plans. He is here to survey the plat and determine if what you want can be done or not. Those kids are from the high school. They all belong to FFA or FHA. By helping out around here, their teacher is going to give them extra credit for community service as soon as school starts. We just have to track their hours."

"What the hell, Sam! You did all of this without discussing it with me? All I asked from you was to figure an estimate! You just step in and take charge of it all! Who do you think you are?" Deborah turned and stomped off as quickly as she could. However, she stopped cold in her tracks when she got to the oak tree. A rope swing with a wooden seat hung from the tree, just as she had wished for yesterday. Even the wood was varnished.

She ran to her house as fast as she could. At the kitchen sink, she put her face as close as she could get to the running water, cupping her hands to bring the cool water to her burning eyes. Why? Why? Why? Why was he doing this? Everything was happening way too fast.

She poured herself a cup of coffee and took a long slow sip as she stared out the window. The hot brew burning her throat as it went down. Sam was obviously in control out there. He had not been swayed by her outburst and neither had Mr. Henderson. They were both talking, pointing this way and that. Some of the kids were pulling weeds from the flower beds on the side of the church, others were raking the yard. After a few more sips of coffee, she knew she had to go back out there and apologize to everyone. She owed that to all of them, especially to Sam. After all, he was only trying to help, and she had asked him for names of people who could help.

First, she stopped and talked to the kids. She properly introduced herself to them and said that she had not gotten much sleep that night. She shrugged it off as being in a strange house and all that. She promised they would never see an outburst like that again and she then headed towards the lake. Thank goodness they could not see her eyes through the dark sunglasses.

Without removing her sunglasses, she looked up to Sam and said, "Please excuse my outburst. I did not sleep very well at all last night and I had not had any coffee yet when I stormed over here. Please forgive me. Sam, I know you mean well and I should not have snapped at you like that. I know you just want to help."

"Mr. Henderson, please don't judge me by what you witnessed earlier. As I said, I didn't get much sleep. You know, strange house, strange bed, and strange noises. I do not typically act that way; I don't know if Sam told you or not that I am a recent widow. Doing something like this is a new undertaking for me and it is suddenly overwhelming. To think, I am just getting started, is downright scary. I am very embarrassed by my childish behavior."

Mr. Henderson replied, "No need to apologize, ma'am. Any time a person takes on a project of this size, it is bound to wreak havoc on their emotions. Trust me, you have taken on a very large project with this one! I would like to show you what I can approve on your plans and what I cannot."

"Yes, thank you, Mr. Henderson." Deborah heaved a sigh of relief.

"Please call me Jim." He said. "We need to be on a first name basis around here, as I am going to be quite involved from this point forward. I will be approving, or not, any and all plans for this project, so we might as well get comfortable with each other."

"Sure. You can call me Deborah.

"Good. First, let me use this laser pointer and show you a few things, and then I will use the spray marking paint to give you an actual outline of where the lake extension can be," said Jim. "You see the raised ridge that runs the full length of the drainage ditch all along the edge of your property there?" Jim said, as he waved the laser beam along the side of the ditch that met up to the main road. "You cannot interfere with that retaining ridge in any way. You must stay at least twelve feet away from the ridge. The closest you can get would be right along this line here." He said as he drew an imaginary line with his laser. "It means you cannot be as wide as you had hoped. What we can do, is make it more of a kidney shaped lagoon design." Again, waving the red beam along an imaginary line on this side of the lake.

"Will I be able to have the footbridge over to the other side?" Deborah asked hesitantly.

"Yes, you can. In fact, it will have a shorter span and it will be easier to build if you start at this point of the bend right around here." He pointed to another imaginary spot. "Then, angle the bridge over towards that clearing over there on the other side. You will be just fine."

Deborah asked him to go ahead and spray paint the lines so she could actually see what he was talking about.

Jim went to his truck and brought out three different colors of spray paint. With the red paint, Jim made long dashes to mark where the extension of the lake could be. With the blue, he made large x's to show the start of the bridge, followed by arrows pointing in the direction the angle would be. The yellow spray paint marked the areas they needed to stay away from.

Deborah walked back and forth trying to visualize what the finished lake might look like. She made a quick apology and said she would be right back. She turned and ran towards the house. Both men looked at each other and shrugged. Neither one knowing why she suddenly darted off again.

Deborah returned quite quickly carrying her camera. Still wearing her sunglasses, she walked along the red marked line, looking through the lens at different angles and different locations. Sometimes squatting down with the camera raised up towards the tree tops. Other times on her knees, and even a few times lying on the ground. She took pictures from every perspective. She knew that Sam and Jim were standing side by side, watching every move she made. She also knew that they could not understand why she was doing what she was doing. When she was almost finished taking pictures of the far side of the lake, she made a quick turn and snapped a few pictures of the two men, catching them off guard and completely unaware that they were a subject in her lens.

Deborah said that she liked what she saw through the lens and that the revised plan looked very feasible. She looked towards Sam and asked, "What do you think? You will be the foreman on this, right?"

Sam looked at her sort of cross-eyed and with a furrowed brow said. "Well, the important thing is, if it works for you, then it will work for me."

Jim replied, "Okay, you are good to go. I will write up the permit and you can hire someone to start the excavating. What else do I need to look at while I am here?"

Deborah told him about the iron archway and the stone pillars she wanted to put at the entrance of the lane. He told her to get an architect to do some drawings for his approval. He told her he had no problems with her idea, but it had to be soundly constructed.

Then, she walked Jim towards the cemetery and told him she would like to have a complimentary iron fence around it, to be sure that it stayed as a place of honor for the deceased, that it would not become a place for kids to run around and play in.

Jim said he was very impressed at her thoughtfulness and concern for the deceased and that he thought it would look quite nice. He said he would study the plans when they were drawn up.

They all agreed that Jim would return at another time to go over the plans for the fellowship hall. Jim got in his truck to leave and Deborah walked to take a closer look at the wooden swing. Sam joined her there as soon as Jim had pulled away. Sam asked, "Is this what you had in mind?"

Deborah smiled and hung her head in shame. She said, "I am so sorry for snapping at you earlier. I had no right to be so rude. This is lovely, but how on earth did you get it made and varnished so quickly? You were gone all afternoon and evening."

"You were checking up on me, were you?" He asked playfully. "When I left here, I went straight to my Cousin Ernie's house over in Flora. He has a barn full of old reclaimed wood that he uses for various projects. I asked for a piece for your swing. I used some quick drying clear varnish. While visiting with Ernie and eating some supper there, I added more stain as each coat dried. If this is not big enough or wide enough, I can go get another piece of wood and start over."

Deborah sat down on the swing to try it out. She leaned back like a little kid and giggled. "It is perfect! Just perfect! Thank You! Thank you also for being such a big help and getting things started around here. Now tell me about those kids over there.

What is the plan?" She asked as she shifted her sunglasses to sit on top of head, not needing them while sitting in the shade of the large Oak tree.

Sam gasped when she lifted her sunglasses. "What on earth?" he asked. Seeing her red swollen and puffy eyes.

"Yeah. Well that's what happens when I spend most of the night crying and not sleeping. This is the ugly truth of what happens on those nights. You might as well be prepared. It won't be the last time I look like this, I'm sure." Deborah proclaimed.

Sam said he was going to go check on the kids and devise a plan of action for them. Deborah said she was going to go get a cup of coffee, since she had never finished her first cup earlier.

※ ※

Deborah looked at the clock on the stove as she entered the kitchen. It wasn't even ten o'clock and yet it seemed as if she had done a half a day's work already, without any breakfast. She thought she should at least eat a piece of toast with her coffee before she herself went over to the church to start working.

While waiting for the toast to pop up, she heard a car quickly pulling into the lane. When it screeched to a stop in front of her garage, she squealed with excitement. It was Andrea and Connie and they had a man with them that she did not recognize. She ran out to meet them.

Andrea screamed, "Thank God you are alright. I have been trying to call you. I've been worried sick!"

Deborah answered, "It has already been a very busy morning. The county inspector was here early this morning and we were going over the plans so he could issue permits. Come in and join me for some coffee. I was just fixing myself a piece of toast. I didn't even get a chance to have any breakfast this morning. Things started happening so quickly."

"Whoa! Wait just one minute, sister!" shouted Andrea.

"You call me in the middle of the night crying hysterically and telling me how afraid you were! I talk to you for over an hour to calm you down and you don't even have the decency to call the next morning to tell me everything is okay? How dare you! I called Connie first thing this morning when I couldn't reach you. Jim Curtiss was at her house and insisted on coming with us to check on you. We stopped at the hardware store and bought new deadbolt locks for you. And everything is just fine and dandy here!"

Deborah realized just how quickly things had changed in the light of day for her and apologized to her friends. She said, "I'm so sorry. I didn't take the time to think things through this morning. I was making coffee when I saw the inspector out there talking to Sam. In fact, my phone is still on the charger in the bedroom. Let me go get it and see how many other calls I have missed."

Jim Curtiss said he would walk to the end of the lane and check things out for the archway that Connie had already told him Deborah was interested in having.

Andrea said she needed to call Gary and let him know that everything was okay. "After all, he had wanted me to call the sheriff first thing this morning when I couldn't reach you! But, thank goodness, I didn't send him out on some wild goose chase, when there was nothing wrong here!"

⁂

Deborah retrieved her phone and discovered that she had indeed missed several calls from both Andrea and Connie. There had also been calls from Davey, Annie and Randy. Everyone wanting to know how she had managed with her first night in her new surroundings. Deborah chuckled, realizing that they really do care. Maybe she had over reacted last night when she had let her insecurities get the best of her.

Sam was at the end of the lane talking with Jim Curtiss, obviously talking about the planned archway. Andrea and Connie were walking around the lawn of the church when Deborah caught up with them. "Once again, please accept my apologies for not calling you first thing this morning, but I honestly didn't give it a thought, with so much happening so quickly this morning." She said above the buzzing noise of the electric hand sanders coming from inside the church.

Deborah filled Andrea and Connie in on the fact that Sam had left yesterday afternoon and met with the county inspector and arranged for him to be here first thing this morning, as well as talking to the high school principal and school counselor to have the FFA and FHA kids here doing some light manual labor for extra credit.

"Look over there at the rope swing! She said excitedly. "I only mentioned wanting it yesterday to Sam and I woke up to find it hanging in the tree this morning. Isn't it awesome? It is picture perfect there, and it is just the beginning of the changes to come!"

Connie said, "I don't know, I think it sounds kind of creepy myself. You don't even know this guy or anything about him. You tell him a few of your ideas and the very next day he is in complete charge, taking control of everything. Acting like he is the one who bought this place. Look down there, will you. Shouldn't that be you talking to Jim Curtiss about the plans for the archway?"

Andrea agreed with Connie. "Deborah, we are worried about you and we want to know more about this Sam Cunningham that is living right here practically under your roof, and you do not know one thing about him, except his name!"

Deborah knew that her friends were right and thanked them for their concern, as she herself had questions.

About that time, two more cars pulled into the lane. It was Aunt Patsy in Marsha's car and Charlie right behind them. Aunt Patsy had a basket of fried chicken and a big bowl of potato salad. Charlie brought a bag filled with potato chips and loaves of bread. Marsha pulled two cakes out of the car. There was also a jug of sweet tea and one of lemonade. Aunt Patsy said, "We didn't want you to worry about lunch and we knew you had a bunch of hard working kids here to feed."

Deborah was overwhelmed at their thoughtfulness. Tears rolled down her face as her shoulders shook up and down. She couldn't believe how helpful everyone was and, of course, having virtually no sleep the night before, her emotions were quite raw. It was this kind of friendship and help that made country living so special. It was what she remembered from her childhood. Family helping each other.

She composed herself and asked them to take the food into the fellowship hall where the kids could go ahead and eat. She wanted to show Andrea, Connie and Jim around the place. She told Sam to go ahead and eat, too.

As Deborah and her friends walked around the grounds and she told them of her plans, they could see for themselves how much she loved being here and that she had thought through what the business would be. It was also obvious she didn't have a clue about the personal side of this undertaking.

Jim spoke first about what was weighing on Andrea and Connie's minds. "Just so you know, Sam and I had a nice chat while we were discussing the iron work for the entrance to the lane. I can tell you he is a smart and sensitive man who truly cares about this place as much as Deborah does. He has had a rough road in life and is looking for calmness, which he had living here alone, being the caretaker, until she came along with her ideas." He chuckled, pointing to Deborah. "Now, don't get me wrong. He likes what you are planning to do and he wants to see you succeed. He said he knows all about starting over, just like you are doing. I also told him that I would be changing out the locks on the house. I told him that it was the smartest thing to do and he agreed. In fact, he said he was going to suggest the very same thing to you today. I really don't think you need to worry about Sam."

They joined everyone in the fellowship hall for lunch and when they were all finished eating, Sam and Jim went to change the locks on the doors of the house.

Sam and Jim both rolled with laughter when they saw the duct taped door frames and the dining room chair propped against the front door. At the exact same time, both men said, "Women!"

Sam added, "And their imaginations!"

As Marsha and Aunt Patsy were leaving, Marsha invited Deborah to come to her house later for supper.

Andrea, Connie, and Jim headed for home, feeling secure that their friend would be okay. They discussed what they could do to help Deborah turn her dream into a reality.

CHAPTER NINE

After everyone had left, Sam suggested to Deborah she should get some rest. He said he would check on the kids and have them wrap it up for the day. "Don't want to wear them out on their first day. We want them to come back."

She agreed that a nap sounded pretty good right now, since she hadn't slept well and it had been a very hectic morning.

Sam chuckled, "Yes, I know." Thinking back to the duct taped door frame and the chair propped up to the door knob. Sam bent down and gave a small peck of a kiss to the top of her head and told her to have a good nap.

Now why in the world did he have to go and do that, she wondered to herself, as her body tickled in a long-forgotten arousal.

※ ※

After a refreshing long nap, Deborah showered and was ready to go visit with Marsha and her husband Chad. It had been a very long time since she and Marsha had spent any quality time together and she had missed those special talks they used to share. Not only were they cousins but they had grown up as very dear friends. Looking back it was sad that they, mostly Deborah, had allowed the decisions of another person to destroy the closeness they once shared. Deborah was looking forward to getting to know Marsha all over again.

Deborah felt uncomfortable and unsure of what to say. So much time had passed since her last visit with Marsha, and she couldn't shake the feeling that she was entering into the house that she had once wanted for her own home.

Marsha was excited to see her cousin walk into her kitchen. She grabbed her and hugged her exclaiming, "I am so glad you are here! It has been far too long! We have so much catching up to do. Come sit at the table. We can talk while I finish up the dinner.

Let me get you some sweet tea."

And talk they did. Non-stop all through dinner. Poor Chad barely getting a chance to speak.

Deborah looked around the kitchen and exclaimed, "I love how you have preserved some of our most precious memories. I love the old wooden picture frame with the inset of yellow gingham fabric topped with chicken wire, showcasing Great-Grandpa Bridge's wood handled cutlery set! That three-tined fork! Those tines are so long and pointed it looks like it could have been a weapon. However, I can still see him sitting at the table eating ham and beans with that fork. Do you remember how he held is fork with an over-handed grip as he scooped up his food? OH, and the water dipper from the old house! That well-water was the best tasting water; it was so cold and refreshing. Remember how we never thought about germs? We all took turns drinking out of the wooden bucket from that old dipper! Life was so much simpler back then."

Marsha said, "That yellow gingham is from Grandma Bridge's kitchen curtains, Remember them? You will have to come over and spend some time going through the old wash house. It is a treasure trove of memories! It is a packed storage shed of history. You know, neither Grandma nor Aunt Dorothy ever threw anything away. There is furniture, pots and pans, bowls, picture frames, old clothes and curtains. A little bit of everything. You may find something to use in the church or the studio."

Deborah said she would love to do that one day soon.

Marsha asked about Lucy and her husband Bill and wondered if Bill was about ready to retire from the Marine Corp.

Deborah sighed. She said she missed her sister dearly. Other than Lucy coming home for David's funeral, they really hadn't had many opportunities to get together. It seemed as if the Marines kept moving them every couple of years, and it was always overseas. Phone calls and computer face to face chats were nice but it isn't the same thing, but grateful for the technology that allowed them to communicate and see each other. She hoped that someday she would be able to make it over to Okinawa to visit them.

After dinner, Chad retreated out to his wood shop to work on a china cabinet he was building for someone across town. Marsha and Deborah took their glasses of sweet tea out to the porch swing to watch the sunset across the empty field. The warm evening air reminded them of their youth when they had run around this very yard chasing lightening bugs, pulling off the little lights and sticking them to their fingers to glow like little green diamonds.

Deborah said, "I noticed, you still have a rope swing hanging between the two oak trees, just like the one Grandpa Bridges kept there for us when we were kids. What precious memories I have of those simpler days so long ago."

Marsha chuckled, "Yes, and you know, even though we put up the big fancy store bought swing set for the grandkids, that wood and rope swing is still their favorite too. Simpler really is better. I hope my grandkids grow up with as many precious memories as we did."

"That is what I want for my kids and grandkids too. Did you notice the swing this morning when you came over? The big old Oak tree between the church and the lake?" Asked Deborah. "Yesterday when I arrived and truly took note of the big tree, I mentioned to Sam that I would like to have a swing hanging there and low and behold, I woke up this morning to find a swing! Tell me, what do you know about Sam Cunningham? He seems to be a bit of a mystery to me," queried Deborah.

"You mean other than being some distant relative? Not a whole lot. He is a bit of a mystery all right. He really keeps to himself and doesn't say much to anyone." Marsha answered. "Our Great-great grandma Bridges was a Cunningham before she married. She and Sam's Great-great grandpa Cunningham were brother and sister. So, that makes us what? Cousins four times removed or something? I don't know. We never knew each other, I don't even know for sure if your dad or mine even knew Sam's parents. Never heard anyone we know talk about them at all. All I know is he grew up out east somewhere."

Deborah seemed puzzled. "So, what's he doing here?"

"He's been here a couple of years now. The talk in town is, he hit a rough patch several years ago. His wife kicked him out of the house, his parents said they were through bailing him out, and it was time for him to make it on his own. I heard he even did some jail time."

Deborah gasped, "Oh, my! Really? Do I need to be worried about him? How and why did he end up here?"

"No, I think he's pretty harmless," answered Marsha. "He has a cousin on his mother's side who lives over in Flora. He took Sam in when the rest of the family turned their backs on him. Ernie told Sam it was his last chance to make something of himself, or he would spend the rest of his life homeless on the streets or in prison. It was his choice to make. Sam worked a few odd jobs helping out people all over the area until the Grace Bible Church hired him as the caretaker for the property. No one has had any complaints about him or his work since he has been here. Why are you so curious?"

Deborah quickly replied, "Well, I think it should be obvious. I have this strange man living on the property I own, and in fact, I have provided the very roof over his head. Not to mention, I will be signing his paycheck to boot! And I know nothing about him! Maybe, I should back up a few steps and do an official job interview with my employee and learn a few things. I am so mad at myself for jumping so quickly. I was so impulsive with buying the church and not looking at the whole picture in front of me."

Marsha looked at Deborah with a questioning smile in her eyes. "You wouldn't be starting to have feelings for Sam now, would you? Are you sure that isn't the real reason you are curious about his past?"

Marsha advised Deborah to go talk to Aunt Patsy. She was sure that if Aunt Patsy would have had any reservations about Sam and his intentions, she would have warned Deborah to get rid of him once she owned the church. Aunt Patsy had always been a good judge of character and she liked Sam and trusted him. Plus, Charlie and Norm Johnson would not have hired him if there were any real concerns about his integrity.

Deborah changed the conversation to the patch of orange Tiger Lilies growing over on the South side of the yard. She remembered her grandparents standing in front of that patch some fifty years ago. They had all just returned home from Sunday services at the Grace Bible Church. Grandma Bridges in her navy-blue and white flowered dress clutching her Bible. Grandpa in a light blue summer dress shirt, with the top button unfastened and no tie. A young ten-year-old Deborah Nelson captured the moment forever with the very first roll of color film she had ever bought for her Brownie box camera. There were only twelve exposures on that roll of film and she chose her subjects very carefully, not wanting to waste any of them.

❧ ☙

As the sun bounced off the pumping oil rig in the field across the road and the crickets were chirping loudly, DK shared a somewhat painful memory with Marsha. "This evening suddenly reminds me of a few conversations I have had on this very porch swing with Aunt Dorothy. You know, after Grandma and Grandpa Bridges died, Aunt Dorothy became the grandma figure to all of us. She had the large German build that Grandma did, her loud robust laugh, and her big full breasts, which made her a good cuddler on cool evenings. More than once I had told her I wanted to live here and every time she ignored me. The last time I tried to state my case was after a quilting retreat that Andrea and I had taken in Dallas several years ago. The retreat house we stayed in was on a farm out in the middle of nowhere, very much like out here. In fact, it took us almost two hours in our rental car to get out there from the airport. The house was specifically designed for hosting retreats of all kinds, but with all the charm and ambiance of an old southern farmhouse. A huge main room with lots of floor to ceiling windows across one wall to let in lots of natural light. A big country kitchen for serving buffet style meals. Two bedrooms on the main floor, both with handicap accessible bathrooms. Upstairs were four more bedrooms and bathrooms. Each bedroom was large enough to sleep four people in their own twin-size beds. I was taken in by the design and set up of the place. I questioned the owner with every question I could think of. There was even a smaller matching house off to the back of the property where the owner lived. I came home from that trip more excited about the house and the possibilities that I could build the same kind of retreat house right over there in that field, than I was of any of the quilting projects we had worked on. David supported my idea completely, knowing that I would not have to live out here full time. I would only have to be here when there were retreats scheduled, and I would be in complete control of the schedule and I would have my own place to live and not interfere with any of the renters. In time, it would have been a perfect retirement place for us."

"Aunt Dorothy would not give me the slightest hope that I could make it work. She said that Orchardville was nothing like any city near Dallas and that no one would come here. She said there was nothing around here to draw people to this area. My first response was that city folks were looking for a place just like this to escape from their busy crazy lives, even if for just a few days. I then tried to tell her that I would be around more to keep her company and keep an eye out on her, with my frequent trips here. Her response to that was that she didn't want to be a burden and she wasn't about to give up any of the land so I could have a bunch of strangers traipsing in and out of her front yard, being all nosey and everything!"

"When I realized that I would never get her to see it from my point of view, I told her, not so nicely, that I was going to go talk to Miss Millie Kraemer and see if I could buy her land. Miss Millie had just moved into a nursing home in Salem and her place was sitting empty. I told her she wouldn't have to see anyone coming and going from Miss Millie's place, since it would be on the backside of her farm!"

"Aunt Dorothy stopped me in my tracks when she said that Miss Millie hasn't owned that property for several years. Her nephew bought it and has let her live there as long as she wanted. He is a career military man and didn't need the house, but wanted to be sure the property stayed in their family. I was heartbroken when I heard that news."

"I left and I never came back here again, until a couple of weeks ago. I don't think you saw me, but I was parked right over there at the edge of that corn field, watching the oil rig and remembering my last conversation here with Aunt Dorothy. When you came out with your grandkids, I pulled away. I wasn't ready to talk to you. All I could see was that you were living the dream I always wanted."

Marsha hugged Deborah and said, "I'm so sorry, I had no idea that you had tried so hard to get the farm. I know what you must be thinking of me and why you have been so distant. Even at Aunt Dorothy's funeral, you barely spoke to me. You had to have thought that I did this to you. Believe me, it wasn't like that at all. Aunt Dorothy sold the farm to my daddy, since he was the youngest of her siblings. She told him to make sure it stayed in the family, you know like most of the old timers around here. They don't want a bunch of strangers moving in on their territory. When Daddy got sick and his medical bills were piling up and he couldn't keep up with the taxes on the farm, Chad and I paid all the back taxes, moved out here and started doing repairs that had been neglected for years. Thank goodness, Chad is handy with almost any kind of tool there is. He has done a lot of work that could have cost us a small fortune."

At last, the tension between them had been erased and both women could now move forward and work together as closely as they had once done, so many years before. They both realized that their future together would work out after all, even if it wasn't exactly like Deborah had originally envisioned it.

                                                 ∞

Deborah woke up just before dawn, refreshed from a good night's sleep and excited for the renewed energy she felt after her visit with Marsha. She was also thrilled that it was Saturday and all her kids were coming to visit. She couldn't wait to show them around and for Jeremy and Jacob to see the lake. Thinking of Annie coming though, did cast a bit of gloom over her. She was sure Annie would find something to criticize or lecture her about. Annie wouldn't be Annie otherwise.

Deborah dressed in a pair of jean shorts and an old work shirt. She pulled her hair into a pony tail at the nape of her neck. She was anxious to get this busy day started. According to Aunt Patsy's phone call last night, it is quite possible the whole town could be converging on the church. It seemed as if everyone was anxious to help get this new business up and running.

The sun was just beginning to rise as the coffee was finished brewing. Deborah quickly poured herself a big insulated cup full and headed out the door. She sauntered across the yard towards the cemetery and made her way to Aunt Dorothy's grave. "Good morning, Aunt Dorothy. We have so much to talk about," said Deborah, as she plopped herself down on the ground, leaning her back against the narrow side of the stone. She kind of chuckled to herself as she remembered her life-long superstition of making sure to never step directly on any grave. She had often watched other people walking all over the cemetery, right on top of where the dead bodies were buried. She, on the other hand, had always made it a point to step around the actual body area. Even now as she was sitting on the ground, she was to the side of the stone, not directly on top of Aunt Dorothy. She tried to remember why she had always done that. Why, of course! It was Aunt Dorothy who had taught her to respect the dead. Aunt Dorothy and Uncle John had been the caretakers of the cemetery for many years. Uncle John had done the mowing and Aunt Dorothy used the weed eater along the headstones. Deborah laughed. All those years she had taught me to never walk on top of the dead. I wonder how she managed to trim the weeds without stepping on the dead. But of course, knowing Aunt Dorothy, she just might have stretched her arms across and really didn't step on them. She was a very superstitious woman. She was probably afraid their spirits could reach up out of the ground; grab her legs and pull her in with them!

"Aunt Dorothy, I guess you know better than any of us just what all is happening around here. For all I know, you could be orchestrating the whole project! You know I have made peace with Marsha and I forgive you for denying me what I had thought I should have had for all those years. It turns out, I am right where I belong at this time. If I had gotten what I thought I wanted so long ago, I would not know the joy of what I am feeling today, here at this church. This church is where Grandma and Grandpa Bridges prayed. This cemetery is where generations of ancestors are buried and starting today, I will teach my grandchildren how to appreciate the history of our family. I didn't know it at the time, and I certainly didn't practice it, but I have come to realize you actually taught me the virtue of patience. I truly appreciate your guiding hand at bringing me here and making this new chapter in my life the dream I didn't know I had. I hope you forgive me for being so stubborn and shutting you out those last few years of your life. I also know quite well that stubbornness runs in the family! I guess

I come by that naturally!"

Suddenly there was no mistaking the smell of musk cologne mixed in with the morning dew. Deborah wiped a tear from the corner of her eye. "Good morning, David, You must be with Aunt Dorothy right now, listening to me ramble. I guess you two are working together up there! I still miss you, but I am beginning to move forward. I wish you were here to work with me. I could use your help and your advice. I need you to keep me grounded. You know I have a tendency to act before thinking, like I did with this place. But I am determined to make this work. I know for a fact, I have at least two guardian angels watching over me."

The musk scent swirled around her and then disappeared. David was gone again, but he would be back. She was certain of it.

∽ ∾

The sounds of cars pulling into the lane broke through her meditation. Deborah got up, wiping her damp rear end from sitting in the wet grass.

She met the boys as they were getting out of the van. With barely a hug, they were off and running towards the lake, shouting, "Wow, Granny, this place is cool!"

Annie gave her mother a hug and said, "They have been so excited. They couldn't wait to get here. You were right. The drive really isn't that bad. I guess it seemed longer when I was a kid, and I thought it was boring to come out here."

Bob gave Deborah a kiss on her cheek. "Good morning, I am anxious to see what you are doing here. From everything Annie has been telling me, it is going to be quite an undertaking."

Randy, Chelsea and Davey were also getting out of their vehicles. Chelsea looked around smiling, nodding her head in approval. Davey said with a robust laugh, "Well, boss lady, we are here to do whatever you need done!"

Deborah told them to be prepared for a huge work party to be taking place today, just as a few more cars pulled into the lane.

When the flatbed trailer with a backhoe secured to it began to make its way towards the lake, the boys came running. "Granny, what is that for?" Jeremy and Jacob shouted in unison.

"What an exciting day for you to be here!" exclaimed Deborah. "They are going to make the lake bigger, give it more shape. You will need to stay up here with me while they get the backhoe off the trailer."

Once the backhoe was on the ground, Sam motioned for Deborah to come over. He said, "I want to introduce you to my cousin, Ernie, and this other man is Clay, Clay Edwards. He owns Edwards Excavating out of Cisne. Ernie works for Clay and they have volunteered to shape up the lake for you. If you are still okay with the plans we drew up, they will get started."

Clay explained to Deborah and her sons that he would start down at the tail end of the extension and work his way over to the existing lake. When they were all satisfied with the new addition, his final digs would break through the wall of the lake, automatically filling in the new addition. It was also noted that before he made the final digs to send the water rushing into the new part, there would be a team of men constructing the foot bridge Deborah wanted. They would set the posts into concrete as soon as they had a clearing to work with. Clay also reminded her that it would not all be completed today. The concrete posts needed time to cure before he let the lake water loose.

While Clay and Sam were explaining the plans to Deborah, more cars were continuously arriving and everyone was bringing baskets of food as well. Deborah put Annie in charge of organizing the food inside the fellowship hall. Andrea and Connie manned the sign-up sheet that listed jobs that needed to be done.

Jim Curtiss and Ed arrived in the "Curtiss Ironworks" truck. There were two iron posts and several bags of concrete. Ed said that today he and Jim would install the support posts in concrete and that he and Gary would come back another time to start building the stone pillars around the posts. Jim informed Deborah he would be back in a couple of weeks to install the archway.

Deborah was overwhelmed with all the activity and so many people all around working to make her dream come true. She hugged Aunt Patsy and cried, "I can't believe all of this. I have never been to a barn raising before, but it has to be something like this!"

Aunt Patsy squeezed Deborah's hand, "Oh child, I know you think this is your dream, but it is the dream of everyone here to see new life in this church. You have brought a vision and a hope that none of us could have imagined. Yes, we want this for you, but keep in mind, it is for us too! This is the heart and soul of our town. This is our heritage here."

Deborah reassured her aunt that she would not let her down.

There was constant activity all day long. Men with floor sanders stripped the church floors, Women and teens finished sanding the church pews. Inside the fellowship hall they limited the work to general mopping and cleaning since the food was in there. The kitchen was scrubbed and polished. Appliances tested to be sure that everything worked properly.

Out at the lake site, Clay Edwards was giving the kids a ride in the excavator. With every couple scoops of dirt, a new child took their place on his lap. He let each one think they were operating the controls and digging the dirt. This kept all of the kids occupied and out of everyone else's way. A couple of the older girls acted as ushers, keeping the kids in line until it was their turn. Not a one caused any trouble for fear they would not get a chance to be the driver.

At one point, while taking a break from all that was going on, Deborah and Randy discussed where she would be setting up her office area. Annie suggested it should be in the front corner of the fellowship hall, not in the house, like Deborah had first thought. Davey and Randy agreed that it was not a good idea to have the clients coming in and out of her home. They said they would bring her desk and computer with them when they returned on Sunday, along with anything else she might want from home.

"As a matter of fact, could you bring your dad's pick-up truck? I have a feeling I am going to need a truck around here," Deborah added.

After everyone had finally called it a day, Annie, Bob, and the boys went into the house with Deborah to relax. The boys set up their sleeping bags in the empty bedroom, and Annie and Bob were set up in the front spare bedroom. Bob offered to grill burgers and hot dogs for their dinner until Debra told him she didn't have a grill here yet. So, they settled for traditional boiled hot dogs and popcorn. It was decided before they turned in for the night, they would all go to Salem in the morning for Mass, get some breakfast at the buffet place in town and go shopping for a bunk bed to put in the boys' room.

As Deborah began to lock up the house and turn out all the lights, she couldn't help but notice that Sam's truck was not in its usual parking place.

CHAPTER TEN

As Deborah headed towards the kitchen to start the morning coffee, her heart fluttered with delight at hearing Jeremy and Jacob giggling behind the closed door of their room. A very sweet sound in her new home. Yes, she would definitely need to get the bunk beds soon, so she could have more mornings like this. Once in the kitchen, her first instinct was to look out the window. Sam's truck was still not home. Had he gone out very early this morning or did he not come home at all last night, she wondered.

Once everyone was dressed and ready to go, they all piled into Annie's van and headed towards Salem. Annie drove while Deborah gave directions. Bob sat in back to roughhouse with the boys.

About halfway through Mass, Deborah was quite surprised and somewhat amused to notice Sam sitting in a pew on the far-right side with a very pretty woman. She hadn't considered the idea that he was Catholic or involved with anyone. She hadn't noticed them come in, but it was very obvious by their closeness, they were together. Once she spotted them, Deborah had a hard time keeping her eyes off them and concentrating on the Mass. Various scenarios played in her head as to who the woman could be. Was she a friend? A relative? Something more? She vowed to make herself seen by them after Mass.

As everyone began to very slowly filter out of the church, Deborah lost sight of Sam. She didn't find him out in the parking lot, nor did she see his truck anywhere. He must have gone out a different door she thought to herself. Disappointment set in. She wondered how she could learn more about the mystery woman.

At the buffet restaurant, Deborah realized she had picked the perfect place for Sunday morning breakfast. Jeremy and Jacob were like two boys who hadn't eaten in a week! They devoured everything as quickly as they could and went back for more. They said they were starving from all of that hard work they had done the day before and they needed more energy for today's work!

As they headed towards the door to leave, Deborah noticed a particular table near the front window. Without hesitation, she walked right up to Sam and said, "Well, good morning, Sam! I was not expecting to see you here! You remember my daughter, Annie and her husband, Bob, and of course Jeremy and Jacob. We just attended Mass and stopped in here to feed these starving boys! Now we are going to see if we can find some bunk beds for these guys so they won't have to sleep on the floor anymore. Maybe you can recommend a place."

She looked directly at Sam and then towards the woman and said. "I'm sorry, we haven't met. My name is Deborah Kingston. I just bought Grace Bible Church over in Orchardville. I guess you could say I am Sam's new boss." Deborah said as she extended her hand towards the woman and asked, "You are?"

The woman smiled as she shyly held out her hand.

Sam quickly interjected. "Her name is Beverly. She is a friend. Lives here in Salem." Sam then gave Deborah the name of couple places that would be open on Sunday and might have bunk beds. Sam then turned his attention to the boys and asked if they were ready to get some more work done later today. He looked at Deborah and said he would be back around one o'clock, which was when most everyone planned to arrive to finish up what they could today. Sam took a long draw from his coffee cup. As he peered over the edge of the cup, he gave her an icy stare.

Deborah nodded and said she would see him later as she nudged the boys towards the door. She tried to not let the sting in her eyes show. It was obvious to everyone she had just been brushed off and that Sam did not want any more questions asked.

SEARCHING FOR SOMETHING SPECIAL

Back at home, everyone quickly changed into work clothes and prepared to welcome all the helpers about to descend upon them.

As they waited for everyone to arrive, Deborah took Annie and the boys over to the cemetery. They walked around the old gravestones, reading the names of relatives who had died nearly a hundred years earlier. As they walked, Deborah reminded the boys to be respectful of the dead and to be sure and not walk on top of any grave. They laughed and asked, "Why, will the boogie-man get us if we do?" She told them there wasn't any such thing as a boogie-man, even if her Aunt Dorothy used to always say the same thing, "Deborah Suzanne, don't step on those graves, or the boogie-man will get ya!"

The boys were intrigued that their granny lived by a cemetery. They asked if she was afraid, or if she saw ghosts at night. She told them no, that it was really quite peaceful living here. She knew there wasn't anyone here who could hurt her and she did not believe in the boogie-man.

Connie and Andrea were the first to arrive. Connie called Deborah to the back of her van to show her what she had brought. There in the back were several bolts of antique Austrian lace. Connie said she had found them in a trunk in her grandmother's attic and that she had used some to make the lace valances for her dining room but Deborah was welcome to the rest of it to use as she wished. She also added that her grandmother would be pleased to know that her treasured fabric would be used for something as special as this place.

Deborah thanked her friend as they carried the fabric into the house. Deborah said she would figure out where to put it later and that she would certainly do something special with it.

The men arrived and started working on the footbridge supports. The sanding commenced inside the church. Davey and

Randy arrived with Deborah's desk and computer which they set up in the front corner of the fellowship hall. Of course, more food arrived with each family that came to help. Deborah was in complete awe and extremely grateful for all the helping hands around her. She had never dreamed of such an outpouring of friendship. She would have to figure out some way to repay everyone who was contributing to make her dream become a reality.

By five o'clock everyone began to call it a day and head back to their own homes. It had been a very productive weekend. Leftover food had been packaged and placed in the large refrigerator inside the fellowship hall. Plenty to feed any workers who might come by during the week.

Deborah walked through the church, taking in the smell of the freshly sanded wood throughout the room. Tomorrow she would be able to start staining and painting the pews with the supplies that Davey and Randy had brought back with them. As she locked the church doors, she noticed Sam driving away in his pick-up truck. She had hoped to talk to him once everyone had left. She wanted to know more about him and Beverly.

It crossed her mind as she headed into her house that maybe Sam had left on purpose. Maybe he didn't want to talk about Beverly. She told herself she would need to approach the subject very carefully since she didn't know Sam very well. As Marsha's words of jail time and that his wife had kicked him out played across her mind, she quickly turned the deadbolt lock on her own door.

       ❦

Deborah walked around inside her double car garage with a sketchpad in hand and a tape measurer hooked to her belt loop. Ideas were forming for her permanent office and portrait studio. The desk setup in the fellowship hall was a good temporary location, but this large garage might be the answer for a permanent office. As she was sketching various options for adding walls and creating rooms and display areas, she thought back to how many times David would tease her about her ideas when it came to building and converting spaces. He always said she was three projects ahead of his hammer. She laughed and said, "Oh Sweetie, if you could see me now! What would you say about all of this?" Her smile faded as she said, "I wish you were here. I wish I was doing this with you by my side. Oh, I know you are here in spirit, but it isn't the same."

Deborah pulled a dining room chair to the garage. She moved it to various locations and sat in it at each point, trying to get a feel of where to place a small conference table for meeting with clients. She needed a comfortable reception area with her desk and computer. She needed walls to hang wedding and family portraits.

The first bay of the garage had a regular pass-thru door on the side that led directly out front, facing the church. Perfect entrance for customers to come in and out of without needing to go through the house, or even the breezeway. Deborah went out through the door and walked along the sidewalk that led to the parking pad and entrance to the overhead garage doors. She visualized, that as clients would drive up the lane and enter onto the actual church property, the double car garage is the first thing they would actually see to the right of the lane. The garage faced perpendicular to the road. If the overhead doors are replaced with large picture windows, the studio itself would welcome them to *The Wedding Belle*.

The space between the sidewalk and the actual garage wall allowed plenty of space to be planted with flowers and maybe a birdbath or a bubbling fountain. More picture taking opportunities, as well as a welcoming entrance to the studio.

Back inside the garage, there was a door that led to the breezeway that connected to the house. Over in the far back corner was a small closet-sized bathroom with just a toilet and sink. It would definitely need cleaning and fixing up, or better yet; gutting it completely and enlarging it. Once Deborah was satisfied with all of the placement ideas, she went inside to convert her measurements to graph paper. David had shown her during one of their many remodeling projects that he could draft them out on the computer with professional results, but she preferred her graph paper and colored pencils. Besides, the computer was over in the fellowship hall and it was getting late.

Early the next morning, with her insulated cup of coffee close by, Deborah was kneeling on the floor of the church spreading the drop cloth under the first couple of pews, preparing to start painting the support braces. She heard Sam's footsteps walking towards her. When he got close enough he said, "You're getting an early start this morning. Do I need to round up some help for you? I think a few of the high school kids might be available."

"Thanks, but this is something I feel like doing myself today. Sort of a break from all the chaos of the weekend. Not that I don't appreciate all that everyone did. I think it is time for me to do a few things on my own. Do you know what I mean?" asked Deborah.

"Yes, I do. It was kind of crazy around here, wasn't it? We got a lot done though." Sam said. Unless there is something specific you need of me today, I need to go help Ernie with a big project he is working on over in Wayne City. Sort of payback for him helping out here over the weekend. Besides, we need to let the concrete cure another couple of days on those supports before we can start building the footbridge.

Deborah told Sam he should go help his cousin. He had been very generous with his time and equipment and if Sam was needed there, she couldn't stand in his way. She wasn't sure if this was an excuse for Sam to avoid talking to her or if he was really needed. She almost asked, but decided against it. But she did say, "Sam, I've been thinking we should talk. We do not really know each other. In fact, I know nothing about you at all. Maybe we could have supper together and get better acquainted? I'll cook."

Sam hesitated but agreed they could have supper together later.

Deborah told Sam to take some of that extra food from the refrigerator for his lunch and to be sure to take enough for Ernie, too.

※ ※

Deborah made a meatloaf for supper. It had always been one of her specialties, baked in an iron skillet, just like her mother and grandmother had always done. It had been one of David's favorite meals. She wondered as she prepared it, if Sam even liked meatloaf. If he did, did he like onions in it or not? She decided that if meatloaf was a failure, she could make scrambled eggs or grilled cheese sandwiches. But what man doesn't like meatloaf? Then she remembered the first day she met Sam and he had told her that Charlie made a good meatloaf. She was confident that he would approve of her dinner choice.

When Sam arrived for dinner, he sniffed the air and said, "I think I smell meatloaf! One of my favorite meals!" Deborah smiled with delight.

Over dinner they kept the conversation light. Deborah didn't want to back Sam into a corner and make him feel like he was trapped. She asked about the job he had been on with Ernie earlier. Sam told her it was a new construction for a strip shopping center. They would be digging sewer and water lines, as well as footings for the walls. It was going to be a big job.

Deborah asked how long Ernie had been in business and

how many employees he had. She finally found a way to work up to what she really wanted to know. "I really should have been asking these questions before he showed up to dig out the end of the lake. But then again, I didn't know he was coming, did I? In fact, I didn't know that more than half the town was going to be here to work. Like I said this morning, I appreciate all the help I had, but it would have been nice to have known what was going on and who was qualified to do what. Sam, I know nothing about you, who you are, what your real line of work has been. All I know is you are caretaker of an old abandoned church. I don't know if you have family or anything.

Sam swallowed hard, took a drink of his iced tea. "Wow! Where do I start?" He took another drink of tea before answering.

"First of all, I'm sorry ma'am. Maybe I did overstep my boundaries somewhat. I really should have talked to you before having Ernie come out here. For that I apologize, but I also knew you did not know who to call or where to start. Which, we did talk about the other afternoon when we walked around here discussing your ideas and plans. I do remember telling you that I knew a few people who could help. The other afternoon while I was at Ernie's making your swing, we were talking about it all and he said he was free this weekend and would be happy to help. No charge. He knew I would work it off by helping him out, too. As for half the town showing up here unannounced, you will have to discuss that with your Aunt Patsy and your cousin Marsha. They would have been the ones burning up the telephone lines, bragging about your plans, and wanting to help you get it going."

Deborah blushed and said, "I guess I am the one who owes you an apology. Yes, you did say you could get some help, I just wish we could have discussed it before everyone showed up. And, I'm sure you are right about Aunt Patsy and Marsha. They are a bit excited about me being here and breathing new life into the church."

Deborah took a deep breath before going on. "Sam, you

know my story and what brought me here. What about you? Who are you and why are you here?"

Sam stood and slowly wiped his mouth with his napkin, which he tossed to the center of his plate. With his hands in his pockets, he walked to the dining room window and stared out towards the church. He nervously rattled the loose change in his pocket as he collected his thoughts. The air between them quiet and somewhat tense. Deborah watched nervously and waited, wondering what she had just stirred up. Unsure if she wanted to hear his answer or not.

After what seemed an eternity, he started with, "I don't know what you have heard about me. I'm a very private person. I don't talk much about me, my family or my past. I try hard to keep my past in the past. I prefer to stay focused on the future. What I will tell you is, that I haven't always been a very nice person; nor one who cared much about helping and doing things for other people. I used to be a very selfish, self-centered person. I liked to hear myself talk and rarely heard anyone else speak. All I cared about was me, and what made me happy, or made me feel good. I seemed to find my biggest pleasures in the bottom of a bottle, I am an alcoholic. That selfishness cost me my marriage, my kids, and my parents eventually washed their hands of me. I ended up here with Ernie who took me in. He and Beverly saved my life. Together they taught me how to be a better, caring man. They literally saved my life. If not for them, I probably would not be standing here today. I am a completely different man from the one who came to town a few years ago. I want to see you succeed in this project almost as much as you do. I know firsthand what rebirth can do to a person's soul. I hope that will answer your questions."

Sam turned to leave, "By the way, Ernie could use me again tomorrow, if you don't need me."

Deborah nodded as tears rolled down her face. She was speechless. She found her voice when Sam reached the door and wished him a good night.

She thought about what he had said, as well as what he hadn't said. She didn't know much more than she did before about the man who lives and works on her property, but on the other hand, she saw a softer side of him. She had also gotten a small glimpse of his dark side, a side she knew he guarded quite closely.

Helplessly, she watched through the window as he headed to his basement apartment. His head hung down, his shoulders slumped as if he had been beaten.

CHAPTER ELEVEN

Reluctantly, Deborah began to prepare herself to attend Aunt Patsy's Bunco night. She tried to get out of going, by saying she had too much to do with work on *The Wedding Belle*. But Aunt Patsy turned on the guilt trip and persuaded Deborah by saying that the ladies who would be attending were all anxious to meet her very smart niece, the brilliant lady, who was going to give their little church a new lease on life.

Deborah, in turn, convinced Marsha to go along as well. Neither lady had ever played Bunco before and did not know what they were getting into. They were both surprised to find nine other ladies besides Aunt Patsy, gathered in the kitchen, dining, and living room. There was a table for four set up in each room. The kitchen counter spread from end to end with an assortment of food choices for snacking. Quick introductions were made before the ladies divided up into three teams of four. There was Charlie's wife Gloria King, Mary Lou Hunter, Betty Martin, June Collier, Rose Adams, Helen Staley, Elaine Roberts, Virginia Albers, and Velma Pugh.

Rose Adams and Helen Staley appeared to be about the same age as Deborah and Marsha. Deborah estimated them both to be in their mid to late fifties. The other ladies could have been old enough to be their mother's and even grandmother's ages.

Deborah and Marsha were split into different teams, so that only one "newbie" was at a table for the first round.

It wasn't long before there was a low rumble of laughter coming from all directions, as well as local gossip, mixed in with the clinking of all the sets of dice hitting each of the wooden tables. Deborah was trying to keep up with the fast pace of the game as well as answering the dozens of questions from the ladies. All of them were wanting to hear more details of her project and offering to help in any way possible. Several offered to help cook and serve food at receptions. Elaine Roberts offered to help as an assistant to Deborah with mailings, phone calls, or any other office work that she may need. With each new round and shifting of partners moving to different tables, Deborah found herself smiling politely and answering the same questions repeatedly.

By the time she and Marsha were headed home, she felt exhausted and had a headache from all the noise and chaos, her jaws hurt from constantly smiling. She knew the ladies meant well, and she appreciated their excitement. But, gee whiz! Repeating herself over a dozen times, made her feel like a broken record.

Over the next several weeks, there was a constant hum of saws and the bang of hammers as work progressed on the deck and footbridge across the lake. Inside, the conversion from a two- car garage to a photography studio was making good progress.

Weekly meetings were being held to discuss the idea of holding a thank you event for everyone who had contributed their time and talent to help build this dream. After much discussion, it was decided that the second Saturday in October they would hold a ham and bean dinner with an open house. It would also bring additional photo opportunities for Davey to include in creating the website and promotional materials. Deborah had been documenting the transformation of Grace Bible Church to *The Wedding Belle* and now it was time to include people and events into the pictures. Deborah said she would offer a free 8X10 picture to everyone who attended. In the invitations, they would suggest that people could dress up as much or as little as they wished for their portraits.

Marsha suggested that they turn it into a surprise birthday party for Aunt Patsy. Her ninety-fifth birthday would be October twenty seventh. Everyone agreed that it was a great idea and Marsha could bake the cake. Together the two cousins would take Aunt Patsy shopping for her dress.

Sam said he could pretend to marry Patsy and Norm Johnson, in order to show that anyone can have a wedding at *The Wedding Belle*, now that he had gotten his on-line license to marry people. Everyone laughed, but Deborah exclaimed. "Sam, that is a great idea! You know how hard it is to surprise her with anything. If she only thinks we are staging pictures for advertising purposes, she would be more willing to dress up real pretty and go along with the wedding idea. Marsha, could you make her birthday cake like a wedding cake? You know, for the pictures! That way too, you can talk to her about her so-called wedding cake, without giving away any birthday surprise."

Deborah asked Sam if he would talk to Steve Abernathy about playing the organ for the service.

Without warning, Deborah suddenly felt guilty for having fun. She realized that even among friends, she was alone. David was not here to share the excitement.

Andrea sensed where Deborah had drifted off to. She reached across the table to touch her friends arm and said, "It's okay, honey. These moments are going to happen when you least expect them. It is only natural, and it is okay to cry if you want to. We will understand."

A tear slipped down Deborah's cheek as she said, "I know he would be happy for me, I just can't help knowing that his death and the money he left me is what is making this a reality. He should be here. It's just not fair!"

Andrea replied, "No, it isn't fair. But David is here, watching over you. He would want you to be doing exactly what you are doing with the insurance money because it is making you as happy as you can be under the circumstances. Besides, you only borrowed from the insurance money. You actually used the inheritance from your aunt Dorothy. You are reinvesting her money into the church that she and your grandparents loved. What better tribute to their memory could there be?"

By the middle of September, it seemed that everything was falling into place and that all the work would be completed in time for the big thank you party. Deborah was anxious to let the community know just how much she appreciated everyone's hard work and support for what she was doing. Of course, it was the main topic of conversation at Charlie's store every day. Neighbors anxious to see their little church coming back to life after being abandoned all of those years.

Just one week before the thank you party, Deborah stopped into the store to pick up a few items for the weekly meeting with Sam, Marsha, Andrea and Connie. Aunt Patsy had now included herself in the weekly meetings. She didn't want to miss any of the details of the big day, which of course made it harder and harder to not give away the birthday surprise. Everyone stayed focused on the mock wedding and appreciation supper. This would be the final meeting and they needed to make sure that they hadn't overlooked any important details.

While Deborah was picking out the deli meats for their lunch, various neighbors were sitting at the tables drinking coffee. Of course, they were all abuzz about the big day coming up. They were asking Deborah one question after another. A couple of them mentioned that they had told a few friends about the celebration and asked if it would be okay to bring them along. Deborah said she didn't see any problem with a few extra people coming, but reminded them that this is supposed to be a thank you party for those who helped with all the hard work in preparing *The Wedding Belle* for business. It isn't meant to be big full blown open house for everyone.

Right at that very moment, Norm Johnson walked into the store and headed straight to the meat counter where Deborah was standing. With a glare in his eyes and stern tone in his voice he said, "Young lady, I'm glad to find you here. There is a big problem with this party you are throwing over there on Saturday and we need to discuss it now. Like, right NOW!"

"Mr. Johnson, whatever could be the problem?" Deborah asked innocently. "I think all of the plans have come together nicely and we have everything under control." She said.

"That's what you think!" he briskly retorted. "Have you any idea how many people are actually coming to this thing? I went to get a haircut this morning in Salem, and every person in there said they were coming. When I went over to get some breakfast at the buffet place that is all I heard from everyone. Why, this town is going to be swamped with more people than you can shake a stick at! That parking lot over at the church will not hold all those cars. Your bathrooms will be overflowing. This thing has gotten way out of hand, Missy! How are you going to fix it? When you started this whole business, you said it was not going to be a circus over there. You promised it would be respectable and intimate!"

Deborah felt like a young school girl being chastised by the principal in front of the whole class. Her lips quivered as she fought back the tears welling up in her eyes. Her body trembled as she searched for a few words to redeem herself.

"Mr. Johnson, I'm so sorry, I had no idea," she started, as her mind raced to find more adequate thoughts. "I don't know how this got so out of hand. I have only invited the people who have donated their time and talents to rebuild the church into something special. I didn't take out any advertising in any papers, nor is it mentioned on *The Wedding Belle* website."

Biting on her bottom lip, she looked around the store at the people sitting at the tables, who suddenly seemed to be ignoring Norm Johnson's rant, but were intent with drinking their coffee in silence. No one was talking to one another, nor looking her way. Their conversations abruptly stopped. The place was suddenly silent.

Deborah had a very profound light bulb moment.

She straightened her back and squared her shoulders, "Excuse me, Mr. Johnson, did you ever tell any of your friends that you would be participating in a mock wedding with my Aunt Patsy next Saturday?" She then walked over to the first table and asked both the men sitting there, "Henry and Walter, what about you two? Did you tell anyone about the party on Saturday? And what about you, Miss Doris and Miss Catherine, I'm sure you told a few people about *The Wedding Belle* and all the plans that we have been making." Each gave a cowardly nod of their head indicating that she indeed was right in her assumptions. As she walked back towards Mr. Johnson, she added, "and Lord only knows how many people my Aunt Patsy told!"

Norm Johnson dropped his head, unable to look Deborah in the eye as he realized who was really responsible for things getting out of hand.

"Mr. Johnson, we are having our final meeting today at noon. Why don't you join us and we can figure out what we can do about this! We certainly cannot un-invite people. Especially, since we have no idea who all has been unofficially invited!"

Charlie handed Deborah the wrapped package of lunchmeat and cheeses and waved her on as he said, "This is on me today. Let me know if I can do anything else to help." With a wink and a grin, he added in a very soft whisper; "You can count on Gloria and me to bring along a big pot of beans and a pan of cornbread to help the cause."

As Deborah started to push open the wood framed screen door, she stopped, turned her body towards everyone in the store and said; "Thank you all for believing in me and supporting my idea! I could not have done this without you!"

ও ৯

Deborah anxiously paced the floor of the church for about twenty minutes. She then went outside and briskly walked along the bridge over to the other side of the lake, where she sprinted along the edge of the water. Sam watched from a distance, his hand nervously playing with the change in his pocket. He had already learned it was best to leave her be. She was obviously working some big issue out in her head and she would let him know what it was whenever she was ready, but in the meantime, it was best to not ask.

The committee members began to arrive for the meeting. Sam met each of them at their cars and said that Deborah would be with them soon. Marsha and Andrea nodded towards where Deborah was pacing the edge of the water. Marsha said, "That is not a good sign. She looks ready to explode. I wonder what has gotten her so upset?" Andrea agreed.

Finally, Deborah made her way back across the bridge and told her friends that they needed to talk before Aunt Patsy and Norm Johnson arrived. Together they all asked, "Norm Johnson? Why is he coming? He's never been to any of our meetings before."

"I know! He and I had a confrontation at the store this morning and I made him eat crow! Now he is going to have to sit at MY table and face me on MY terms, whether he likes it or not!" Deborah declared.

The group looked at each other and shrugged their shoulders and there were a few mutterings of "Oh my!" and "Uh-oh!" and "Wow!" as Deborah marched fearlessly ahead of the group heading towards the breezeway entrance to her house.

Deborah quickly filled them in on what had happened at the store with Norm Johnson and that they were about to be inundated with a countless number of people. They quickly put their heads together and devised a plan of action. They all wanted to show Mr. Johnson that they would not be beaten by this news. They wanted to prove that they could handle the situation.

Sam got on his cell phone and made a couple of calls. Andrea, Connie and Marsha did the same, while Deborah continued to pace between the living room and dining room. By the time Norm arrived with Aunt Patsy, they knew what they were going to do.

The school parking lot would serve as the parking lot for out of town folks coming from the West, since it would be the first major business folks would see upon entering into town. From the East, folks would park at the tractor supply store. Gary and Ed would each be stationed at the locations to provide shuttle service to *The Wedding Belle* via a horse drawn hay wagon or carriage, which also provided more photo opportunities for Deborah. Clay Edwards would have port-a-potties delivered to the school, the tractor supply parking lot, and *The Wedding Belle*. Sam concluded with the statement, "As it says in the Bible how Jesus served the crowds with loaves and fishes until they were filled. We can only pray that we will have enough beans and cornbread to satisfy our crowd as well!" To which Aunt Patsy added, "Yes, God will provide! He always does!"

The day before the ham and bean dinner, Deborah and her crew were quite busy with the last-minute preparations. Annie took charge of getting the ham and beans cooking on the stove. Sam, with the help of Jeremy and Jacob, made sure the grounds were trimmed and raked. Hay bales had been delivered and placed in various areas throughout the churchyard for seating. Corn stalks tied in bundles and accented with jumbo sunflowers were attached to the support beams of the footbridge and deck, as well along the step railings to the church and the fellowship hall. Potted mums of all colors filled in around the bases.

Bob assisted Andrea and Connie with draping bolts of sheer organza fabric and strings of tiny white lights between the wooden beams in the ceiling of the fellowship hall. Marsha set up Aunt Patsy's birthday cake on a round table in the front left corner of the room. She had done a beautiful job creating a fall looking wedding cake. Four tiers were decorated with ivory colored frosting in a basket weave pattern with small clusters of fall colored flowers anchoring the draped frosting trim. The top tier, elevated on crystal pillars looked like a basket full of large frosting mums cascading over the top. The autumn gold and cranberry colors were taken from the accent colors in Aunt Patsy's dress.

The florist in Cisne arrived with the bouquets for the church and centerpieces for the hall. A box of boutonnieres and corsages were left in the refrigerator to be handed out the next day.

Before going to bed, Deborah checked her emails one last time. Of course, there was one from Lucy sending her love and wishing she could be there to share in the festivities.

With all the final details completed, the big day was here at last. Deborah woke up early and started her day over at the church. She sat in the front pew, drinking up the quiet solitude feeling grateful. Looking up to the single stained-glass window with the sun shining through; her camera in hand she captured the ripples of light as they danced from the colored glass to the highly-polished wood floors. Deborah thanked God for allowing her to make His home a part of her own. This little white church had held a special place in her heart for as long as she could remember and now she hoped it would be a special place for generations yet to come.

As she left the church, Deborah took notice of the blooming mums at the foot of the steps. She picked a couple of stems before she walked over to the cemetery. Placing the burgundy colored mums on each of her grandparent's grave, she reminisced about the earliest memories of being in this very place with them. Who would have ever guessed that the little six-year old girl would one day become the owner? What little girl ever thinks of owning a church? Next, she went over to visit Aunt Dorothy and Uncle John. She took a whiff of the mum's before placing them on the graves. They didn't have the usual smell of a mum, they smelled more like...like musk! Of course, David would be here too! He wouldn't miss this occasion. She thanked her guardian angels for everything they had done to make this dream a reality. She said she could not have done this without their help and that she knew for a fact that there had been a whole lot of Divine intervention happening in the past three months and was quite certain that there would be more to come. A sense of peace like she had never felt before came over her and she was ready to face the day, and welcome her guests that would soon be arriving.

&

Sam looked very handsome in his black preacher suit with the knee length duster jacket. Deborah envisioned Sam Elliot playing the role of a country preacher in a movie. When she asked him about the suit, he said that Beverly had helped him find it on line. He said it was called a western duster. Holding a Bible in the crook of his arm, Deborah posed him on the top step in front of the walnut stained double doors of the church. She then took him inside and took several more poses of Sam, including a few of Sam with Beverly. Deborah shuttered when Sam kissed Beverly intensely for one of the pictures. Was that a streak of jealousy that jolted through her body as she realized they were more than just friends?

It didn't take long for the place to be buzzing with people walking around and admiring the work that had been done. They drifted from one area to another. Interestingly, but not completely surprising, almost every one of the local friends who had worked so hard to prepare the church for today, also arrived with pans of cornbread and big pots of beans. When Deborah first noticed Miss Doris and Miss Cynthia with their pans of food, she quickly thanked them but also said this was supposed to be her gift to the community for all they had done for her. But they both hung their heads and said it was the least they could do, since they had helped to spread the word about today's party. They said that after they had heard Norm Johnson talking about how many people could be here, they knew they had to help feed some of the folks. And so it went with most of the women in town. Deborah was truly amazed at how giving and thoughtful everyone had turned out to be.

Davey had been put in charge of escorting Aunt Patsy to the party. They arrived promptly on time for the so called four o'clock wedding. Her dress was an ivory colored satin with a separate jacket that had long sheer sleeves. The collar and cuffs had machine embroidered flowers in burgundy, beige and copper.

As soon as Sam had finished the pretend ceremony with Aunt Patsy and Norm Johnson, several other couples took turns with their own pretend ceremonies. All had dressed for the occasion. Needless to say, word had spread throughout the neighboring communities and there were quite a few people who had come to see for themselves what *The Wedding Belle* was all about. The thank you party had grown into a full-fledged advertising campaign on its own. As Deborah took pictures of each couple in the church, Annie took notes and gathered information for getting their free picture mailed to them. Davey also had created release forms that everyone had to sign, stating that their pictures could be used in any advertising literature and website.

Once all the pretend weddings were over, Deborah announced that it was time to head over to the hall for the reception pictures. Earlier, she had instructed Davey and Randy to detain Aunt Patsy and Norm as long as possible, so that Aunt Patsy would be one of the last to enter the reception.

The hall was full when Patsy made her entrance, with her "groom" by her side. She looked as radiant as if she really was a bride. They were directed straight to the cake table where they posed and cut the cake. Norm even made the first attempt to feed the bride and Patsy followed suit. Deborah capturing everything with her camera. At that point she nodded to her boys who then asked everyone to join them in a toast to Aunt Patsy. With that, everyone began to sing Happy Birthday to her. Aunt Patsy's jaw dropped. She couldn't believe what was happening. They had succeeded in surprising her after all. She cried tears of joy as her nieces hugged her and told her happy birthday. The party was now officially started and dinner was served. Many of the guests took their food outside to sit on the hay bales and enjoy the crisp evening air as the sun was setting.

Randy asked his mother to join him outside. He had some photo ideas he wanted to share with her, something he thought would be a good publicity shot. He urged her to hurry and to meet him at the bridge. He wanted her to catch the sun setting on lake. Chelsea was on the bridge waiting for them. Randy said, "OK, Mom. Get the camera ready!" as he bent down on one knee and handed Chelsea a ring. When she said yes, fireworks went off on the other side of the lake. Deborah moved the camera away to see Sam standing there with Jeremy and Jacob. Talk about secrets and surprises! Apparently, there had been a lot of that going on by everyone.

After all the hugs and congratulatory wishes were given, there were more pictures to be taken of the newly engaged couple as they embraced each other on the bridge, and as they played on the wooden swing together. First, Randy sat in the swing with Chelsea on his lap, then she sat on the swing while he sat draped sideways across her lap acting all silly. They stood on the swing together and in another shot, Randy pretended to push Chelsea in the swing.

During their photo session, Chelsea told Deborah that, of course, their wedding would be here sometime early next year. She would have liked to be the first real wedding at *The Wedding Belle,* but seeing the response of so many people here today, she was quite certain there would be several weddings here long before she could be ready.

Photo opportunities were in abundance all evening. There were the candid shots of close family and friends laughing and having a good time. There were group shots of people sitting in the hay wagon and the carriage. Even Gary and Ed had dressed the part of carriage drivers, wearing top hats and tails, adding to the authenticity of the event. Deborah thinking she barely recognized Gary without his maroon SIU baseball cap. Wouldn't David love to see this!

It was delightful to see many of the elderly women taking a turn to sit in the wooden swing and smile like young girls again. Of course, there were pictures taken at the bonfire as guests made s'more's and sang songs together. It became quite clear that it would be difficult to choose a handful of pictures for the website from the hundreds that were being taken.

The biggest surprise of the evening was when Norm Johnson approached Deborah and said, "Young lady, I don't know how you did it, but you really pulled this thing off. Everyone is having a good time. There haven't been any problems and there was even enough food for everyone.

A sharp voice spoke up from behind him, "Norm, didn't I tell you that God would provide? You never listen, do you?" scolded Aunt Patsy. "God sent her here to save this church and this community! It is high time you start respecting her and her ideas!"

"Yes Ma'am," he replied sheepishly.

CHAPTER TWELVE

Word had spread about *The Wedding Belle* and the website was getting continuous hits and email inquiries. Deborah was kept busy scheduling appointments for wedding consultations as well as family portraits and engagement photos. There were more requests for anniversary celebrations and marriage renewals than she had anticipated. She had anticipated this venture would be slow to get going and would build gradually. She never expected this original burst of business. Then of course, she feared, this original big bang would fizzle out and become a big dud. What would she do to redeem herself and her pride?

Deborah found it increasingly difficult to get away and go home to Belleville for more than a day or two. For now, the house was being taken care of by both of her sons. Davey had moved into the basement while Randy remained in his old room upstairs. They shared the duties of the yard and maintenance on the house.

Decisions were going to have to be made soon about the house. Deborah hesitated to sell it, but she also didn't want Chelsea to feel obligated to move into her mother-in-law's house. She knew very well that a new bride would want a home of her own. She was going to have to find time to go as often as she could and start deleting clutter and prepare to sell the house. She felt it was time to say good-bye to the home that she and David had shared their whole married life. It also meant that both Davey and Randy would have to find places of their own. She began to realize a part of her had successfully moved on with her life, but she was also afraid to completely let go of the past.

∽ ∾

Deborah's trips to Belleville were scheduled to coincide with the boy's school activities. She needed to prove to Annie that she could still be an involved grandmother to Jeremy and Jacob. She made sure she was there for school plays, soccer and softball games, along with special dinners and treats of ice cream after all such events.

With the holidays approaching, Deborah and Annie decided, with Davey and Randy's blessing, that this Thanksgiving would still be held at the family home just as it had always been. Annie snidely retorted that it would probably be their last holiday together as a family, since all their lives were changing. Deborah tried to reassure the dramatic girl that would not be the case. She reminded her that everyone would be coming out to the country for Christmas. She wanted a real old fashioned country Christmas and she also wanted to have the boys stay with her during the first part of their Christmas break so they could help with the preparations. She wanted to make sure they all had a very special and memorable Christmas this year.

∞ ∞

There was an email from Lucy:

"Hey Sis, I have been following all the chatter on your website. The pictures are awesome and it looks like things are going well for you and your wedding chapel. So proud of what you have accomplished so quickly. I can't wait to see it in person. Love Ya!"

And an email from Connie:

"Are you free anytime tomorrow? I want to come talk to you about something very important."

After a quick glance at her calendar, Deborah responded that she was free anytime and to come whenever she could. She told Connie she would have the coffee on or lunch ready, whatever she preferred. The truth was, there were several things on her calendar, but she would rearrange things to accommodate Connie's schedule. Something must really be wrong for Connie to reach out and want to talk so urgently.

An email arrived from a young lady by the name of Melissa

Peterson it read:

"Good morning Mrs. Kingston, I had the privilege of meeting you at your open house a few weeks ago, and I want to thank you for the beautiful picture that you took of my fiancé and I out by the lake. We would like to come meet with you and have more portraits made and to also discuss having our wedding at The Wedding Belle at the earliest possible time available. My Great Aunt, Millie Kraemer, used to be a member of the Grace Bible Church and we would like to honor her by having our wedding there. Her health is declining and it would mean a great deal to all of us if she is able to attend our wedding. Please let me know when we can schedule a meeting to discuss the details. I can be reached at the phone number below."
Melissa Peterson

After checking her calendar, Deborah called the young woman to see what arrangements could be made for pictures and setting a wedding date. The young lady was so anxious to get things moving she said she and her fiancé could be there later that very afternoon.

❧ ☙

The young couple arrived precisely at three o'clock and were prepared with a couple of changes of clothes. Deborah apologized and said she did not remember seeing them at the open house, but then again, there were so many new faces that day that she had never met before. She asked, just how exactly they heard about *The Wedding Belle*.

Melissa said, "As I mentioned in my email, my Great Aunt Millie Kraemer was a member here, when it was a thriving house of worship. Some of her friends visit her regularly and they told her all about you. Aunt Millie told my daddy about a lady who came to town and bought the church and was turning it into a wedding chapel. Daddy knew I was planning my wedding and looking for a special venue. We did some internet research and liked what you were doing with the church. We thought it would be very fitting to get married here. Then daddy heard about the open house. He couldn't come, but Brad and I were here. Oh, look! There is our picture on the wall," she said as she pointed to a large collage hanging on the wall. The collage had a thumbnail copy of every picture Deborah had taken that day.

Together they compared calendars and schedules to determine a wedding date that would work for all parties involved. The first date that was agreeable to everyone would be the day after Christmas, which would be on a Saturday. Deborah said the church would be decorated for Christmas and would make a beautiful background for the pictures. She said it would also save her some money on flowers and decorations. Melissa was very excited about that prospect and said she could picture a Christmas wedding. She said, "Aunt Millie will love it too!" Then she asked about Sam performing the wedding but what she really wanted to know was if someone else would be allowed to perform her wedding.

"I saw on the website and observed at the open house that Mr. Cunningham is listed as the on-sight officiant. However, I have always dreamed of my daddy performing my wedding. It didn't work out the first two times I was married and I would like the third time to be the charm. In more ways than one!", she said, as she gave her fiancé a nudge and a wink. Melissa added, "He is a retired Air Force Chaplain, and has presided over many other weddings. Now I would like it to be mine!"

"Well, yes, of course we can do that!" responded Deborah. "I look forward to meeting him and working out the final details. Now, let's start taking some pictures of you two, shall we?"

Deborah had lunch ready when Connie arrived. She could tell that something was weighing heavily on Connie's heart. After a bit of formalities of friendly chit-chat and talking about the business, Connie finally asked, "How do you do it? How have you been able to move on so quickly after David's death? I have tried for over ten years to get on with my life after Chrissy's death and no matter what I do or what I take on, I feel like I am still sinking into a deep hole that I can never escape."

Deborah sucked in a deep breath. She was not expecting anything like this. She studied Connie's face as she searched for the right words. She herself was not sure how she had moved on, or if she really had. Oh, yeah, maybe on the surface, but in reality?

Finally, she found her voice. "Connie, I don't know what to say to you. I don't have to tell you that everyone grieves differently, and that everyone has their own time frame for moving forward, there are some who never do. Even when we do move on and try to get past the grief of losing someone, I think in the end, we will still die with a broken heart."

Connie told Deborah that she had been watching her all these months working to build *The Wedding Belle* and taking control of her life. She said she had been admiring her strength and courage and wishing she could be more like her.

Deborah took Connie's hand and said, "Come with me." They walked across the gravel parking lot and went into the church. Connie hesitated and attempted to pull back from Deborah's hand. "No, I can't go in there." Deborah refused to let Connie back away. Once inside and sitting in the front pew, Deborah said, "Here is where I find my peace and my strength. I can't really explain how or why I am able to do what I do. I know from past conversations, you blame God for taking your daughter. Please try to let go of some of that anguish. You will begin to feel better if you do. I know she was young and you want to know -

why. But, we cannot always know - why. I miss my David as much today as I did the day he died; probably more so now. I'm sure I always will. I understand the deep hole and the inability to escape, that you talked about. I was there too, but I was lucky, I realized rather quickly David would not want me sinking deeper into that hole. He would want me to live a meaningful life. David himself helped me out of that hole. I believe that he and his band of angels up there with him, such as my parents, grandparents and Aunt Dorothy and Uncle John, along with the angels here on earth, like Aunt Patsy, provided this outlet for me to discover who I am for myself. I firmly believe that a higher power than just little old me pulled this off. Come, let's walk."

They went outside and walked towards the lake. As they reached the foot of the bridge, Deborah stopped to pick a couple of flowers. Handing one to Connie, she said, "This flower is a gift from God, along with everything you see here," she stated as she swept her hand across the open air. When they were standing on the bridge, Deborah tossed her flower into the water and said, "Watch it float. It bobs up and down with the waves but it doesn't sink. That is how I feel. Every single day, I bob up and down. I kid you not, some days it takes a real effort to not sink. It takes work!"

Connie had tears rolling down her face. "That is what I want too. I want to bob up and down, I am so tired of just sinking deeper and deeper. I know Ed is worried and my brother Gary is very concerned as well. I've tried therapy and even pills, but I keep losing ground. I thought when we bought Grandpa Jack's place I would have a new purpose, but the truth is I can't stop sinking!" Connie surveyed the ground along the edge of the lake and suddenly darted towards the end of the bridge. Deborah was uncertain if she should follow or call out to Connie. She wasn't sure where Connie was going or what she was going to do.

Connie ran to the base of the bridge, bent down and picked up a rock. Throwing it into the water, she shouted, "There that's me! Sinking straight to the bottom of the lake!" Deborah dashed to the edge of the lake, also picking up a rock as she got closer. "Connie Dear, you don't have to sink. Here skip across the water like this!" Deborah did a side handed throw of the rock into the water. One little hop and the rock sunk. They both laughed. "Well, okay, that wasn't a very good example of what I meant to do." It was supposed to skip across the water before sinking. Sweetie, if you could just do a little bit of skipping before floating, you will start to feel better."

Connie tossed her flower into the water and watched it float peacefully. She turned to Deborah and asked for her help.

Deborah bent down and picked up a couple more rocks. Handing one to Connie, she said, "Here, let's take care of this first." Both women took turns picking up rocks and skimming them across the lake. Laughing and having a good time as they tried to see who could skip their rock the furthest. This bit of mindless child's play, helped to lighten Connie's somber mood.

Deborah embraced Connie and said that all she could do would be to give her some advice, but it was up to her to take it to heart and pull herself out of the hole. Treading very carefully, she asked Connie about Chrissy's re-created room at the farm house. "Does that room give you comfort or heartache? I know it causes Ed heartache and he will not go in there. What about you?"

Connie sobbed and shook her head; "Actually, both. There is heartache in seeing all of her stuff and knowing she will never walk into that room, but there is an even bigger heartache in thinking about disposing of all her stuff and acting like she never existed."

"Whoa! You don't need to get rid of everything, especially all at once. Take little steps. Chrissy did exist. She had a big heart and always wanted to help others. She had clothes that could be donated to the less fortunate. Her prom dresses can be donated to the non-profit group that collects them for the girls who can't afford prom dresses. Her stuffed animals can be donated to the children's hospital. Those are just a few ideas and, even with that, you don't have to get rid of everything. You need to keep some mementos. Pick out a few of your favorite clothes of hers. We can piece them into a quilt that you can wrap around you, instead of looking at them hanging lifeless in the closet. Keep one of her favorite stuffed animals and spray it with her perfume. Keep her scent alive when you hug that stuffed bear. Take it one step at a time."

Deborah continued, "I have heard of some kind of horse therapy, I don't know the correct title of it, but if you could get certified, it could be good for others as well as yourself. Lean on God, your Grandpa Jack, and Chrissy too. She'll help you, if you let her."

Connie said that it was equine therapy and it is something she has thought about, but not actively pursued. Just boarding other people's horses and giving trail rides have not brought her the comfort she had thought it would.

Deborah went on to tell Connie about the teenage son of a friend of hers in Belleville. The young man was having a terrible time adjusting to his mother's death. He was actively causing trouble at school and at home. He was starting to hang out with the wrong group of friends and his father was quite worried about the influence all of this was having on his younger siblings. She said the father is considering sending him off to boarding school or to a group home before he ends up in jail. "Connie, do you think equine therapy could help him? Do you know of a facility that I can recommend to my friend, since you are not certified?"

"Let me do some research on the subject and see what is involved with getting certified. I will also see if there is something available now for your friend. Thank you, Deborah, for listening to me and for giving me something to look forward to. It has been a long time since I have felt like I might have a purpose. I love you. You have always been a very special friend." Connie hugged Deborah and left; feeling that the burden she had been carrying for years was a bit lighter as she drove home.

※ ※

Throughout the final weeks of October and the early weeks of November, both Sam and Deborah were kept very busy with their hectic schedules. Sam performed as least one wedding each weekend and sometimes two. Deborah had family portraits during the week that clients were wanting to give as Christmas gifts. With the autumn leaves of every color imaginable and the bales of hay still stacked in various places, every portrait taken was unique, in its own way. She had even set up a Christmas room inside the studio for those who wanted that background for their pictures. Deborah was very conscientious that every client had a unique setting. At the end of the long days, she and Sam both wondered what things were going to be like once more people were aware of what they were doing in this little country town, that most people had never even heard of before. They laughed and proclaimed that they were about to put Orchardville on the map.

Deborah had quickly grown comfortable with the computer programs that Davey and Randy set up specifically for the business. She was elated that she could flip from various screens within the program and know exactly when each client was scheduled and what settings they wanted, and who had paid deposits or not. In other parts of the program she could track the expenses versus the income and was surprised and quite excited to see that she was already operating with a slight profit. Hope for even larger profits in the coming year ran high as the appointments kept coming in. It was still too early to gloat, but she was confident that her investment from Aunt Dorothy's inheritance money was going to turn out exactly like she had hoped it would. If only David could see what all she had been doing and learning in such a short time. She smiled and realized that, of course he could, and most likely was by her side and helping her. She knew she was not alone.

An email arrived from Connie:

Dear DK,

Ed and I have had some long talks about your suggestion for using our ranch for equine therapy. I am in the process of getting certified, but in the meantime, I have contacted your friend Patrick Collins. Last Saturday he brought his son Quintin out for a visit. He immediately bonded with our Sugar Bear. We went for a trail ride and when we returned, he was very conscientous of every detail of brushing her down and grooming. He wanted to know how soon he could come back. Surprisingly to me and without hesitation, Ed told him to come back next weekend and stay the whole weekend. Ed told Quintin he could be his shadow for the weekend. I think Ed enjoyed having him around just as much as Quintin enjoyed it. Mr. Collins will be bringing Quintin late Friday afternoon to stay with us. I made sure to stress that we are not certified, that this is just friends helping friends. Thank you again for the suggestion.

Oh yeah. I have taken down a few of Chrissy's posters and boxed up a few of her most favorite clothes that will one day be made into a memorial quilt. Slowly, the others are making their way to the local family shelter.

I couldn't have done this without you!
Love and hugs,
Connie

Deborah slept in until about ten in the morning. Totally exhausted from Saturday's schedule, she leisurely padded around the house in her pajamas as she gathered items to pack for her week away. She was looking forward to some quality time with her family in her Belleville home and preparing for Thanksgiving Day. As she packed a box of home grown and canned foods that many of her neighbors had brought her as gifts, she smiled at the kindness they had showered on her. She would be sharing their bounty and kindness with her family on Thanksgiving. While she was very thankful for all that God had brought into her new life, this Thanksgiving would definitely be bittersweet without David at the head of the table. She had so many new things to be grateful for, she couldn't help but feel joy, as well as remorse.

Once she was dressed, packed and had the car loaded and ready to go, Deborah went into the church for a few minutes of prayer and thanksgiving to God for all that he had bestowed upon her in the last few months. She also walked over to the cemetery and placed flowers on everyone's grave and thanked each of her guardian angels for watching over her. As she walked back to her car, she picked up Bandit who was sitting on the church steps waiting for her. Together they headed to their other home in Belleville.

Tonight's family dinner would be home-made pizza bar. It was a family favorite for casual dinners. Everyone, rolled out their own mini crusts and added their preferred toppings. With the built in double ovens, several pizzas could be baked at one time. Of course, more personal pizzas were in the works while the first ones were baking. There was lots of laughter and conversation going on at one time. It was definitely a kitchen filled with love. Deborah stood back and observed her family with great pride. She beamed at seeing and knowing she and David had done a good job of raising their children to be strong independent adults who enjoyed being around their siblings and they were teaching the next generation what it meant to be a family. David would be proud to be standing here and observing this love along with her. Instead of feeling sad, Deborah felt genuinely warm and at peace.

They discussed who was bringing what for Thanksgiving dinner and made plans for attending the early Mass together as a family. Of course, there had to be cinnamon rolls for breakfast while the parade was on television! That ritual was a long-standing family tradition for generations and no one was going to allow that to change.

Deborah showed Annie and Chelsea some of the home canned goods that she had brought from Orchardville. Of course, Annie began to protest that there were family recipes that needed to be served. It just wouldn't be the same without Grandma Kingston's Cranberry relish and Grandma Bridges' Sweet Potato Casserole. Deborah agreed that they would continue with their usual traditions, but the gifts from the country would be nice additions. Besides, she was sure there were a few things in the box that Jeremy and Jacob had never had before. It would be interesting to see what they thought of some of the things in the box.

After Deborah finished her grocery shopping and put everything away, she headed downtown to meet Chelsea and Randy for lunch. They said there was something they wanted to talk to her about in private before Thanksgiving Day.

Chelsea started the conversation, "Deborah, I hope you will like the idea that I am about to propose to you and I want you to know that it is completely my idea. Randy did not talk me into this. We would like to buy your house. We want it to stay in the family. We want that house to always be the hub for family dinners and most importantly, we want you to know that you will always have a home here with us if you ever need it. You will not need to get rid of everything in order to sell the house to some stranger."

Deborah was nearly in shock. She had not expected anything like this.

Randy added, "We have mentioned the idea to Davey and have told him he can continue to live in the basement as long as he wants. Of course, we will start charging him rent! But the house is big enough for all of us. When you come into town to visit, you will always have a place to stay."

Deborah asked both of them, "Are you sure about this? Chelsea, don't you want your own home, one that is of your choosing?"

"Yes, and I choose this one. I know the love that lives in this home, and I know that it was built with love. If you sold it to some stranger, they could never appreciate it like we can. We want this house. Please say yes."

Before she could say yes, Deborah shot off a list of questions. "Randy, I guess you know what kind of paperwork will need to be done, but how do we come up with a fair price? What about Annie and Davey? My will is set up that the three of you would benefit from the sale of the house. There is a lot to consider. I think we should discuss it with them. You said you mentioned it to Davey, but did you talk to Annie?"

Chelsea answered with, "We are pretty certain that Annie will be delighted with the idea. She has been consumed with worry that everything in her life is changing. Deborah, I believe that if she knows the house is going to stay in the family and that she can come there at any time, she will be a lot happier. It will be one less change for her to have to accept."

Deborah sighed as she took a deep breath. "You might be right. We have endured a lot of change this year, and this just might give us all something to hold onto. I guess we should talk about it Wednesday evening when everyone is together for turkey dinner prep-work night. We will need to have the house appraised."

~ ~

Wednesday evening before Thanksgiving had always been as much a family tradition as the actual turkey day dinner. There were three crockpots of different soups along with homemade biscuits and cornbread. An easy dinner that people could help themselves to whenever they were hungry. Left over biscuits and cornbread would be crumbled and allowed to dry out to be added to the two loaves of torn up white bread for the dressing. It was Grandma Nelson's recipe. She let nothing go to waste.

Davey, Randy, and Bob were playing video games in the basement with Jeremy and Jacob. Annie and Chelsea were chopping celery and onions for the dressing, while Deborah was stirring the cranberries cooking on the stove. Deborah was not quite sure this was the right time, but wondered, when exactly would be the right time? She watched her daughter and daughter-in-law to be, laughing and talking like two best friends. She was confident that everything was going to be okay. But then again, where Annie was concerned, one just never really knows for sure.

Deborah cleared her throat, "You know, I really enjoy watching you two together. Chelsea, I am so glad that Randy found you and realized that you were the person he wants to spend the rest of his life with."

Annie agreed, "Yes, he has brought home a few that I would not have wanted to spend holiday dinners with. Chelsea, you are different from anyone else he has brought home. I am glad that you are going to be a part of our family. Too bad we won't be having any more dinners in this house. I guess we will have them at my house, or you and I can take turns when you guys buy your own place."

Deborah turned off the burner on the stove and joined the girls at the table where they were chopping. She sat down and looked at Annie and said, "What if there is a way that dinners can continue to be held here? What would you think of that?"

Annie frowned and asked, "How can that ever happen, unless you aren't going to sell the house? Are you going to keep it?"

"Not exactly, dear." Replied Deborah. "But, Randy and Chelsea have informed me that they would like to be the ones to buy the house. They want to keep it in the family and continue to have holiday dinners here like everyone is used to having. But you and Davey have to agree to let them buy it. I won't do it unless you all agree."

Annie squealed with delight. "YES!! That is the best news I have heard in a long time!" She swiftly wiped her hands on a towel and gave Chelsea and Deborah a hug as she ran towards the basement stairs shouting, "Davey, Randy, we need to talk!"

※ ※

At last the turkey was placed on the dining room table. This year, Davey would take over the carving duties. It was a somber moment as he stood at one end of the table, with David's empty chair at the other end. However, it didn't take long for the conversations and laughter to break the silence and turn dinner into a joyous occasion after all.

Of course, most of the conversation centered on Randy and Chelsea buying the house and the possible changes they were going to make. Chelsea apologized to Deborah for planning to make changes before they had even talked about the paperwork.

Deborah tried to ease Chelsea's mind by saying, "I know you want to make this place your own, as you should. There are some things that would definitely need updating. Besides that, if I sell the house to a stranger, they would most likely make changes as well. Honey, it will be your house to do as you please. However, I would like to ask if I can dig up some of the flower bulbs out of the beds and take them back home with me to plant there. Now is the perfect time to move the bulbs. Kind of ironic that some of the original flower bulbs came from Orchardville, and now they will be going back."

Annie questioned, "So what kinds of things do you have planned to do around here? Change the carpet, right? That gray Berber should have gone a long time ago!"

Everyone laughed. To which Deborah retorted, "At least it's still not the old green shag carpet we started with! It would still be here if your dad would have had his way. He did not want to pull that up when we did."

Davey added, "Yeah, I remember that. The truth was, he didn't want to spend the money and he said there wasn't anything wrong with what was there."

Randy said that they have kicked around a few ideas, but nothing real specific. Most likely cosmetic stuff such as pulling up the carpet and putting down hardwood or laminate floors throughout the house, maybe, upgrade the kitchen cabinets.

Chelsea turned to Deborah and said, "Deborah, with the floor plan that you and David designed with your master suite on one end of the house and the remaining bedrooms and bath at the opposite end, we want you to keep your bedroom as it is. We will not change anything there, unless you decide you want it done. We can convert two of the bedrooms into one large one for us and that way, when you come to visit, we both still have our own separate space, we want you to always feel at home here."

Before Chelsea could say anymore, there was a sudden groan from Jacob as he asked, "What are these nasty looking green things in this bowl?" Everyone laughed, but they also wondered what it was. It was something that had never been on their dinner table before.

Trying to control her laughter at the face that Jacob was making, Deborah started to explain that it was a very old country recipe. She said her grandma called them Mangoes, but they were nothing like the fruit that the boys liked to eat. They were pickled peppers stuffed with shredded cabbage. Jeremy added his disgust at the new dish by announcing, "Eww, I'm not eating any of that!"

Deborah cut one of the peppers up into smaller pieces so they could each have a small taste. She told them that since they like dill pickles and those nasty gummy sour candies, they should like this too. She went on to tell them that both her grandma and great grandma used to make them every year when they had an abundance of green peppers from the garden. She told them it was one of her favorite dishes from the country. She had always asked her grandma for the recipe, but was told there wasn't a recipe. They just made them with a pinch of salt, a scoop of sugar, another pinch of pickling spices, some vinegar, and packed into the jars. That's all there was to it! When Mrs. Abernathy brought her a couple of jars a few weeks ago, it was a reminder of her grandma and she couldn't wait to taste them again. It had been so many years since she had had them, she had completely forgotten about them.

Both boys still said they weren't eating those green globs of stuff.

Annie, being the teacher, suggested that the boys should think about the true meaning of what Thanksgiving dinner was all about. They should think about the first Thanksgiving and what was important about it.

The boys looked at each other and thought about it for a few minutes. They took turns giving their answers. That the pilgrims and the Indians shared their food and that they both ate things they had never had before. The farmers share their food with their families and friends. Together they said that Thanksgiving was about sharing and family. With a bit of coaxing, they did try a bite of the stuffed pepper and decided it was good, and even asked for more.

After dinner was over and the kitchen cleaned up, Davey and Randy brought up the artificial Christmas tree and dozens of boxes filled with ornaments. The guys put together the tree and hung the lights, while Deborah and the rest of the family began to sort through and unwrap everything. It was bittersweet for Deborah as she reminisced about her entire life stored away in these boxes. Each and every ornament held a memory of her life with David and the many years they had shared together. The boys were intrigued by the stories, even though they had heard them before. Somehow, they had a deeper meaning this year. Deborah said, "I guess this year as we take the tree down, we should divide the ornaments up so you will each have them for your own trees at home. Be thinking about which ones each of you want."

Annie added, "Of course, there will be some special ones we will want to fight over, so we need a fair way to decide who gets what!"

In unison both brothers proclaimed, "Yes Annie! You don't get all the good ones!"

CHAPTER THIRTEEN

The days had grown shorter, the weather a bit brisker, and the trees were nearly void of their leaves. This change in the season altered the time available for outdoor pictures. Most pictures were now taken inside the studio, except for a few nice sunny afternoons. The phone continued to ring for scheduling spring weddings and photo shoots. Deborah and Sam both enjoyed the quiet lull from the chaos they had experienced when *The Wedding Belle* first opened. Even Norm Johnson had settled down and was not quite so gruff whenever he ran into Deborah in town.

Deborah began to make plans for when Jeremy and Jacob would be arriving for their Christmas break, which was only a couple of weeks away. She spent evenings working on the quilted gingerbread wall hanging to go in the kitchen. She called Andrea and thanked her for the book and supplies that she had given her last summer. She told her that she was enjoying focusing on the project and even creating a few ideas of her own, such as Gingerbread themed stockings to hang on the fireplace, along with placemats and table runner for the dining room table. She also told her that when the boys arrived they would be making cookies and gingerbread houses and potpourri balls from oranges. They were also going to go over to Marsha and Chad's farm and cut down their own Christmas tree. Surprisingly, she was looking forward to a very special Christmas this year, after all.

Deborah also told Andrea that between Steve Abernathy, the school choir director, Aunt Patsy, Marsha, and Sam, there was going to be a Christmas pageant on Christmas Eve in the church. It would be the first Christmas celebration in almost four years for the church.

Andrea said that she hoped that the news stayed within

their own community and that it didn't explode into the monster that the opening thank you party turned out to be.

Deborah laughed and said, "Oh, me too! I am not preparing for anything like that at all! I want this to be a quiet, low key event for our town and their immediate families. I want my boys to experience a real country Christmas. It would be nice if it would snow just enough that a sleigh ride after the pageant could be included. Sam said he can borrow a sleigh from someone he knows. Besides I have a wedding here the day after Christmas, I don't need a thousand people to be here on Christmas Eve."

It was a crisp but bright, sunny morning, Deborah was catching up on emails and other paperwork in the studio. A tall, muscular, clean shaven gentleman with a close crew cut, sort of half knocked on the door with one hand as he pushed open the door with his other hand.

"Excuse me, I'm not sure if I'm supposed to just walk in, or knock and wait for you to answer the door. There isn't a sign that says, "Open, please enter, nor is the door locked to keep anyone out."

Deborah laughed and said, "Come on in. That's what most people do around here. I'm Deborah Kingston and welcome to *The Wedding Belle*. What can I do for you?

The man reached over to shake her outstretched hand. He said, "Chaplain Kraemer, ma'am. Oops. Sorry. Old habits die hard. I keep forgetting that I am retired now. Please call me Daniel, my daughter Melissa has talked to you about me performing her wedding ceremony here the day after Christmas. I happened to be in town today and thought I should come meet you myself and look at what you have done here. I've heard a lot of good things."

Deborah seemed a bit puzzled, "Umm, Melissa Peterson, correct?"

"Yes, that's her," he said. Don't let the last name confuse you, she's been married before."

"Oh, yeah. Right. She did tell me that. She also said you are a retired military chaplain.

"That's correct, Air Force. Served my country for almost thirty years. Decided it was time to finally slow the pace down and begin to enjoy life a little bit. Going to start right here where I grew up and hopefully get my daughter on the right track with this new husband. She hasn't had it easy being shuffled around all her life. I hope to make it up to her," he explained.

"You grew up here?" asked Deborah.

"Sort of, but not exactly. My Aunt Millie raised me when I was little after my mom died. A few years later when dad remarried, he came and got me and took me to live with him and his new wife. I left there the day I turned eighteen and ran straight back to Aunt Millie and the farm. It is the only place I ever felt safe and secure. But you don't want to hear all of that. We need to talk about Melissa's wedding."

"Aunt Millie? Kraemer? OH, MY! Now it is all coming together! Miss Millie Kraemer! Her farm connects to the back of my grandparents' farm. You probably knew my grandparents Otis and Ruby Bridges and my Aunt Dorothy and Uncle John Harper."

"Yes, of course I did. I remember your grandparents from when I was a kid living here. However, your aunt and uncle I didn't know very well. Mostly saw them when I came to visit when I was on leave from service," replied Daniel.

"Well, this small world keeps getting smaller, doesn't it? I spent lots of summers with my grandparents when I was a kid. Funny, I don't remember ever meeting you. Did I?" Deborah asked.

"I can't say that I remember meeting you either, but then again that was a long time ago. Of course, there were various events at church and at different people's houses where there would be gatherings of people that I didn't know. Could be that our paths have crossed and we just don't know it," he said.

"So, would you like to go over and see the church and the hall? We can discuss the plans that Melissa and Brad have talked about, then I'll show you around the grounds. Let me grab my jacket," she said.

"Yes, please." Daniel stepped towards the door and held it open for her.

Daniel was very impressed with the refurbishing of the church and the hall. He said she had done a very good job, and had quite a vision for the place. He said he could never have imagined anything like this happening here. He told her that she had certainly been a God-send when this town needed it most. He told her that he has heard nothing but good things in town.

He said, "I know that you have the pageant already planned for Christmas Eve and I do not want to interfere with what Steve and Sam have already been working on, but I would like to contribute by adding a short sermon, if you are agreeable."

"Oh! That would be lovely," she replied. "No, wait, that would be perfect! A real honest to goodness church service here on Christmas Eve! You sir, are the God-send! The town will be delighted!"

They then walked around the grounds as Deborah showed Daniel the changes she had made to the lake. They walked through the cemetery pointing out each - others long lost relatives. Daniel asked if she was ever bothered about living so close to a cemetery. She told him no, that she actually finds comfort and solace being near the cemetery. She said, "I know you are going to find this crazy, even though he is not buried here, I often smell my husband's musk cologne when I am out here. Especially, when I am troubled, or apologizing to Aunt Dorothy for some of the stupid things I have done in the past. David always seems to let me know he is near and approves of what I am doing."

Daniel said, "On the contrary, I do not find it crazy at all. I have always believed that our loved ones do reach out to communicate with us. The big problem is most of us do not recognize the little things, like a song on the radio or an unexpected hummingbird visit, as a visit from a spouse or parent.

Our problem is we are all too busy to take the time to notice these things and appreciate them for what they are. Nor, do most people talk about it for fear that others will think they are crazy. Right?"

Deborah let out a little snicker and agreed. She knew very well that he was right.

When they reached Daniel's truck, he thanked her for the tour as well as the opportunity to preach on Christmas Eve. He said he would be in town now through Christmas, working on Aunt Millie's farm and that if she needed any help with anything, she should give him a call. He said he would be happy to help with anything. He handed her a card with his cell phone number.

❧ ☙

Annie would be arriving with the boys later in the afternoon. Christmas was officially about to begin! Deborah was putting the final touches on all of her newly quilted decorations. The house was beginning to look like a winter wonderland full of gingerbread themed decorations and with the boys help over the next couple of weeks, it would soon smell and sound like Christmas too.

Annie and the boys arrived just before sunset. The boys ran around the yard and danced and giggled like a couple caged animals who had just been set free. They ran to the lake and skipped rocks across the water. They chased each other across the bridge to the other side and climbed up a tree to a branch hanging over the water. Annie yelled at them to be careful and not fall in, for they would freeze in the cold water. It was fun watching them explore and be curious little boys. Sam came out to join the boys in their wanderings. Annie and Deborah went inside to have a cup of tea and watch from the window.

Annie stayed for the entire weekend. She and Deborah wrote out the guest list for Christmas dinner and planned the menu. They both agreed it would just be their immediate family, not a lot of outsiders, this first Christmas without David. Deborah said she was certain that both Sam and Marsha would be spending Christmas with their own families. No need to think they should be invited anyway. Together they shopped for the non-perishables and frozen items for the dinner. They purchased all the ingredients for the cookie baking and gingerbread house making days that were about to start.

Annie decided she could stay a couple of days longer than planned. She wanted to be included in some of the cookie baking too. Of course, Deborah was delighted to have her daughter stay.

The first day of cookie baking was a day of mixing and prepping. The group mixed up eight different kinds of dough and stored them in the refrigerator and cleaned up the mess before going into town to eat dinner.

The second day was the start of the actual baking. One by one the various doughs were brought out and baked per instructions. The boys had a hard time getting the cookie press to work properly but they never gave up and eventually had perfectly shaped butter cookies with colored sugar sprinkles on them. They had fun rolling the little balls of hot baked dough into the powdered sugar for Grandpa's all-time favorite Snow Ball cookie. They knew very well that it wouldn't be Christmas without the Snow Ball cookies.

Tins and plastic containers were filled with all the sweet confections and put away to save until Christmas. After the kitchen was cleaned up, they enjoyed mugs of hot chocolate by the fireplace, then called it a night.

∾ ∾

Annie left for home and Deborah and the boys talked about how they wanted to spend their time in the country. They asked if they could go hunting and fishing. Deborah had not given those ideas any consideration and said she was not prepared with guns and fishing poles.

Jeremy reminded her that Sam had fishing poles. Surely a man living out in the country would have guns, too. Deborah said they could talk to Sam later about that and suggested they go over to her cousin Marsha's house and go for a walk in the woods. They could look for their Christmas tree to cut down later. "Oh, yeah!" they both shouted. She said she would call Marsha and let her know they were coming and told the boys to bundle up well since it was cold outside.

Deborah grabbed some large five-gallon buckets from the storage shed and put them into the bed of the truck. She told the boys she wanted to gather up some pine and cedar boughs and boxwood cuttings to create swags for the church.

❧ ☙

When Deborah pulled into the lane at Marsha's house, Chad came out to meet them. He directed them to go past the pond and to take the lane to left and over the ridge. They would find some nice trees to choose from. He gave her several of strips of bright yellow fabric and told the boys to tie the fabric around the trunks of the trees and he would help cut them down in a few days. He said it was too early to cut right now. Chad said they should pick out a couple of trees for the church and the fellowship hall, too. "Pick one out for me while you are at it. Okay?"

Off they went bouncing and bumping on the rough trod lane. The boys exaggerating their bounces much more than necessary. Giggling saying, "Granny, this is as much fun as a ride at Six Flags!"

They found a good clearing to park the truck, and the exploring through the woods began. Deborah took to clipping branches from various trees to create the decorative swags, and the boys hauled them to the truck. They checked out various trees to cut down. Deborah had to remind the boys that they couldn't pick the tallest ones that they were choosing. They needed to remember that the tree had to fit inside their house and the church, so they needed to look at smaller ones. At one point, the boys started into having a leaf fight, scraping up the leaves from the ground. Of course, Deborah was prepared with her camera to capture the memories. They were all laughing and having so much fun that at first, they did not hear the voice coming from the other side of the trees.

"Hello? Who is over there?" came a loud shout.

The boys stopped and looked at each other, then took off in a mad dash heading to the other side of the trees.

Again, a deep voice bellowed, "Who is there? Call out!"

The boys yelled out in unison. "I am Jeremy!" and "I am Jacob! Who are you?"

By now the boys had made it through the trees and on the other side of the fence was a man sitting on a horse. Again, the boys asked, "Who are you?"

Deborah caught up with the boys and stood next to the fence as well. "Well, hello there! Good morning!"

There sitting high in the saddle of his horse was Daniel.

He tipped his hat and said, "Good morning to you, too. I couldn't figure out who was out here in the woods. But, from the sound of the young sounding giggles I heard I didn't think they were out here alone."

He said he was out surveying the property and seeing what kind of repairs he would need to be working on over the winter. She told him they were out looking for their Christmas tree and greens to use for the church decorations. He told Deborah that next year she could pick the trees from his farm. He said he had been working his tree farm for several years and next year they should be ready to go.

"Hey mister, can we pet your horse?" both boys said in unison.

Daniel moved his horse closer to the fence so they could

reach her. He threw a couple of apples to them and said, "Here, you can feed her these. Her name is Candy and she loves a good snack."

"Can we ride her too?"

"Well, we have a problem with that idea, there is a fence between us."

Instantly, both boys started to scramble up the metal wires of the fence. Deborah grabbed both of them by the seat of their pants and insisted that they wait.

Daniel said that if she didn't mind he could take them one at a time for a short jaunt around his field. Deborah agreed and let Jeremy go first. She and Jacob watched from their side of the fence. Deborah snapped pictures of Jeremy delighted to be sitting in front of Daniel atop the chestnut mare. There were close-up shots of Jacob hanging on the fence drooling with anticipation. When both boys had had their turn at riding, Deborah thanked Daniel for his patience and time with the boys.

Before Daniel rode off, Jacob yelled, "Do you have any guns at your house? We want to go hunting and Granny doesn't have any guns!"

Deborah tried to shush Jacob and wave Daniel off. "That's enough, young man. Quit bothering Mr. Kraemer. He's got work to do, and so do we."

Daniel chuckled and told Jacob that indeed, he did have some guns and they could see about hunting on another day.

Jacob was grinning from ear to ear and gave his brother a high-five as he proclaimed, "Cool, dude!"

※ ※

Back at home, Deborah filled the buckets with lukewarm water and recut the stems of her greens, placing them in the buckets and putting them outside to keep cool. She told the boys this would keep them fresh until she was ready to wire them together into long ropes for the church railings. Then it was time for hot chocolate in front of the fireplace along with a game of cards.

The next morning, as soon as breakfast dishes were cleared away, it was time to mix up the gingerbread dough and get it in the oven. The boys told Deborah they had been drawing their own pictures of what they wanted their houses to look like. They ran to their room and got the pictures to show her. She was very impressed with their creativity. While the dough was baking, she had the boys set up all the decorating supplies on the dining room table, so the boys could see what all she had gotten for them. She said, "You check and make sure I have everything that you need, or let me know if we need to go shopping for anything else."

The boys compared her supplies to their drawings and proclaimed that they were ready to decorate as soon as the dough was finished baking. Jeremy said, "There are a few changes I will make to mine because we don't want to have to stop and go shopping. We have enough stuff here to work with. Is it ready yet?"

~ ~

Early morning of December twentieth, Deborah had the boys bundle up really good for going out. The air had turned bitter cold, but they needed to go help Chad cut down their trees. Sam was outside with his chain saw, waiting to go with them. The boys were all excited about cutting down their first Christmas tree. Chad was at his house sitting in his truck with the engine running while he waited for them. When they arrived, he let Deborah take the lead in her truck since she knew which trees she wanted.

"Here's the first one!" shouted the both boys. "Can we do the cutting?"

Sam said, "I don't think so, but you can yell timber when she starts to fall. We have to warn anybody who might be out here hunting or something, Okay?" Sam let them stand close by and watch as he made the first wedge cut on one side of the tree. Then he told them, "Now, we are going to move to the other side of the tree and cut over here, then the tree will fall down over in the direction of that first cut. I'll tell you when to yell. Be ready!" Sam powered up the saw again and made a few cuts into the tree. "Okay, now!"

As the tree cracked they both yelled as loud as they could, "T-I-I-I-M-B-E-R" and the tree plopped to the ground. Chad and Sam loaded the tree into the back of Deborah's truck. They moved on to the other two trees making short work of the job. Sam thanked the boys for their help and told them they had picked out some mighty fine trees. He said they were going to look quite nice inside the church.

❧ ☙

Deborah and Sam were busy getting the church decorated inside and out when Steve Abernathy arrived driving the school bus bringing the kids to practice one last time for their pageant. Jeremy and Jacob watched intently from the very first pew. Steve, kindly invited Jeremy and Jacob to join the pageant. He said they could be additional shepherds and told the boys to go grab some costumes from the box in the back of the church.

Very quietly, Daniel Kraemer and his daughter, Melissa, slipped in to watch from the back of the church.

Daniel and Melissa were waiting for the rest of the wedding party to arrive for their rehearsal, but they wanted to get a sneak peek at the pageant first. Steve Abernathy came over to shake Daniel's hand. He said he wanted to assure him that he was perfectly fine with Daniel preaching after the children's pageant and he thought it would be a great addition to the night.

Sam added, "I am not a preacher, I just officiate at weddings here for Deborah. So, if there is ever a time you want to offer a service, or perform a wedding, do not ever feel that you are hurting my feelings any. I prefer a lawnmower and outside work, myself. Believe me, I have no hard feelings about you performing the wedding for your daughter, or anyone else. I was drafted into the position of performing weddings. I will be happy to step aside any time."

⁂

Christmas Eve morning arrived and Deborah's family would be arriving later that afternoon. The house was decorated and ready. The aroma of the fresh pine tree by the fireplace filled the air. Two amazingly crafted gingerbread houses took center stage on the dining room buffet table. Boxes of cookies were ready to give to friends, along with small loaves of homemade fruitcake. Deborah had made the fruitcakes right after Thanksgiving and had been keeping them wrapped in whiskey soaked cheesecloth all this time. Her fruitcake had become one of David's favorite holiday treats even though he had previously claimed he never liked fruitcake. Eventually, it rated right up there with her Snow Ball cookies.

Before everyone arrived, however, she and the boys were going to go out and deliver the baked goodies to her friends. She filled two large wicker baskets and loaded them into her car. Their first stop was to her cousin Marsha. Marsha said she was very excited about seeing the pageant later this evening. Marsha said that she and her family would be going over to her daughter's house for dinner on Christmas day.

Their next stop was to Daniel Kraemer's house. Deborah asked him about the two large camping trailers parked on his property. He said they were for Brad's out of town family who were coming for the wedding, but would not be arriving until late Christmas day. Deborah asked him about his plans for Christmas dinner. He said he didn't have any real dinner plans except to spend time with Aunt Millie so she wouldn't be alone and that

Melissa would be with Brad's family for dinner and then bringing them here in the evening. Deborah exclaimed, "Then you must join us for brunch! We can't have our preacher giving his first service here on Christmas Eve and then eat alone on Christmas Day. That's just not right. You have to join us and bring Aunt Millie!"

"I don't want to intrude on your family. I will fix us something to eat and spend some time with her."

"Nonsense!" she said. "I won't take no for an answer. Bring Aunt Millie along, she needs real food and family on Christmas. We will plenty of both, food and family!"

Their next two stops were to Charlie and Gloria King's house, and then to Norm Johnson's house. Old Mr. Johnson's eyes lit up when he saw the fruitcake. He took a whiff of the package and smiled. He said it reminded him of the ones his dear sweet departed Henrietta used to make. He told Deborah that if her cake was half as good as Henrietta's was, well... she would certainly be all right in his book!

On their way home, Jeremy asked Deborah about inviting Mr. Kraemer and his Aunt Millie for dinner. He reminded her that she and his mom had said they were not inviting anyone else for Christmas dinner. That it was only going to be family this year.

Deborah stuttered around a bit as she remembered that conversation with her daughter. She said, "Yes, we did say that, but this is a special circumstance. Your mom will understand when I tell her that Mr. Kraemer didn't have any place to go for Christmas." She then mumbled under her breath, "I hope!"

Once they were back home and eating lunch, they went over the sleeping arrangements for the night. The boys said they could sleep in their sleeping bags on the living room floor and wait for Santa to arrive. Uncle Davey and Uncle Randy could sleep in their bunk beds. Deborah agreed with Davey and Randy sleeping in the bunk beds, but they could not sleep in the living room because they would never go to sleep. They needed to be in another room. She offered the floor in her room, to which they agreed.

Davey arrived first, followed closely by Randy and Chelsea. The boys were getting anxious waiting for their mom and dad. They were afraid that Annie and Bob would end up missing the pageant. When at last, their van pulled into the lane. Annie jumped out quickly and ran to her mother and said, "Quick! Turn around and close your eyes. I have a surprise for you. I'll tell you when you can turn around." Annie had her hands held across Deborah's eyes. She added, "No peeking, Mom!"

Deborah heard a commotion and shuffling around going on behind her, she heard both of the boys' gasp, and start to say something, but it was obvious that someone had clamped a hand across their mouths to keep them silent. At last Annie removed her hands from her mother's eyes and told her she could turn around and look.

"SURPRISE!! MERRY CHRISTMAS!!" shouted everyone.

Deborah could not believe her eyes. It was Lucy! She ran to embrace her sister and said, "What are you doing here? I can't believe this? Where is Bill?"

"Bill couldn't get any leave, so I am here on my own. I'm staying for two weeks. I want to take my time looking around here and see what you have done. We have so much catching up to do. Annie did a great job of keeping a secret, didn't she?"

Deborah could not believe that her sister was standing right here in her living room. It had been years since they had spent a Christmas together and now here she is. Deborah realized that her daughter had gone out of her way to make sure that this Christmas had to be special for her mother. She had rallied as much of her family together as she possibly could. Deborah knew that Annie was trying to fill the void left by David's death. Deborah's mood became bittersweet, she fought off tears as she went over and hugged Annie and thanked her for the best Christmas gift she could have given her.

They shared a light supper before getting ready for the pageant.

CHAPTER FOURTEEN

The church was filled to a standing room only crowd. Folding chairs from the fellowship hall had been carried over and placed along the walls to accommodate as many people as possible. The school choir stood up front singing traditional carols as they waited for the pageant to begin.

Two of the older kids had been chosen to play Mary and Joseph. As they entered the church, Joseph was leading Mary astride on a donkey that had been loaned by Norm Johnson. The choir began to sing "Silent Night" and all the people joined in. After Joseph had helped Mary from the donkey and settled her in the front corner where a temporary stable had been built, a young man portraying a local villager quickly escorted the donkey back out of the church and into a portable pen outside. Steve and Fern Abernathy's newborn granddaughter, Heather, had the honor of portraying the baby Jesus who was lying in a cradle built by Marsha's husband, Chad. Children of various ages portrayed the kings, shepherds, and villagers who had come to see the newborn king. Included in the pageantry were a couple of sheep, rabbits, and chickens. One little boy brought his dog, another carried his prized rabbit. Annie and Bob beamed with pride at seeing their boys included in the play. The choir ended the pageant with everyone singing, "God Rest Ye Merry Gentlemen" and "The First Noel."

≈ ≈

Daniel stepped up to the pulpit to make his debut sermon at *The Wedding Belle*. The newly revised house of worship held life-time members of the former Grace Bible Church and their remaining family members, as well as newcomers to the community, some returning to their ancestral roots, which many had come to believe was by Divine intervention to keep the community growing strong.

Sitting in the front row to the right of the pulpit was Aunt Patsy with Lucy, Deborah, and Annie. Behind them sat Bob, Davey, Randy, and Chelsea, followed by Norm Johnson, Sam, and Beverly. In the front pew, directly in front of the pulpit sat Melissa Peterson with her fiancé Brad along with Aunt Millie Kraemer sitting in her wheel chair in the open aisle. Behind them were Marsha and Chad with their extended families, followed by Charlie and Gloria and their family. Everyone in town had arrived for this very special Christmas Eve service.

    Daniel opened the service by saying, "We have just witnessed a beautiful joy filled musical reenactment of the birth of Christ. Luke 2:7 says that, *'she brought forth her firstborn son and wrapped him in swaddling clothes and laid him in a manger, because there was no room in the inn.'* Luke reminds us that there was something special brewing on the planet earth and that there was hope to come. The Book of Matthew 1:1-17 tells of the ancestry of Jesus, fourteen generations of man that had led to that one miraculous night. In numerous other works of the Bible, we read stories of women who have become widows and lost children and yet, turned their lives to God and were rewarded."

    "How are these various scriptures related, you ask? What do these other verses have to do with the purpose of being here tonight, on Christmas Eve? As with everything we do, and what generations before us have done, realize it or not, everything has been the work of God. Being here, gathered tonight, was all part of God's plan. When did, this plan start? Last July when a lonely widow drove into town and later, that night had a dream for this building? Or was His plan in motion long before that? Could it have been in the works for generations?"

    "When Mrs. Deborah Kingston drove through town last July, little did she know what life held in store for her. Little did she know that she would be sitting here tonight as hostess of the largest gathering this church building has seen in years. Oh, she knew she wanted to preserve the memories of her youth when her grandparents were members of the Grace Bible Church, but she did not know the extent of her heritage and lineage. You see, during some of the remodeling and new construction done here at the church, a time capsule was uncovered. Besides the numerous photos taken of the early community members, she found several documents that proved she did indeed belong here in this town. In fact, she does indeed belong right here on this very property! First of all, as everyone knows, Orchardville is in Wayne county, named after the great general, 'Mad' Anthony Wayne. Deborah had known all her life that her maternal great-grandparents last name was Wayne and that she was a direct descendent of the famed general, but she had never made a connection between her maternal ancestor and this county named Wayne, as also being named after the general. She never realized that her connection to being here, actually stems from both sides of her family tree. Coincidence? Wait, there is more!"

"There was also a property map that was dated in 1910. The map shows all the property lines for each and every property owner in the town of Orchardville at that time. It is marked with little churches and schools that were scattered throughout the area. You can see on the map how, even today, our heritage is still connected, even as the generations have evolved and moved on. In fact, every person here tonight, knows my Aunt Millie Kraemer. She is ninety-three years young. She was born as Mildred Cox, and has lived on her father's two hundred and forty acres her entire life, as did her grandparents before that. I will carry on that family tradition now and pass the property on to my daughter and grandchildren when the time is right."

"The map shows that my two hundred and forty acres, backs up to the original eighty-acre farm, where Marsha and her husband Chad currently live. Deborah, several of us have gone together and had that map preserved and framed. It is now hanging over in the fellowship hall for everyone to see. However, you are free to move it into your home or office, or wherever you would prefer it to hang. The community wants to thank you for your vision for this church building. You did not allow it to decay and rot away in the field like an old deserted barn."

"But, the most important paper proving that this woman does indeed belong here, is a letter and a certificate of ordination dated July 25th, 1916. Deborah's third great grandfather, Alvin Bridges was the original pastor of the Grace Bible Church. Now, one of his own will breathe new life into the community and continue the work that he started more than a century ago."

He went on to say, "I vividly remember the first time I met Deborah Kingston. Her energy and love for this place was contagious. I, too, fell in love with being here. While we are sitting here this evening with a new gas furnace keeping us warm and toasty, I remember the day that Deborah was showing me the changes. When we walked into this church, she told me to inhale deeply, to savor the smell of the smoke that had permeated the wood from all the years of being heated by a wood burning stove. She likened the aroma to a mystical incense of history. While we have the gas heat, if you inhale deeply, you smell history. She kept the wood burner in the back, not only as reminder from the past, but as a back- up plan, if it should ever be needed.

He then thanked the community for opening their hearts and minds to Deborah Kingston and her vision. He said he was looking forward to being able to preach here from time to time once he is completely relocated. He reminded them that he is retired, and not looking for a full-time job. In the meantime, he would be available by appointment for any special occasion, whether it would be to perform a wedding or anniversary celebration, to welcome a new child into the world through baptism, or to send a loved one home to the Lord with a funeral. He gave a brief resume of performing these blessings while serving in the military in many different countries, and looked forward to the opportunity to do them in his former home town. Daniel wished everyone a Merry Christmas and a wonderful day with

SEARCHING FOR SOMETHING SPECIAL

their families. He then asked Deborah if she would like to say something to the congregation.

Deborah stepped up to the pulpit. With tears in her eyes and a trembling voice, she thanked everyone for accepting her ideas and for all their help in making this dream come true. Not only for herself, but their dream came true as well, with the arrival of Daniel Kraemer. She added that she could never have imagined that this first Christmas without her husband could end up being such a special one.

❦

When the service was over, there were cookies and punch for everyone in the fellowship hall. Santa was there for picture taking and listening to last minute requests from the little kids. Christmas carols added to the spirit of the evening. As the guests started to leave, they stepped outside to a brightly star filled sky where they found a gently falling snow was beginning to cover the ground. It was a beautiful silent night.

When Deborah and her family returned to the house they discovered that Santa had arrived. All the stockings were filled and there were gifts for everyone. Deborah herself was quite surprised to see that there was a stocking and gifts for Lucy, too. It was obvious that her arrival had been thoroughly planned and indeed had been a well-kept secret.

Their celebration lasted into the very early morning hours. Davey proclaimed that if they didn't get to bed soon, they may as well stay up until it was time to go to Mass in Salem. They all agreed they needed a couple of hours of sleep to get through the next day. However there needed to be a change in the sleeping arrangements. Lucy would sleep with Deborah, just like they used to do as kids. Jeremy and Jacob would sleep on the living room floor like they originally wanted, only they wouldn't be waiting and watching for Santa to arrive.

CHAPTER FIFTEEN

Christmas brunch at Deborah's was more of a full-blown feast instead of a brunch. A bevy of breakfast casseroles along with a baked ham and sweet potatoes covered the dining room table. The breakfast bar was lined with vegetable side dishes of every kind and taste to please any picky eater, not to mention the buffet table full of assorted cakes, pies and cookies.

Daniel arrived helping Aunt Millie in with her wheel chair. They both thanked Deborah repeatedly for the invitation. Deborah noticed Annie giving her a nod of approval for the extra guests. She hoped it also meant that finally she was okay with Deborah's decision to move to Orchardville.

Lucy and Daniel had much to talk about together: his career in the Air Force and her years of being a Marine wife. They compared notes of various countries and places they had each been stationed. They both agreed that Okinawa was probably their favorite of all places.

Jeremy and Jacob clamored all over Daniel, wanting to know when they could go hunting with him and ride his horse again.

Sam and Beverly dropped in on Deborah's brunch. He said they were on their way to Beverly's family for dinner and not going to stay long, but that they wanted to bring Deborah a gift and to wish her and her family a Merry Christmas. Beverly insisted that Deborah open her gift right away. Deborah urged them to have something to eat and drink while she opened her gift. It was a custom-made jigsaw puzzle, made from one of her pictures of the church. The church was in the center surrounded by a collection of pictures taken at the thank you party and mock wedding for Aunt Patsy and Norm Johnson. There were pictures of people sitting on the hay bales, one of Sam at the top of the stairs looking all preacher like, and the twins playing on the rope swing. Many glorious memories from the very first event held at *The Wedding*

Belle. Deborah loved it, gave them both hugs, and thanked them profusely. Of course, she wanted to know how they had acquired all the pictures.

Davey quickly chimed in with, "It's a secret, don't ask so many questions."

Deborah realized that her son had been in on the gift idea and with his building the website and creating the brochures he had access to all her pictures. In fact, he probably gave Sam the information that she enjoyed jigsaw puzzles and where to get a custom one made. Sneaky kids, she thought to herself.

Davey, Randy and Bob were in a corner of the kitchen talking with Daniel. They welcomed him to *The Wedding Belle* family. Then, questioned him about his plans now that he was retired. Daniel was eager to share his thoughts. He told the guys how he had been planning for this since he was eighteen years old. He briefly told them about the difficult relationship with his father and step-mother. How he had resented their marriage and the fact that he had been pulled away from his Aunt Millie and her farm. He vowed from that day forward, that he would return to the farm and that he would always take care of his aunt. He told them about his first wife dropping his daughter, Missy, off with Aunt Millie while he was on a deployment.

He went on to tell them it hadn't been an easy life for any of them, but they made the best of the situation and were a very close knit family because of the struggles that they had overcome.

Daniel had bought Aunt Millie's farm when she could no longer keep up the taxes or the maintenance on the two hundred and forty acres. He promised her she would always have a home there. His long-term plan had always been to operate a Christmas tree farm. Several years ago, he found two partners in town who were able to manage the day to day work of getting the first fifty acres prepped, planted, and ready for production. The trio were now into their tenth year of growing and trimming the trees. They were all looking forward to the next holiday season and seeing the benefit of their long hard labor. This year was the first year that they had begun to harvest a few of their trees and were looking forward to next year when there would be more opportunities, since Daniel would be living here full time and working the tree farm with his partners.

Aunt Millie was excited about the new venture that "my boy," as she liked to call him, would be home and putting the land to good use once again. She only hoped to live long enough to see him prosper and enjoy the land. Millie and Patsy sat together in the dining room bragging about their young people and the difference they were going to make in this town. Neither one of them would have guessed that something like this would ever happen here, in their lifetime.

Norm Johnson also arrived unannounced with a big basket of fruit. Said he just wanted to say Merry Christmas and to officially thank Deborah, Sam, and Daniel for what they were doing. In a humble sort of way, he was apologizing for the doubts he had had in the beginning. He told Deborah she was doing a good job and to keep up the good work.

Deborah made her way to the far corner of the living and observed her immediate family along with her new extended family, laughing, talking, and truly enjoying each other's company. Everyone was completely engaged with one another and filled with the spirit of Christmas. She hoped that this peaceful and beautiful day was a new beginning for herself, her family, and her new friends. Of course, she was taking plenty of pictures to mark this joyous occasion.

※ ※

The morning of Missy's wedding arrived along with a beautiful blanket of fresh fallen snow. Sam was out on the tractor clearing the gravel parking area in front of the church. The trees and bushes were picture perfect, with the tufts of snow tucked between the branches. Guests began to arrive and take their places inside the church, but no sign of the bride or Daniel. Deborah paced nervously, waiting with her camera. Then she spotted on the road, through the bare tree branches, a horse drawn sleigh turning into the lane. Daniel was steering the sleigh, with Missy snuggled under the cover of a white fur blanket.

Daniel walked his daughter down the aisle, handed her off to Brad, and then moved into his place to perform the ceremony. Aunt Millie beamed with pride from the very front row at watching the magical moment between her nephew and his beautiful daughter.

Following the ceremony, everyone gathered in the fellowship hall for a dinner that had been prepared by the friends and neighbors of the town under the leadership of Marsha; now, lovingly called, The Bunco Bakers.

There was an unmistakable twinge of tension at the reception when Daniel introduced his father and step-mother to Deborah and Sam. They had driven in from Indiana for the wedding. George Kraemer seemed reserved and Nancy appeared bored with the whole thing, however, they said they wouldn't have missed this wedding, no matter what. Nancy did compliment Deborah on what she had done with the transformation of the old Grace Bible Church. "Why, I would have never guessed that the old church would ever become such an attraction." She said with a slight sneer.

Daniel offered sleigh rides to anyone who wished to go. Folks waited in line in the falling snow, to ride, including George and Nancy. Deborah made sure that their picture included Daniel at the reins. He gave a glaring look, revealing his distaste for that shot, but Deborah knew she was recording a moment of family history, whether he liked it or not.

It was fun to watch the couples who snuggled together under the furry blanket, and the kids who laughed and waved at everyone they passed.

As the sun began to set, Daniel called out to Deborah that

she had not yet been for a ride. She eagerly climbed into the seat next to him. Off they went, down the lane and out onto the snow-packed road, crossing into the next pasture. With her camera in hand, she was snapping pictures of the sun setting on the snow-white fields, as well as close-ups of her driver in his top hat.

The rush of the holidays and the wedding were over. Everyone had returned to their own homes and life took on a sudden quiet that Deborah had not realized since the day she first moved to Orchardville. From day one, there had been construction work and people clamoring all over the place. This was actually the first time of total peace, quiet, and serenity. The first time she was truly alone with her thoughts.

On the first Sunday in January, Sam invited Deborah to join him and Beverly to have breakfast after Mass. They chose to go the café on Central Street instead of the noisy all you can eat buffet place. He said it would be quieter and they could talk much easier. Sam's hand trembled as he lifted his first cup of coffee up to his lips. His left leg doing a nervous bounce under the table. His eyes looked troubled. Beverly reached over and placed both of her hands on top of his free hand lying on the table. With understanding eyes, she consoled, "It's okay, Sam. It is time. It is a new year and we need to start fresh and honest."

Deborah glanced back and forth between them, trying to read their faces and guess what was going on.

Sam stammered around trying to find the right words. Again, taking a sip from his shaking coffee cup. "I don't feel like I have been one hundred percent honest with you Deborah. I feel really bad about that, but I couldn't tell you my whole story when you asked me. Remember back at your house at dinner, several months ago? I couldn't tell you all of my story without telling you Beverly's story, too, and it wasn't my place to tell you her story. It is her story to tell, and we have now reached a point in our relationship that she wants you to know everything."

"Are you two getting married? Why are you so nervous? I think it is wonderful!" Deborah exclaimed with delight.

Beverly quickly responded, "No, we are not at that point, yet. However, someday, is not out of the realm of things. What Sam did not feel he could share with you, is that I am an alcoholic. Sam and I met an AA meeting a couple of years ago. We saved each other's lives."

Sam interjected with, "I told you that night, I was an alcoholic, and that Beverly had saved my life, but I could not tell you that she was one, too. We attend meetings together regularly. We support each other and keep each other on track. I don't know what I would do without her help."

"Sam, you know I can't make it without you, either," Beverly added.

Sam continued to tell Deborah the whole story of his time in Iraq and how he had gotten really messed up while fighting over there. Booze and pills seemed to be the only way to cope. He thought he would be fine once he came home, but he wasn't. In fact, things got worse. He couldn't understand why he came home in one piece and so many others did not. The booze helped to numb the guilt, and even more booze numbed the memories that he wanted to erase. He thought he had hit rock bottom when he began hitting his wife whenever she tried to confront him. During his drunken binges, he thought she was the enemy in Iraq. The night she ended up with a broken nose and two black eyes, she had him arrested. The next morning she and the kids left town. He didn't know where they were or how to contact them. This only made him want to drink more, since now, he had more things he wanted to forget. When his mother found him passed out in a drunken stupor, she had him put in a rehab center to get sober and then told him that she was done with him until he could prove to her that he was finished drinking. Having lost his wife, his kids, his job, and now his mother too, he packed his bags and showed up down here at his cousin Ernie's house, asking for help.

Beverly told Deborah, "That is when we met. It was his first AA meeting and he looked like a lost puppy who needed a friend. I introduced myself and we have been friends ever since. I came by the disease naturally. Both of my parents were drunks and several other relatives as well. I made a vow to myself and to God, that the alcohol gene would end with me. I had no intention of being a part of that hereditary line. I never married. I did not want to have kids to pass that gene on to. I have been downright drunk in the past and I have lost jobs over it, but I have been sober for ten years and have sponsored and helped many others. Not everyone can be helped, but only because they do not want to be, or are not ready to be."

She went on to add, "I do not sugar coat things. In the meetings, I tell people I am an alcoholic, but I used to be a drunk and there is a difference. I am now proud of who I have become and I want to stay that way. I want to stay true to myself. I like my life now. I have an honest job as a cashier down at the Piggly Wiggly. I pay my bills and I go to church. But even with all that, it does not mean that a day does not go by that I do not want a drink. I can taste that warm amber liquid in my throat and wish that I could have just one little taste but, thankfully, I remember what I stand to lose if I do. I knew when I met Sam, he was ready and wanted to be helped. We connected and have been good for each other."

"Wow, what a story!" Deborah exhaled. "I had no idea. I am very proud of both of you for staying so strong. You should not be ashamed. You have a disease and I am honored that you trust me, and care enough to want to tell me your stories."

Sam reached down into his left front pocket and pulled out a handful of coins. "Deborah, I know you have noticed that when I am nervous, I jingle the coins in my pocket. Well, it is not money." He pulled out a handful of coins, "These are my chips marking my sobriety. I fiddle with them when I am nervous, as a reminder of how well I have been doing and how far I have come."

❧ ☙

January brought not only peace from construction noises and the constant flow of people in and out of her life; it brought gray skies, howling winds, and random snow blowing through the fields. January also brought dread. The first anniversary of David's death was approaching quickly. In the previous six months, she had pushed the reminders of that awful day aside during the hustle and bustle of being overwhelmed with work and preparations for the opening of *The Wedding Belle*. But, now with the rush over and the weather too gloomy to venture out and about, she had nothing but time; to think back to that day when her life was turned upside down.

While trying to think ahead to the spring weddings scheduled, including Randy and Chelsea's June date, she could not overcome the sadness that seemed to be taking control of every thought in every minute of the day.

Early on the morning of January tenth, the florist from Cisne arrived with a bouquet of flowers from Davey and Randy. Later a plant arrived from Gary and Andrea along with one from Annie, Bob and the twins. Of course, there were phone calls from everyone, asking how she was doing. Every time the phone rang, she checked the name on caller ID before answering. If it was someone close to her who would be concerned if she didn't answer, she answered and tried to put on a brave front. Of course, she was sad, but reassured them that she would get through the day and no, she did not have any plans for dinner. Nor, did she want any plans for dinner. If she could ignore a caller or postpone them to another day, she did not answer. She remained curled up on the couch in front of the fireplace, sipping her tea, wrapped in David's tattered brown terrycloth robe.

At some point in the day, she pulled out the old photo albums and thought back to their early college days when they first met. There were the pictures of the children when they were babies, and the day they became grandparents to Jeremy and Jacob. Her cup of tea was later exchanged for a glass of wine at dinner time. Dinner for one in front of the fireplace. As the flames danced and the embers crackled, the tears gently slid down her face. "Oh, my dear David, I miss you so much! There are days like this when it hurts to even breathe without you. I know you are in a good place surrounded by unimaginable beauty, and glorious love, but I wish you were here with me. I know I am being selfish, wanting you here. The boys are growing so quickly. I know you are their guardian angel and watch over them daily, just as you watch over me. I keep trying to move forward and for the most part, I think I am. Life is just not the same without you here to share this with. I know you would be proud of what I have accomplished, but I want to hear you say it. I want to feel your arms around me as you tell family and friends how proud you are, or what a good job I have done. I will never again hear you say those words to me. Somehow, some way, I must go on alone."

Throughout the gloomy month of January, she dawdled and began to give thought to the spring weddings. She was thrilled that Randy had found someone as thoughtful and caring as Chelsea. She could not have found anyone more suited for him, if she had handpicked the girl for him. And was looking forward to having Chelsea be a part of the family.

Mostly though, she was looking forward to January being over.

With things being slow at *The Wedding Belle*, Sam was

spending most days working with Ernie over in Flora. One day at lunch, Sam was talking to Ernie about his wedding plans and how he was looking forward to creating a home with Beverly.

Ernie cleared his throat, and said, "I'm happy for you too, man. You were quite a mess when you arrived here a couple of years ago, I wasn't sure you were going to make it."

"Well, that makes two us! I didn't have much hope left when I came knocking on your door. Thank God, you didn't kick me to the curb, too."

"Sam, you do know why your mother did that, don't you? I know she told you it was 'tough love' and she was done with you and you had to find your own way, and she wasn't going to bail you out anymore. But, Sam buddy, you gotta know, she didn't want to watch you kill yourself anymore. She didn't want to sit by helplessly, and watch you die."

Sam hung his head, "Yeah, I know that now, but I sure as hell didn't know it then. All I knew was that she wanted nothing to do with me. Just like when Elizabeth took the kids and disappeared. She walked out of my life and never looked back. Mom did the same thing; I haven't heard from her since that day."

"Your mom would love to talk to you, but she doesn't want to upset you. She is afraid that if she contacts you; you'll slip up and go back to your old ways. She has been waiting for years for you to call her, and since you haven't; she is content in knowing that you are doing well."

"So, you been giving her reports on me, huh?" Sam asked.

"Yes, I have been keeping her informed of how you are doing, and I told her that you and Beverly are engaged. She is very happy for you. Think about calling her, okay?"

CHAPTER SIXTEEN

During the first week of February, Aunt Patsy came down with pneumonia and was hospitalized in Mount Vernon. Everyone was certain that the spry, strong willed woman would bounce back quickly, but her tiny body, just couldn't seem to shake it off. After several days, she called Marsha and said she wanted to see her and Deborah together, as soon as possible. They both dropped everything and drove the twenty-five miles to see her.

"Thank you both for coming so quickly. I don't know how much time I have left here, and there are some things I wanted to say to both of you." Patsy struggled to talk, taking deep labored breaths between every word. "I am so proud of both of you for mending the fences between you, and the way you are working together to bring new life to our town. Deborah, you and your ideas were a gift from God, at just the right time. Never doubt what your purpose in life has been. When my time here is over, please be sure that I am buried there in the cemetery where I know you will watch over me and Sam will take proper care of the grounds. Oh! Be sure that the handsome Daniel Kraemer handles the service. His Aunt Millie and I have been friends since we were kids and he is a caring and kind man. I'm glad he is now an important addition to *The Wedding Belle*. Deborah, you two will be good partners. One more thing; you should contact my attorney's office, Porter and Powell, in Wayne City for the details of my will.

Both women began to strongly protest. "Quit talking such nonsense! You are going to snap out of this and be home soon. You just need to rest and get your strength back."

Deborah added, "No more talk of wills and such!"

Patsy drew both the girls over to her for hugs. She told them that she loved them and treasured them as if they were her own children. She dismissed them and reminded them to be true to themselves and to continue doing what they were doing, and everything would be just fine.

That night, Patsy died peacefully in her sleep, content with knowing that her girls would be strong enough to continue the mission that had been presented to them.

At her request, Daniel performed the funeral service to a packed church. Amazing Grace and the Old Rugged Cross were sung harmoniously by everyone gathered for her final farewell. Patsy's casket was carried over to the cemetery on a horse drawn cart, to her final resting place, among the rest of the family who had gone before her.

Deborah, Marsha, and her husband, Chad sat in the attorney's office together. The other remaining cousins had chosen not to make the trip to Wayne City, figuring there was nothing in it for them. After Mr. Powell entered the room carrying the folder that held Aunt Patsy's Last Will and Testament, he took his place behind the large dark walnut desk. The over-stuffed, black leather chair enveloped his tall frame.

"Good morning Ladies, Chad," said Mr. Powell, as he nodded towards each of them. "Marsha and Chad, I have known both of you for years. Deborah, you have made a place for yourself in our community and we have benefitted from you sharing your ideas and talents with us. You have helped all of us to not only survive, but to grow and prosper. Your Aunt Patsy was a pillar here and she will be deeply missed. If you don't mind, I think we can dispense with all the legal and technical wording and just hit the high points."

They all agreed.

"First, Patsy was thrilled when you two women reconciled and worked together to build the church into the prosperous venture that it has become. She had always hoped you would become the close cousins again that you once were. Which, is why she has left everything she owns to both of you to equally divide and do with as you wish. That includes her house and property, her furniture, jewelry and bank account."

Their jaws dropped as they looked at each other in total surprise.

Mr. Powell went on to say. "As you know, Patsy had no children of her own and her nieces and nephews were the only remaining family, but you were the only two who showed any interest in keeping any ties to Orchardville. You cherished the family bond and looked after Patsy, both before and after she needed serious care. She treasured your loyalty and wanted to show how much she appreciated all that you had done for her, for so many years."

Deborah and Marsha leaned over and hugged each other, Marsha turned to hug Chad. Tears flowed from both of the women. Deborah turned to Mr. Powell and said, "Tom, you know, we did not see this coming at all. We loved Aunt Patsy dearly and she was a joy to be around. We weren't with her for this, not to get her money!"

"Yes, Deborah, I do know and so did she, which is exactly why she did it. Deborah, there is one more thing for you, well actually, two things. Here are two keys to safe deposit boxes at the bank next door. They are both in your name and the contents are yours," said the attorney.

"I don't understand. Why do I have keys? Not both of us?" questioned Deborah.

"Deborah, this key, with the tag ending in the number ninety-five, is to a small box that you are to open first. Use the other key only after you have the contents from the first box," Tom instructed.

૪ ૭

The trio walked next door to the bank and asked for the first safe deposit box. They were ushered to a small room with a table and a couple of chairs. Once the box was placed on the table, the bank teller told them to ring the buzzer whenever they were ready and she would return to put the box away.

They all looked at each other, laughing with curiosity. What could be the big mystery? Chad said, "This is like out of a TV movie."

A single white business size envelope sat in the bottom of the box. The front of the envelope had her name written across it in beautiful script. Deborah Suzanne Bridges Kingston. Deborah picked it up slowly and cautiously, as if she was afraid to touch it. She studied it and knew it had been written by Aunt Dorothy. She turned it over, and saw the floral sticker sealing the back flap. She held it up to the light to see if she could read through the envelope, but of course she could not. Marsha nudged Deborah, "Open it already!"

Deborah scowled, "I don't know if I can. I'm afraid. What can it be?"

Marsha snatched the envelope from her, "I can. Let me!"

Deborah grabbed it back. "No, it's mine, I'll do it." She hesitated. With her hands shaking, she lifted the colorful floral sticker and opened the flap to reveal a second envelope. This one, also addressed to Deborah, had a floral flap that matched the sticker from the outer envelope. Inside, was matching floral stationary. Yes, very typical of Aunt Dorothy and the beautiful stationary she always liked to use. Deborah started to scan over the letter in silence, wanting to quickly discover the big mystery.

The letter was dated August 18, 2007

My Dear Deborah,

"If you are reading this, it means that my dear sister Patsy has joined me on the other side of God's Golden Gate to heaven. It also means that all of my siblings are no longer on earth. There is

no one left who knew my secret. A secret that I swore I would take to my grave, and I kept that promise to everyone. The few who knew, also kept their promise as well. There is no one left for you to question, and trust me my dear child, I know you would hound anyone to death with your unending questions. You are stubborn like that, but you come by it naturally!

When I was a young girl, barley fifteen years old, I fell madly in love with a young boy and foolishly thought we would be together forever. I never saw, nor heard from him again, once I told him I was with child. Devastated and ashamed, I did not know what to do. I was much too young to raise a child and I wanted more for you than the farm life I had grown up with. Times were very different back then, not at all like they are now. Not only was an unwed mother put to shame, but a fatherless child was marked for life as a bastard. I wanted more than that for you."

Deborah was trembling as she read the words and was beginning to comprehend the meaning of the letter. The air in the room suddenly felt intensely hot, her chest tightened and her throat seemed to close, she started to feel faint. She dropped the letter to the floor and covered her mouth with her trembling hands, saying, "No, it can't be...I can't ...I can't read anymore!" Her body crumpled. She buried her head in her arms on the table and sobbed. There wasn't any need to read more. She had it figured out.

Marsha picked up the letter and asked if she should finish reading it.

Deborah said, "No, there is no need." And yet in the next breath, she whispered to Marsha to go ahead and finish reading it. Marsha read out loud:

"Your mom and dad had only been married a few months when the Army sent Bert to Oklahoma. They had rented a small two-bedroom duplex off base. My mom and dad, your grandparents, sent me to live with them. No one here in Orchardville knew I was pregnant. Everyone thought I was going to go spend the summer with my big brother at the Army base. I *got a job at the local dime store so I could contribute in some small way for my room and board. Mom and Dad sent money from time to time. I tried very hard to stay out of the way of the newlyweds. They were very kind and understanding of the situation. Together we talked to adoption agencies and visited homes for unwed mothers. We talked to churches who handled private adoptions. I loved you more than I could ever think possible. The more my belly grew, the more I loved you. I wanted you to have more opportunities than I ever had. It didn't take very long for us to devise the plan. They would adopt my sweet little baby and raise it as their own. Keeping it in the family and telling no one, ever, that the baby was not theirs. This way, too, I could watch you grow up. I promised to never interfere in your upbringing as long as I could maintain a relationship with my new little niece or nephew.*

Knowing that no family member would ever go to Oklahoma to visit while they were stationed there, Clarice announced by letter to all our family and friends that she was pregnant. She sent regular newsy letters on the progress of her pregnancy, getting first-hand knowledge directly from me. I know it was hard on my brother, having to take extreme precautions to avoid Clarice from really getting pregnant, or our plan would not work. But the good Lord watched over all of us and presented us with the most beautiful baby girl we could ever ask for. I, of course, stayed longer than the summer break. I needed to help Clarice take care of the baby while Bert worked long hours on duty.

We all returned home later that fall. Thanksgiving was especially meaningful that year as we celebrated your new chance of a good life, my ability to watch you grow into an adorable little girl and the announcement that you were about to quickly become a big sister. Of course, there were the teasing comments from the brothers and uncles to slow down the baby making and the advice from the aunts and sisters that it would be good to have the babies close together.

You were a loving sister to Lucy when she was born and the two of you were very close. It was a joy to watch you together. As much as I ached to tell you I was your mother, I knew I had done the right thing for you.

I was able to watch you grow and become the smart, well-educated woman that you are today. You married well and have raised your own beautiful family; all of the things I wanted for you.

It broke my heart every time you talked of living here near me, wanting some of the land to call your own, wanting to watch over me. You had no way of knowing how blessed I felt by your genuine love and concern. Oh, how I knew that your desire to belong here was bred in you from the day you were conceived. This has always been your home and so shall it remain.

As you know, Marsha and Chad are owners of the original farm and they do own it free and clear. However, there is a separate forty acres across the road from the farm. You know, where you wanted to build a retreat center house, close enough to keep an eye on me, you said. My dear child, that forty acres is in your name. It has been for years. When the oil well went in, a bank account was set up for direct deposit for all income from the well. That account was used to pay taxes on the property, but with interest compounded over the years, there should be a nice little nest egg for you to live comfortably for a good long time. Patsy was the manager of the account and she took very good care of my investment for you. A separate safety deposit box should hold all of the bank statements as well as the deed to the property. You are now free to build your retreat house or a nice retirement home for you and David. Whatever your heart desires, at this time in your life.

Never doubt how much I loved you and please try to understand why I couldn't tell you."

My never-ending love,

Your Mother, always and forever!

Deborah's head laid on top of her folded arms across the table. Her shoulders shook as she silently sobbed. She didn't utter a sound. Marsha came and wrapped her arms around her and tried to bring comfort without really knowing how. What could she say that could possibly help? The very core of Deborah's entire life had just been ripped apart and turned upside down.

Deborah whispered, "Please take me home."

Marsha reminded Deborah that there was another safety deposit box that she needed to look at. Deborah shook her head and said she couldn't handle anything more, but Marsha insisted. Marsha pressed the buzzer for the bank attendant to return. Marsha handed her the remaining key. The attendant pulled out one of the largest boxes in the vault. Together Deborah, Marsha and Chad began to sort through the stack of papers and envelopes. Just as Aunt Dorothy had said in her letter, there were bank statements and investment letters from the company who processed the oil well. Deborah said she would have to turn all these papers over to Randy for him to process and explain in detail just what all of this was worth. She told Marsha and Chad that she would leave all the papers right there in the bank box where they were. There was no need to carry them all home right now. Just as they were putting the papers back into the box, Marsha discovered a padded envelope with Deborah's name on it.

"Here, Deborah, I think you should open this and see what it is," instructed Marsha.

On top of the medium sized, padded, manila envelope was taped a smaller white envelope. Deborah removed the smaller envelope and discovered a letter from Aunt Patsy. It said the items inside had belonged to her sister Dorothy and that she had wanted Deborah to have them, but did not want to show favoritism at the time of her death. She didn't want other cousins questioning why Deborah had gotten them. This was the only way she could be sure that there would never be any hard feelings among the others.

Deborah opened the manila envelope and pulled out a

petite ivory cameo with a caramel color background in a gold setting. There were matching earrings and a ring. Deborah gasped as she held the precious jewelry in her hands.

Marsha exclaimed, "They are beautiful, Aunt Dorothy only wore them on very special occasions! Like weddings and funerals and things like that!"

Deborah was trembling as she fingered the delicate carvings of the cameos. "I know! The necklace was a gift from Grandma and Grandpa Bridges when she graduated high school. She and Aunt Patsy were the only two siblings to go to high school. None of the boys went to school past the eighth grade. Uncle John gave her the ring when they got married, but I do not know when she got the earrings or who gave them to her. Do You?"

Marsha said she did not know either. In fact, she said she never remembered seeing them before.

Deborah put the cameo jewelry in her purse and then called for the bank attendant to put the big box of papers away. She said she would bring Randy to the bank at a later time.

Chad drove home while Marsha sat in the back seat with Deborah. Deborah sat silently staring out the window while Marsha held her hand. When Marsha asked if she wanted to talk about it, Deborah, simply shook her head, no. She never uttered a word the whole way home.

A heavy snow began to fall and the roads were slick, which made the drive seem to take even longer than normal, but at last they were at Deborah's house. Marsha offered to stay the night with her, but Deborah waved her off and said she would be okay. She just needed to be alone, and did not want to talk now. She told Marsha she would call her in the morning.

Chad and Marsha watched as Deborah ever so slowly made her way into the house. They noticed Sam was not at home or they would have asked him to keep an eye of Deborah. They hated to leave her alone like this, but she had insisted she needed to be alone with her thoughts.

Deborah dropped her purse in the chair closest to the door. Without even removing her coat, she made her way to the bathroom. She looked in the mirror at her tear stained, red blotchy face with swollen eyes that reflected emptiness. Mascara smeared like a raccoon mask. Her usual well styled hair was tousled in total disarray. She asked, "Who are you? What now? Your whole life has been a lie! You don't even know your own father's name! How do we fix this? David!! Please help me. I don't know what to do!" She turned and walked away from the haunting reflection in the mirror.

The next thing she knew, she was in the cemetery, at Aunt Dorothy's grave. She slumped to the ground, lying directly on top of where the casket would be, not a thought of fear about stepping on a dead body. She beat the ground with her fist shouting, "Why! Why! Why!" Then sobbing in the next breath, "I do understand why you did what you did, and I thank you. NO!! I hate you!! I HATE YOU!! Do you hear me? I hate you! Why could you never tell me the truth! Why did you lie to me? I loved you with my whole heart!" Beating the ground again with her fist. "I loved you and I know you loved me. I know now, why we had such a bond my whole life. I just wish we could have talked about it." She cried, and sometimes screamed at the top of her lungs, and wailed out loud like a dying animal, until she was totally spent and could not shed another tear.

CHAPTER SEVENTEEN

When Sam pulled into his usual parking spot, his headlights caught sight of a snow-covered mound lying in the cemetery that he knew should not be there. He pulled his truck closer to the fence to get a better look. It was a motionless blob that he assumed must be an injured or dead animal. Grabbing a shovel out of the truck box, he walked over to investigate further. He was shocked to discover it was Deborah, lying face down, covered in snow, nearly frozen to death.

Dropping the shovel, he grabbed her up from the ground and ran as fast as he could to his truck. He knew at that very moment; his truck was the warmest place. He grabbed his cell phone with one hand, dialing 911 and rubbing her face and hands with his other hand, shouting for her to wake up. He advised the emergency operator that he was heading towards Wayne City with someone who had been lying in the snow for quite some time. He didn't want to wait for an ambulance to come all this way. He said he would meet the ambulance on the road. He would have his emergency flashers on and would be honking as soon as he saw the ambulance. He begged them to hurry. He was certain that she was nearly dead. Sam ripped off Deborah's snow covered coat and grabbed a blanket from behind the seat to cover her. He yanked off her shoes and socks and put her cold bare feet between his legs. Without taking time to unbutton his flannel shirt, he pulled it up and over his head, using it as a towel to dry her wet hair. Randomly taking time to make frantic attempts at mouth to mouth resuscitation. He turned the heat up as high as it would go, turned his truck around and headed down the road. Steering with one hand, alternating between patting Deborah's face and rubbing her toes with the other, pleading, "Come on, sweetie! Please wake up! Deborah! What in the world were you doing out there?"

About eight miles down County Road 13, Sam spotted the red lights flashing through the falling snow. He found a spot on the side of the road where he could safely pull over. He proceeded to honk his horn and flash his headlights to garner their attention. The ambulance pulled over and circled around behind him.

Sam quickly filled in the attendant with what little bit he knew, saying that he didn't think she was breathing and he couldn't find a pulse. The attendants quickly transferred Deborah to the ambulance and started prepping her for transport while communicating with the hospital. Sam followed the ambulance the rest of the way, staying close behind and praying that she would be okay. Once Deborah was in a treatment room, Sam remembered to call Marsha. He's not sure exactly why, but he called Daniel to come, too.

Marsha, Chad and Daniel, arrived simultaneously. They found Sam pacing the hallway, holding a Styrofoam cup of coffee. He nearly broke down when he saw their faces. He explained where and how he found her, along with his fears that she was nearly dead. If he had been any longer getting home, she would have been for sure!

Marsha's knees buckled as her face went flush and she broke out in a terrified sweat. Chad grabbed her before she collapsed. "I should not have left her alone! This is my fault!"

"No, dear. It is NOT your fault," stressed Chad, as he ushered her to a chair in an alcove close by the treatment room.

Daniel handed Marsha a cup of water as he and Sam gathered near her and Chad. They both wanted to know how this could be her fault.

Marsha looked at each of their faces, then considered Chad's eyes, looking for a way to answer their question. She dropped her head, as tears fell down her cheeks. Feeling torn and helpless, she uttered, "I wish I could tell you...she made me promise... I can't. Not right now." She sobbed audibly. Chad sat and wrapped his arms around his hurting wife, pulling her closer to him.

A doctor came out and said that Deborah was stabilized,

but still unconscious. He said that they could all go in and visit for a few minutes. Maybe their presence and their voices would help to bring her around. He said they would be monitoring her for pneumonia and other complications, but, for now, they are waiting for her to regain consciousness. The doctor commended Sam for his quick thinking and told him that he literally had saved her life. He went on to say that if Sam had been any later, well, they would be having a different conversation right now.

Marsha grabbed Deborah's hand and pleaded with her to wake up. Everyone joined hands and circled around her bed as Daniel led them in a prayer. Deborah's eyes fluttered but she did not wake up. The three men left the room and gave Marsha some time alone with Deborah. Marsha assured her that she would not tell her secret, but reminded her that she had to wake up and deal with this. "Don't make me live with this all alone. Remember Aunt Patsy's words, we have been given a mission to run; *The Wedding Belle.* Everyone needs you! We need your vision and drive! Please wake up!" There was no response from Deborah.

Marsha went out in the hall to talk to the men. She handed Chad her cell phone and asked him to call Deborah's kids and Andrea. She then asked Sam to go be with Deborah so she wouldn't alone. She wanted to talk to Daniel privately.

Marsha stated, "I know you are not a Catholic priest, but I hope, that as a man of God... I umm," she stuttered. "I need to talk to you, with the confidence that it will remain between us and God. I really must talk to someone."

Daniel suggested they go to the hospital chapel to talk.

They sat side by side in the very first pew. Daniel turned slightly and took Marsha's hand. "Please, I want you to feel safe with me. Tell me whatever you need to lift this burden you are carrying."

Marsha sobbed, "But, I promised! We have learned of a lifetime of lies. Ironically, all well intended, but lies, just the same. Deborah wants to be the one to tell her family, as she should.

But what if she can't? Should I? If she dies, does the lie die with her?

Daniel said in a soothing tone, "Now, now, no one has said anything about her dying. She is going to pull out of this and the two of you can discuss whatever the problem is. It could be a bit of time before she is well enough to talk, but I trust in God, that she will. You know, I have grown quite fond of her in the short time I have known her. I am praying just as much as you are that she will be okay."

        ❦ ❧

Hours turned into days as they waited for Deborah to wake up. They all took turns keeping vigil. Davey, Annie, Bob, Randy, Chelsea and Andrea were beside themselves with worry. Of course, Annie said this would have never happened if her mother had not come up with the crazy idea to move out here to the middle of nowhere. Immediately, her brothers chastised her for her comments, saying that until they knew why she was out in the cemetery in the middle of a snowstorm, they could not comment on why or how this accident happened. They just needed to pray that she would wake up soon.

By this time, the doctors were saying that it was strictly up to Deborah and God to pull her through. She was completely stable and all of her vitals were good. They said she just needed the will to wake up. They encouraged her family to keep talking to her and encouraging her to open her eyes.

        ❦ ❧

At long last, one day while Andrea was taking her turn at sitting by Deborah's side and talking, she opened her eyes and started crying and trembling. Andrea jumped up to hug her, while pressing the call button for the nurse at the same time. "Thank God! You are awake! We have all been so worried about you!"

Deborah just shook her head and softly whispered, "I know." After the nurses and doctors had checked her vitals and welcomed her back to the living world, they left the room. One of the nurses said she would be back with some juice.

Deborah looked around the room and asked Andrea, "Where is everyone else?"

"They went home for now. We are taking turns sitting with you. I will call them and tell them the news. They will want to come see for themselves."

Deborah reached out to stop her from using the phone. "No, not yet. I am not ready for them. I need time to think."

"Think? Think about what? Sweetie, you nearly died. They will want to know that you are awake and talking," Andrea pleaded.

"NO!" Deborah screeched as loudly and as forcefully as her weakened voice could muster.

Andrea looked at her friend in disbelief. "You don't want to see your kids? What is wrong?"

"I can't. Not yet. I have to adjust my own mind first. You know, I didn't really want to wake up. I did not want to be a part of this world anymore. I liked where I was, but David insisted that I had to come back. He said that I had a new life waiting for me here and that it would be a good life. He said that he wanted me to be happy in my new life."

Andrea held her friends hand and gasped. "Are you saying that..."

"Yes, I saw David and he sent me back here. I saw my mothers' too. They agreed with David and said it was not my time to be with them. She said I had to return and face the world and right the wrongs that had been done. She hugged me and told me she loved me more than life itself, and that I should never forget how much she loved me, and how much she sacrificed for me. Then there was this iridescent rainbow like glow that got brighter and whiter around them, but it seemed to slowly drift away from me. I didn't want to wake up. I didn't want them to go away." Deborah started to cry uncontrollably.

Andrea called for the nurse again and explained what was happening. The nurse left and quickly returned with a shot of a mild sedative. She said it was just enough to calm her down but it would not knock her out.

※ ※

As the calming sedative began to take effect, Deborah asked Andrea to close the door so they could talk in private.

Deborah swore Andrea to secrecy. She said she needed to talk, but was not ready to discuss it with her children just yet and she did not want them to accidently walk in and overhear what she was about to tell her. Slowly, in between jags of crying, Deborah told Andrea the whole story. She said she would have to come to grips and understanding the full impact on her own, before she could lay all of this onto the kids. There was so much to think about and right now, she just didn't have the strength to think it all through. "And then there is Lucy. How on earth do I tell her that she is not my little sister? She is my cousin."

"Lucy may not be your sister by parentage but she is your sister in every sense of the word and you do essentially have the same blood running through your veins. She will always be your sister and you know it. I am here for you, whenever you need to talk. Now let me call your kids and tell them you are awake"

Deborah smiled and nodded in agreement.

※ ※

When the kids arrived, there were tears of joy mixed with questions and concerns about why she had been out in the cemetery on a snowy night like that.

Deborah reassured them that she would answer all of their questions in a few days. She said she was tired and just not up to talking at the moment. She asked for their patience. After much protest, they agreed to give her the space and time that she was requesting. She thanked them for their prayers and vigilance but it was time that they return to their homes and jobs and resume a normal life again. She promised she would rest and take care of herself and would fill them in on what happened very soon.

❧ ☙

Two days later, Deborah was released from the hospital. Marsha and Chad were there to take her home. On the way home, she informed Marsha that she had told Andrea the whole story, and she would be telling her kids in a few days. She was still struggling with how to tell Lucy and felt that Lucy should know as quickly as possible.

After Deborah was settled in at home, with a few containers of chicken and dumplings and fresh biscuits from Marsha, she promised she would call if she needed anything. Even if it was just to talk, or a shoulder to cry on. She also promised she would not be going out to the cemetery either. Feeling reassured, Marsha and Chad went home.

Immediately after they left, Deborah called Daniel and asked if he could come to the house. She even offered to share her chicken and dumplings.

When Daniel arrived, he kissed her cheek and told her how good it was to see her up and about. Deborah took the biscuits out of the oven where they had been warming, and dished out the piping hot chicken and dumplings. When they sat down to eat, Deborah got right to the point of why she had asked Daniel to come over. She said, "I remember at Christmas, you and Lucy were talking about Okinawa. How long is the flight? I need to go see her. What do I need to know about making the trip there? What about going through customs?"

Daniel replied, "Well, first of all, you need to get stronger before can think about flying half way around the world. It is a long flight with several changes in planes. Then there is the long slow line at customs. You are not up to dealing with all of that right now. Give it some time. Okinawa is a beautiful place and Lucy is going to be there at least another year. You have got plenty of time to make that trip. You need to make sure you are strong enough to enjoy it."

"No, Daniel. I know you do not understand, but this is extremely urgent and I need to go now! Can you drive me to the airport in St. Louis?"

"Now? Why the urgency?" Daniel questioned.

Deborah snapped back, "Sorry, if it is too much trouble, I'll ask Sam to drive me."

"Slow down and tell me what is going on with you. I want to help you, but I could use some more information." Daniel pleaded.

In exhausted frustration, Deborah replied, "Fine!" But this stays between us, okay? Promise me you will not repeat what I am about to tell you."

Daniel knew instinctively that it had to be what Marsha was referring to, that first night at the hospital. He pledged his loyalty to her. She filled him in on the fact that her birth mother was her Aunt Dorothy and that Lucy was not her sister. She said that Lucy deserved to hear it from her in person, and not over the phone, nor some computer face to face video chat.

Daniel acknowledged that it was a serious issue and agreed that a trip would certainly be the best way to deliver the news. He did however point out that a trip of this magnitude should be more thoroughly planned and that she should plan on staying a couple of weeks, not only because of the cost of the trip, but she would want to stay with Lucy for a time, so they could both adjust to the news together. Besides, she should make sure that Lucy would be home and let her know that she was coming. With Lucy's adventurous spirit, she could easily be traveling around to some other islands or countries in the area. He also pointed out that her kids deserved to know the story just as much as Lucy. If she was going to be gone for a few weeks, she would have some explaining to do to them for leaving so abruptly after the accident.

While Deborah was mulling over everything Daniel had said, he took her by surprise, when he said, "If you will take another week or two of taking care of yourself first, I will accompany you on the trip for moral support and to help you through the various airports if you get tired."

Deborah was not expecting that response. But after a few moments of consideration, she agreed, with one stipulation: "You must let me pay for your airfare. It is the only way I will agree to let you go." With a chuckle she added, "I can certainly afford it, with everything that Aunt Dorothy left me! Why, I can probably afford a private jet. What do you think?"

Daniel laughed, "I am glad to see you make a joke about the situation already. But a private jet is not necessary."

"Okay, then we have a deal. Next Monday, we will fly to Okinawa to tell Lucy the news. We will plan on staying for two weeks. Is that enough time, you think? Or should I buy one way tickets and keep the return trip open, just in case. You can preach on Sunday, as scheduled, and be sure to announce that you won't be available for any kind services for a couple of weeks or until further notice."

"My, my! You must be feeling better. Listen to you taking control and making all the plans," Daniel responded.

❦ ❦

After Daniel left, Deborah called Annie to tell her that she was home and had just finished a large bowl of chicken and dumplings with biscuits from Marsha. She told her she was glad to be home and was feeling much better. She added that she was looking forward to sleeping in her own bed, just as soon as they finished talking. "Oh, Sweetheart, if you could arrange a family dinner for next Sunday afternoon, I would like to meet with all of you and discuss what happened. Just let me know which house it will be at. Yours or mine, or should I say, the boy's house?"

Annie squealed with delight at the thought of a family dinner. "Of course, we will have a family dinner here at my house! I will tell the boys and Chelsea. I'll take care of everything. You get some rest and we will see you next Sunday. Jeremy and Jacob are going to be so excited!"

"Annie, one more thing. Can you set an extra place, please? I will be bringing Daniel with me," Deborah added.

"What?... Why?" Annie questioned.

"Good night, dear. I am really tired. I will talk to you later. Love You!"

Early the next morning, as Sam was getting into his truck to head over to Charlies' for his morning coffee with biscuits and gravy, he spotted Deborah walking around in the cemetery. At least she was properly dressed for the blustery morning he thought to himself. She had the drawstring of the fur trimmed hood cinched tightly around her face. The heavy parka hung well below her knees. Surprisingly, she was not standing in her usual spot at Dorothy's grave. Instead, she was walking from grave to grave and with her gloved hands, was ferociously brushing away the snow from the headstones. Almost, as if she were on some kind of a mission. He watched for a few moments while the truck was warming up, trying to figure out what she was doing. He then left the truck running while he went over to join her. "Hey, Deborah, what are you doing out here? No need to clean off the headstones, there is more snow coming later today. Besides, you just got out of the hospital. I don't want to have to take you back there again."

She looked at him blankly, and then searched around at the

graves as she contemplated his questions. "Well, I umm... I was looking for something, or I guess more like, someone."

Sam wrapped an arm around her shoulders and turned her towards the cemetery gate, as they walked, he asked her to join him for coffee at Charlie's. He said it would be good for everyone to see that she was out of the hospital and doing well and it would do her good to see some friends. As he opened the passenger door of the truck to help her in, he wondered what she had meant that she was looking for someone. He also knew that he could not leave her alone out there in the cemetery, for fear of a repeat of the last time he saw her there.

The store was crowded with folks drinking coffee and catching up with each other, while the skies were clear. They were all delighted to see Deborah out and about. They exclaimed how worried they had been about her. She thanked them for their concerns, while studying each and every man who might be over seventy years old. She studied their eyes, their jaw-lines, their chins. She wondered if any of them could be her father. More importantly would she ever find out? And how? Did anyone else around here know her secret? Who could have been friends with Aunt Dorothy as a young teen? Did they know that Dorothy had gotten pregnant? Did they know the scheme she had devised to stay close to her child? Did anyone know who she was? Was there someone in this store looking at her thinking, "I know your secret!" As various conversations swirled in the background around her, she watched Norm Johnson and how he moved and talked. She looked at Charlie just as intently, Walter and Henry too.

"Earth to Deborah, Hello! Are you listening?" asked Sam.

"Oh, I'm sorry, I was just thinking about something."

"Yeah, apparently. You were a million miles away," replied Sam. "I was asking if you needed to go into Salem and get a few things before today's snowstorm hits. I need to stock up on a few things and you can certainly ride with me and get some stuff, as well." Sam said as he rose from the table to leave.

"Gee, I don't know. I haven't been home for a while and I didn't look around last night when I got home."

"Okay, then, you are going with me. I'm sure there are a few things you need or will pick up once you are in the store."

CHAPTER EIGHTEEN

Daniel arrived on Sunday morning with his packed bags secured in the trunk of his car. He had left emergency contact information with Aunt Millie's caretakers at the skilled care facility and informed Missy where he was going and why.

Deborah gave Sam some last-minute instructions, not that he needed any. He knew what was expected of him. The only thing he was to tell anyone who asked was that business was slow right now, and that she was taking this time to go visit her sister in Okinawa.

When Daniel and Deborah arrived at Annie and Bob's home, Annie gave her mother a puzzled look at seeing Daniel standing by her side. Deborah dismissed the look and directed her attention to Jeremy and Jacob. They were delighted to see their granny, but more excited about their additional guest. "Hey, Mr. Daniel! Thanks for bringing our Granny to dinner. Don't forget, we get to come ride your horse and you are going to teach us to hunt. Summer will be coming soon, and we will have lots of time to stay with Granny!"

They all enjoyed a very pleasant pork roast dinner with mashed potatoes and golden pork gravy, green beans, and applesauce. Annie was quick to point out that it was one of their father's favorite meals.

Not to be intimidated, Daniel responded politely, that her father had good taste and he would be proud of her cooking skills. He told her the meal was delicious and that he appreciated being invited.

Annie gave a half snide and half-hearted retort, "Uh, thanks."

When dinner was over and the lemon cream pie had been served, Deborah said she would like to discuss the accident and what had happened and why. Annie started to dismiss the boys off to the basement, but Deborah asked for them to stay. She wanted them to know the truth of what had happened and she preferred that they hear it directly from her. If they were to have any questions, she wanted to be able to answer them.

She explained everything that had happened from the reading of Aunt Patsy's will to the reading of Aunt Dorothy's letter. She told them about being in a total state of shock and having a complete emotional meltdown in the cemetery. She shared the days that she was in a coma, how she had witnessed going to the other side, even if for a little while. The beautiful sights she witnessed and her conversations with David and her mothers, both of them: her biological mother and the mother who raised her to be the woman that she is today. They both told her that it was not her time to be with them yet. She still needed to live and to love and to share her life with others.

Of course, the boys didn't care about the whole biological mother part of the story, but they did want to know more about her talking to ghosts and what it was like. They asked if the 'boogie-man' had grabbed her while she was laying on Aunt Dorothy's grave. They wondered if she would be seeing more ghosts and boogie-men.

Deborah's children were speechless for a short time. Looking from one to another, trying to digest all she had told them, the implications, and what the fallout would be.

Finally, Annie asked, "What about Aunt Lucy? Does she know about this?"

"No, she does not know yet. I don't expect anything to change between us. She will always be my sister," replied Deborah. "Yes, for a while we will both have to adjust to the news, but it shouldn't change anything. No matter what, we are bonded for life."

Deborah further elaborated, "Another reason I asked for this dinner today was so that I could tell you that I want to go tell

Lucy myself, in person. It is not something I want to share over the phone with her so far away. I will take Aunt Dorothy's letter and let her read it for herself."

Davey and Randy simultaneously agreed that it was a good idea and a trip would be good for her. Chelsea said she would be happy to make the travel arrangements for her.

Deborah swallowed hard before stating that she had already made all the plans and that she would be flying out first thing in the morning.

"What?" Was the resounding question from around the table.

Deborah stood firm in her response, "Yes, I do not want to put it off. I have my doctor's permission and Daniel is going to accompany me on the trip so I do not have to be alone. Also, since he and Lucy got along so well at Christmas and have a shared love for Okinawa, together they will be great tour guides!"

There was complete silence. No one wanted to come right out and say what was on their minds. But, the reality that they were now going to have to face, was that their mother was about to go on a trip half way around the world with a man who was not their father. A man that they had met briefly, just a few months earlier. The other reality was, they knew they would not be able to change her mind.

Finally, Davey rose from his chair and came over to hug his mother. "I love you Mom, and I understand that you have a difficult job ahead of you. You and Lucy will be fine. I hope you will have a good trip." He then turned to Daniel and reached out to shake his hand. "Sir, take good care of our Mother."

Chelsea asked how long they would be gone.

"Well, actually, I bought one way tickets. I wasn't sure if two weeks would be enough or if we would need more time to talk. I don't want to be rushed. So, as soon as I see how it goes, I will decide when to return home. There isn't any work scheduled until the end of March, so, of course, I will be home by then," she chuckled.

Annie looked directly to Daniel and asked, "I wonder, sir. I do not believe that my aunt's base apartment is very large. Where will you be staying? If I may ask?"

Daniel smiled, and internally, enjoyed her protectiveness of her mother. Even though Annie was trying to come off as stern and in control, he knew that the little girl inside was testing him.

"I still have some friends stationed there that I will be bunking with, except for when Deborah needs me for moral support and official tour guide," replied Daniel while trying to stifle a laugh.

Annie exhaled deeply before continuing her questions. "So, you fly out tomorrow morning. From St. Louis? What time is your flight? How early will you have to leave Orchardville to get to the airport?"

Daniel and Deborah exchanged looks before answering. It was now Deborah's turn to take a long deep breath before exhaling. "Actually, the flight is at seven in the morning. So, to save time, we are booked at an airport hotel."

"Separate rooms, of course!" Daniel added with a grin. "You need not worry about your mother. I care for her and have a very deep respect for her. I would not do anything to jeopardize our friendship, nor yours."

Before Deborah and Daniel left, Annie said there was one more piece of business that she needed to take care yet. She went to the living room and removed a manila envelope from her purse. She handed the envelope to Annie and said, "These very special pieces of jewelry belonged to …to…my Mother. I want you to have them. I remember seeing her wear them on special occasions. I know how much she treasured them, but I don't think I could ever wear them. It would hurt too much."

Annie hugged her mother and asked if she was sure about this. When Deborah shook her head, yes. All Annie could say, was, "Thank you, I will take good care of them for them for you."

                                    ~ ~

As Deborah and Daniel settled into the comfortable soft black leather seats and were buckling their seatbelts, Daniel exclaimed, "I didn't think you meant it when you said you were going to buy first-class tickets. This is a bit much, don't you think?"

Deborah grinned and said, "Well, when you told me how long the flight was going to be, I knew I wanted to fly in comfort. I can afford it now, remember? Besides, it was a new experience for me to book airline tickets on line! I've never done anything like that before! Nor, have I flown half way around the world. This is pretty special. I think I deserve first-class!"

"Yes, I remember that you have suddenly come into a great deal of money, but that is no reason to squander it away. I would never have pegged you to be someone to just blow an inheritance." Daniel was stern and poignant with his comments as he scowled at her.

"No, of course not," she replied. "It's just that, right now, I think I deserve a bit of luxury and pampering for all that I have been through in the past year."

Deborah stopped to acknowledge the hostess standing near them to take a drink order. "We'll have Mimosa's, if you have them? Please." Deborah then turned her attention back to Daniel. "Actually, it is kind of hard to put my life into perspective when you think about this past year. First, I lost David, then my Aunt Patsy, I nearly lost my own life after learning I am not who I always thought I was, and now I have to fly half way around the world to tell my sister that she is not my sister!"

"Deborah, yes, I agree, you have lost a lot in one year, but look at what you have gained! You must put it all into perspective!" Exclaimed Daniel.

"Oh, yeah, nothing like a big fat bank account and an oil well to put life into perspective, all right!" Deborah retorted.

"No! I am talking about the strong independent woman who took on the strongest willed members of the town, and won them over with her ideas and business plans. And, you just said it yourself, about booking the airline tickets. Think of the new computer skills you have learned. Why, I don't think there is anything you can't do if you set your mind to it. You are creative and full of unique ideas. I'm sure that Orchardville has not seen the last of your creative mind! You have grown in more ways than you realize."

Deborah giggled, knowing he was right. David used to always tell her she was always full of ideas.

"Well, Chaplain Kraemer, we have several hours to talk and get better acquainted. All I know about you, is that your mother died when you were a toddler, you were mostly raised by your Aunt Millie. Your wife up and left you with a young daughter. Now you are retired and starting up a tree farm. Would you care to fill in some details?"

"That about covers my life," he replied quickly. When the stewardess brought two more mimosas. He contemplated the glass in his hand, as if he would find the words in his drink. "I don't often talk about myself. Especially, telling my story. Not really much to tell. You know all the highlights."

Deborah peppered Daniel with questions. "How did your mother die? How old were you? Do you remember her?"

Daniel paused while still staring into his glass, "I was four when she was killed in a car wreck. It was pouring down rain and the car in front of her stopped suddenly, she swerved to avoid hitting them and lost control on the wet road. Her car flipped into the ditch. They say she didn't suffer, but who knows for sure. I have always wondered what her final thoughts were and did she know what was happening as she swerved."

"Oh, Daniel, I am so sorry. I didn't mean to bring up such

bad memories. We do not have to continue this. I brought cards, do you want to play rummy or something?"

"No, it is okay. My dad did not know what to do with a four -year old boy. He tried to go to work and take care of me too, but it was too much for him. So, Aunt Millie took me in until he could get himself straightened out. He would come out to the farm on the weekends to visit, but those visits became fewer and fewer after he met Nancy. When they got married, she tried to put on a good front and be the caring step-mother. I think I was a constant reminder that her husband loved someone before her and she resented being second; and I think I was in the way of her relationship with my dad. Especially, after she got pregnant with her own child. I was never as good as her son Joe. I was always pitted against him.

As soon as I turned eighteen, I left and never looked back. I ran straight to Aunt Millie's, it was the only place I ever felt safe and secure. For several years, I floundered and got mixed up with the wrong bunch of guys. We worked hard all day helping various farmers get their crops in and we partied even harder at night. There was lots of drinking and plenty of girls to spend our free time with. Aunt Millie would drag me with her to Grace Bible Church every Sunday morning. She was certain that between her and the preacher I would become a better man come Monday morning. Eventually she told me if I didn't get right with the Lord, she would kick me off the farm forever.

That's all it took. I started talking to Reverend Carter every day. I went to college and got my Divinity Degree, then decided to join the Air Force so I could travel the world and spread God's Word with others.

Missy was born while I was on one of my many overseas deployments. Her mother dropped her off with Aunt Millie; said she didn't sign up to raise a baby all alone. She said she was too young to spend her days changing diapers and night's walking the floor with a crying baby without any help from a husband. She sent me a letter, told me where to find Missy when I returned and she was off to have some fun. We haven't heard from her since. Don't know where she ended up living. Missy has tried a few times to try to find her, but hasn't had any luck. I hope she doesn't. No need to open up those old wounds."

"I wanted Missy to know her grandfather, even if he and I never had close and loving relationship. For Missy to get to know George, she had to know Nancy, too. They were married and it was a package deal, whether I liked it or not. Just because I had issues with my step-mother, I tried not to let that interfere with their relationship with Missy. Nancy is his wife and she is the only grandmother that Missy knows and should be acknowledged as such, no matter what my feelings were. They have grown to care for each other, and I have learned to be a little more accepting of Nancy, as well. Your turn. Tell me who you are."

"David and I met in college. I was a freshman; he was a junior and captain of the football team. We met in an antique store over a cast iron skillet. He bought me lunch and taught me about football. I dropped out of college and became a hairdresser. Following graduation, he carried on as the third-generation owner of the Kingston Accounting Service. He built me a dream house, we raised three children and he died of a massive heart attack. I have been searching out what to do in the next chapter of my life and how to go on without him. Just when I thought I was beginning to find myself, I learn that I don't have a clue who I really am!"

Daniel chuckled, "Aren't we a pair? We have both had some interesting hardships. I have been a vagabond my whole life traveling the world trying to escape my personal reality and that carried over to my daughter who has never had a stable home. I guess that was my fault. Whereas, you my dear, grew up in a secure family, you married into the same environment and have raised your children with those same values. You have been a good role model for your children. Now for both of us to end up here in Orchardville at the same time, looking for…for what? Calmness? Serenity?"

Deborah contemplated what Daniel had said, "I think we are both looking for something special…maybe it doesn't have to have a name. Maybe it is just something different than what we have known before. Maybe it is just…to be."

✌ ✍

Lucy met Deborah and Daniel at the airport, they stopped at a nearby café on an oceanfront cliff to have a light dinner. Bill was working late and would not be home for several hours.

As soon as they were settled in their seats, Lucy started babbling endlessly, reporting on all the places she wanted to show Deborah and the things they were going to do. When the waitress brought their coffee, Lucy asked her to please bring lots of coffee white, she knew Deborah would need more than what was on the table. Deborah looked at Lucy and asked, "Coffee white?"

"Oh, for you, that is creamer. Here, it is called coffee white," she giggled. "I am so thrilled that you decided to come for a visit! I was a bit surprised too, since you just got out of the hospital. So, tell me about the accident and what happened."

Deborah reached under the table and grabbed Daniel's hand for support. He squeezed her hand and rubbed his thumb gently back and forth across her knuckles.

"Well, it is a rather long story and quite personal. I would rather not talk about it here. Can we wait until we get to your house and we can sit comfortably and talk? Right now, I just want to enjoy being here with you."

Lucy examined both Deborah and Daniel's faces looking for some sort of clue when she noticed their hands under the table. She laughed out loud and said, "Sure thing! That will be fine. How about in the meantime, you tell me about this," she said, as she swirled her right hand around in a circular motion towards them.

"This, looks like a very interesting story, right here!"

Quickly both hands were up on top of the table. Deborah briskly stirring her coffee, her face blushed red. Without looking at Daniel she rambled, "There is no, "this," we are just good friends. Daniel has been helping me through a very difficult time and did not want me to travel so far alone. You know, since I just got out of the hospital. And, well, since you two got along so well at Christmas, I thought that together you would be great tour guides."

"Yeah, sure," snickered Lucy.

After their food arrived and Lucy continued to talk nearly non-stop, Daniel sat silently and observed at how very different they were. He also wondered how much he was imagining their differences. While Deborah was smart and creative, she was much quieter and reserved. He felt she studied a situation before talking or acting on anything, whereas, Lucy was more vivacious and bubbly. She talked without thinking. It was easy to see how well their personalities complimented each other. He could see the close bond they shared, sometimes finishing each other's sentences and laughing at old family jokes that only they could relate to. Daniel said a silent prayer that this relationship would not change once Lucy knew the truth.

Deborah's first car ride in this big city was a little bit unnerving. It wasn't enough to experience riding as a passenger on the opposite side of the car, but also to be watching Lucy steer from what is normally the passenger side. Not to mention being on the wrong side of the road and watching traffic whizzing by, going the wrong way, in her mind. But there was just so much traffic! All traveling so quickly!

"Thank goodness it is dark outside and you cannot see the full scope of the traffic right now," Lucy exclaimed. "Wait until daylight when you can really see the traffic! I just may have to give you some motion sickness pills!"

"Oh, great! Maybe I should sit in the back so I can lie down and not watch," replied Deborah with a forced smile.

When they arrived at Lucy's military base apartment, Bill had gotten off work earlier than expected and he was waiting for them. He had the table set with fruit, an assortment of cheese and crackers, and a bottle of wine. He told them that he hoped they were not too tired or too full to sit and visit for a while before going to bed.

Daniel shook hands with Bill and introduced himself. He said he would love a glass of wine, but he needed to call his friend and tell him that he would be a bit later than expected.

There was an awkward silence in the room for a few moments before Lucy finally asked Deborah if she was going to tell her the big story or not.

Deborah was not sure if she wanted to hurry up and talk right now and get it over with, or wait until morning, after she had some sleep. She grabbed her wine glass and took a long gulp.

Daniel reached over and squeezed her shoulder. "I'm right here for you, but it is your story to tell, when you are ready."

"Well, that sounds very ominous! Out with it sister! Whatever it is, I am dying to know! Are you two getting married? No wait! That would be a good thing! That wouldn't explain why you nearly froze to death and then made the trip here." Deborah, please tell me!"

Deborah slid her chair closer to Lucy and took both of her hands in hers. "What I am about to tell you is going to come as a shock and there is no easy way for me to do this. I have played this conversation over and over in my head for a couple of weeks now. One time I think I should just blurt it all out, or do I just show you the letters and let you find out the same way I did. Or maybe, not tell you at all and just keep life exactly as we have known it to be. We don't have to change a thing, but I can't do that. I can't let this lie go on any longer."

With a trembling voice, Lucy said, "Deborah, you are scaring me. What lie? You are not making any sense to me."

Deborah hung her head and turned to look into Bill's face

and then Daniel's before turning back to Lucy. "Like I said, there is no easy way to do this." Deborah drew a deep cleansing breath and exhaled loudly. "I am not your sister. I am your cousin!" Deborah immediately broke down and cried.

Lucy sat dumbfounded, her mouth unable to close. She looked at Bill and to Daniel. Daniel nodded, yes. Lucy squeezed Deborah's hands intensely and said, "Sweetie, I know there is more to this, but no matter what you are saying, I AM your sister." Deborah continued to sob uncontrollably.

Daniel reached over and placed his hand on Deborah's back, patting it gently as she sobbed. Bill got up and walked over to Lucy and placed his hands on her shoulders. Deborah looked up to Lucy, who appeared to be lost and confused. "Our mother, I mean your mother, Clarice is not my mother. My real mother is Aunt Dorothy. Bert is not my father. I don't know who my father is. I am just a bastard child!"

Lucy dropped to her knees and grabbed Deborah and hugged her tightly. "NO! It can't be. No! Bill, Daniel do something! Tell her this isn't true! Where did she get such an idea?"

The two men pulled the women apart and held each of them tightly. Daniel cleared his throat before speaking. "Lucy, I am afraid that what Deborah is saying, is true. She has the letters to prove it and she did bring them with her. Dorothy is indeed her biological mother. Clarice and Bert took Dorothy in while she was pregnant and then adopted the baby and raised her as their own."

Deborah composed herself enough to continue with the story and told Lucy and Bill the whole story to the very end, when she had the complete breakdown in the cemetery and ended up in the hospital. Lucy and Deborah moved to the living room sofa and held each other and continued to cry together.

Bill pulled Daniel into the kitchen and asked if he could stay the night. Bill was not so sure about being left alone with two very upset women. Daniel agreed that it might be a good idea, if he slept on the couch. He called his friend and told him, he would check in with him the next day.

※ ※

As the conversation continued into the wee hours of the morning Bill called for a shift in the sleeping arrangements. Knowing the girls would want to talk for some time to come, Bill suggested that they go ahead and retire to Lucy and Bill's room. They could talk or cry as long as they wanted. Daniel was told to take the spare room and Bill would sleep on the couch. The two men held a brief argumentative conversation. Daniel finally gave in and retired to the spare room.

Over morning coffee, Bill and Daniel got acquainted and shared military stories while they waited for the girls to eventually wake up. Bill said that he had taken off the rest of the week so they could all explore the island together. Now, with this news, he was very glad that he had decided to do that. He wanted to be around for Lucy if she needed him.

※ ※

Lucy was right when she had warned Deborah about the daylight traffic. It did look completely different. The roads appeared smaller and the buildings taller and closer together. She was surprised to see familiar American logos and signs; such as McDonalds and KFC. Even if she couldn't actually read the words, she knew what they were. Deborah laughed hysterically when driving down a very narrow road and Bill pushed a button on his dashboard and both side mirrors folded in towards the car so as not to scrape the vehicle in the other lane. "Now that is way too close!" she squealed.

Most businesses had tiny parking lots right on the main roadway with no place to turn around. When they backed out of the spot, they backed right into traffic. "Oh, my! I could never drive around here. Toto, we are not in Kansas anymore!" Deborah squeaked with a fearful laugh.

Lucy chuckled, "Just wait until we start climbing up the winding mountain roads later! Talk about narrow!"

When they arrived at Okinawa World, Deborah immediately set her camera to work taking pictures of the different Shisa Dogs. She especially loved the huge topiary ones at the entrance gate. Lucy explained that Shisa Dogs were an Okinawan mythology They appear to be a cross between a lion and dog and they are placed in pairs on the rooftops or flanking the entrance to a home or business to ward off evil spirits. The female is placed on the left. Her mouth is closed to keep in the good spirits of the home. The males with their open mouth is placed on the right to scare off evil spirits. She went to say that it is really bad luck to reverse the sides of the male and female. Deborah then took on the task of taking as many pictures of all the Shisa Dogs she could find.

They walked through one of the largest caves she had ever seen. There were shops of every kind from pottery to glass blowing and weaving. There were outdoor dance shows that included the traditional Eisa Drummers in their brightly colored costumes. When they arrived in the building that housed the snake show, Deborah insisted on sitting in the back row, as far away from the creatures as she could get. When the show was over, against every excuse she could give, she gave in to Lucy's insistence to have their picture taken together with one of the snakes. The biggest, fattest snake was wrapped around their shoulders. Lucy held his head while Deborah held the tail. Too afraid to squeal out loud, Deborah tensed at feeling the strong muscles of the snake pulsing on the back of her neck. Daniel snapped several pictures of her squeamish facial expressions.

Keeping true to his word to Deborah's children, Daniel slept at Phillip's place every night, except for that first emotional night for Deborah and Lucy. During the days, Daniel divided his time between going on outings with Deborah, Lucy and Bill and spending time with his friend Phillip Jones and a couple other Air Force buddies. Phillip and Daniel had served together at various times over the years and had developed a long-term friendship. Phillip was preparing for his own retirement in a few months and was curious about how Daniel was enjoying his newfound freedom. Daniel invited Phillip to visit Orchardville once he was out of service.

Lucy and Deborah spent an equal amount of time with one on one girl time, discussing the events of their lives and how this latest revelation was not going to change things between them. Deborah kept repeating how on one hand she could understand why Dorothy did what she did, but on the other hand, she didn't understand the life-long lie. Why must everything be secretive? She would have liked to have the opportunity to talk openly about her life.

While exploring the island, Deborah noticed several things rather quickly. There were Coca-Cola machines everywhere: on the beaches, in parking lots of nearly every business, built into retaining walls, and in fields out in the middle of nowhere. One never had to go very far to get their favorite drink. Why, even the local motorcycle shop had one with their own logo on the machine!

Then there were the Peace Poles scattered in various places. Each white pole contained the words, 'May Peace Prevail on Earth,' written in a different language on each of the four sides of the pole. They were placed in strategic places as a reminder to how many lives had been lost in the war.

So, between the Shisha Dogs, the Coca-Cola machines and Peace Poles, Deborah was constantly asking Lucy or Bill to stop or at least slow down so she could get another picture. It became a big joke as they would tell her that they may never get to their destinations, but she was going to have one awesome scrapbook!

At night, alone in the spare room that faced the ocean, Deborah opened the windows and as she laid in bed, the cool ocean breezes swept across her naked body. The sound of the crashing waves lulled her to sleep. The natural elements combined to caress her in calmness and comfort like she had never experienced before. A serenity that she desperately needed.

~ ~

It was a fast paced, two weeks, with lots of ocean views, beautiful gardens tucked everywhere and historical sights to treasure. There were all the new foods that Deborah was coaxed to try, from Sweet Red Bean Soup to Sushi and slurping Soba Noodles. She also mastered the art of using chopsticks, but she did not like the mochi balls that were in the bean soup. The pretty pastel colored balls looked like little puffs of cotton candy floating on top of the white creamy soup, but the rice paste balls did not taste anything at all like cotton candy, they tasted like paste!

Sadly, it was time to return home and get back to work. At the airport, Lucy thanked Deborah for making the trip to tell her the news in person, and reiterated, it did not change who they were. They would always be sisters. Lucy then told Daniel to take good care of her sister.

"I intend to do just that," he said with a smile.

After another round of hugs by everyone, Daniel and Deborah headed towards their terminal.

Settled once again in their first-class seats, Deborah gave Daniel a puzzled look as she leaned over and sniffed the air. She asked, "You smell different, when did you change your brand of aftershave?"

He looked at her, pulling his head back, eyes wide open, "I haven't changed my aftershave. I have always been an Old Spice man, have never worn anything else. Why?"

"Oh, maybe it was someone else walking by. I thought I smelled musk."

"Not me, I didn't smell anything."

Deborah settled back in her seat, and looked out the window towards the sky, a smile of contentment crossing her face.

❧ ☙

Deborah had promised her kids that she would stop in Waterloo on her way home from the airport, before going back to Orchardville. She was thrilled to find a simple dinner of sloppy joes, French fries and coleslaw waiting for them. She savored every bite! Annie confessed that Daniel had sent her a text message earlier, suggesting some simple American food would be greatly appreciated. There was vanilla ice cream and brownies for dessert, which was the perfect topping to the meal.

Deborah talked endlessly about all the places they had seen and the foods she had tried. Jeremy and Jacob could not believe that their granny had held a real live snake. Even looking at the pictures, they still had a hard time believing it. Deborah was most excited to show off the fancy artwork that she had on her toes. Delicate hand-painted cherry blossoms on every single toe! She told Annie that the pedicure was probably the highlight of the trip, a total spa-like experience. She said she was going to try to make it last as long as possible, that she absolutely loved looking at her toes, and it was a bit too far to go to get another one anytime soon.

Directing the conversation to the twins, Deborah grabbed a couple of specific pictures, "Look at these pictures of the bathroom toilets. You won't believe them…they are either a hole in the ground, or a throne fit for a king! In one you just squat above the hole and go. In the ultra-modern one, there is a console with a push button system for sanitizing the seat before you sit down, you can also spray wash your bottom when you are finished and then hit the dryer button to dry it off! Oh, yeah, there is a music button to keep you company while you go potty too!"

Both boys were giggling hysterically. Jeremy said, "It sounds like a car wash for your butt." Jacob added, "And the music is so no one else can hear you fart!" As he giggled even harder.

Annie reminded the boys that they were at the dinner table and to please choose nicer words or they could leave the room.

"Yes, Ma'am," they both replied. Then turned to Deborah, "Can we go with you the next time you go see Aunt Lucy? We want to see the king's thrones!"

"That does sound like fun, and I think you would enjoy it. There is so much to see and do. We should give it some thought. I think it would be educational, as well. Maybe next year."

Somehow without her knowledge, Daniel had talked to the boys about getting Deborah out of the room so he could talk to the grown-ups privately. Once they had gotten her to go to their room to show off their latest school projects, Daniel told Annie, Davey, and Randy that he wanted to reassure them that this trip had been very good for both Deborah and Lucy. He said that there had been a lot of tears and a whole lot of talking about life and the connections people make, whether by blood, or by bonding.

"Which brings me to the bonding part. Your mother and I have been good working partners in the short time we have been working together, and we share the same values. When she nearly died in February, I was scared to death that I was going to lose her. I knew I had found the woman I had been waiting my whole life to find and it almost ended before we had a chance to get started.

During this trip, we did our own bonding and have become very good friends. She is fun to be around, and has a great sense of humor, and an infectious laugh. I think we can become so much more. I can bring companionship as well as love to her life. I want to protect her and take care of her. In time, I would like to ask her to marry me, but I will not even consider that possibility without your blessings. If you cannot give us that, I would remain her friend and working partner, I would never want to cause any discord among any of you. But, I want you to know, I do love her!"

There was a long moment of silence as each of them looked to the other in various looks of disbelief and yet a sense of knowing that this might have been coming. Surprisingly to everyone, Annie was the first to speak.

"Daniel, I'm sure you are well aware of my reservations of you being personally involved with my mother. I loved my daddy very much and I cannot imagine anyone ever taking his place in my life, or my mother's. He was our whole world. However, that being said, I see a sparkle in her eyes now that I have not seen in a very long time. I think you are good for her and I believe you will do right by her. I want her to be happy. I trust you, and I believe you would have reached this decision regardless of the recent events and her inheritance. But, I must add, that none of us know very much about you. Does my mother know anything about your past life, other than you being a retired Air Force Chaplain and your wife walked away from you and your daughter? Now you are a part-time minister and tree farmer. That about sums up all we know about you."

Daniel became a bit overcome with emotion listening to Annie talk. "Annie, I would never try to take your dad's place, but I do care very deeply for your mother. I knew it the very first time I met her when we were planning Missy's wedding at *The Wedding Belle*. That was long before her inheritance. I will insist on a pre-nuptial agreement, of course, so there is no misunderstanding about my motives. As for my personal past, you are right. We both have had a past life, which we talked about at great length on the plane to and from Okinawa. I think we know each other pretty well by now. My life is an open book. Feel free to ask me anything, anytime."

Davey and Randy went over to shake hands with Daniel. "Welcome to the family," they said in unison. "You have our blessing."

Davey added, "Mom is always full of ideas and she can be very stubborn when it comes to getting her own way about things."

Daniel laughed, "I have already figured that much out!"

They were all standing, chatting and laughing when Deborah and the boys returned.

"What is going on in here? It sounds like a party!"

Daniel replied, "We are just getting better acquainted, that's all."

~ ~

Daniel sent a bouquet of flowers to Annie's house, and a plant to the offices for Davey and Randy with a card that read: "Thank you for letting me be a part of your family. Daniel."

CHAPTER NINETEEN

Sam and Beverly had had numerous discussions over the previous months regarding him contacting his mother. He wanted to call her, but was anxious about making that connection. He was an only child and he wanted his mother back in his life, but he was just as nervous to open those old wounds, for fear of letting her down again and slipping back into his old ways. If he never makes that call, he won't have to face the disappointment in her eyes again. He wants to remember the days when her eyes sparkled when she saw him, not the hurt that he had so often caused.

Beverly encouraged him to do what he felt best without pressuring him. She also reminded him that Helen was aging and he may one day regret not making that call.

Sam eventually made the call and he could hear the joy in her voice, as well as the tears she tried to hide. After about thirty minutes, he invited her to fly out to spend some time with him and Beverly. He told her he did not want to wait until the wedding for her to meet her new daughter in law. He also wanted to introduce her to Deborah, the other woman who had given him a new lease on life.

❧ ☙

Deborah asked Sam, Charlie and Norm to come to a meeting at her house. She told them that Marsha and Daniel would be there as well. She explained that she wanted to discuss some further plans and ideas that she had.

Almost immediately upon arrival, Norm Johnson was already being true to form. "Young lady, you know I have went along with the wedding chapel and other ideas that you have presented. You also know that we do not want this town to outgrow our own people's needs. We don't need any more of your ideas. I like you and I want to keep it that way!"

Deborah grinned at his familiar rant. "Mr. Johnson, if you

please. I have some news that I must share with you and I thought it best to share it with all of you at one time. I didn't want any of you to hear it second hand before I could tell you personally. She drew a deep breath and her bottom lip quivered.

Daniel and Marsha each grabbed one of her hands. Marsha, patting the top of her hand saying, "It's okay honey, take your time."

The other men looked at each quizzically.

"You all know how much my Aunt Patsy and Aunt Dorothy have meant to me and I think you all know how much I love Orchardville. I'm not sure if you are aware that I have wanted to live here my whole life. Did you know I used to fantasize to my Aunt Dorothy about building a retreat house on the property across from her farm?"

"I knew it! Another one of your big business ideas!" bellowed Norm Johnson. "Next thing you know, there will be a business at the corner of every farm in town! I think you have done quite enough, young lady!"

"Uh, no sir, I mean, yes, sir… uh, no not exactly… oh, Gee! She pulled her hands free from Daniel and Marsha and ran them through her hair, in anguish, while she thought about what she needed to say. "It's not anything like all of you are thinking. Not at all. Oh, how do I do this?"

"Sam, Charlie, Mr. Johnson, the open land across from the farm, my aunt Dorothy left that forty acres to me in her will. As I said, I used to fantasize about a retreat house there, a quiet place where groups could book a week or long weekends to work on quilting, painting, business or church groups to get away from the city for in-depth meetings or workshops. My friend Andrea and I have been to similar places with quilting groups. It is a get-a-way for studying a craft or team building with like-minded people." Deborah paused while waiting for their response.

Charlie spoke first, "I don't understand why you haven't presented this idea before. Miss Dorothy has been dead for several years."

Deborah inhaled deeply, then exhaled very slowly. "Because, I just learned about the will in February, after Aunt Patsy died. She was in control of the estate. You can read Aunt Dorothy's letter telling me about the land, and that I should build the retreat house of my dreams, now. She did not want me to know about the land until...until all her family were gone. She didn't want me asking any questions."

She looked around the table and saw the confused looks on each person's face and knew she had to continue with her story.

"You see, I learned something else in this letter." As she picked up the folded stationary. "I learned that my dear Aunt Dorothy was not my aunt after all. She was my biological mother. Her brother Bert and Clarice were my adoptive parents and raised me as their own daughter. In the letter, she said that no one except the immediate family knew. Norm, you have known the family forever, did you know? Do you know who my father is? Is it possible? Could you be my father?"

Norm stuttered, "Whoa, that is pretty heavy stuff there! Uh, no, I mean, I would have to do some thinking back, but right now, no. I don't know who it could be. I know it is not me! I am really caught off guard here. I never knew that Dorothy had been pregnant. Wow! You are Dorothy's daughter!"

Deborah pushed forward, "I'm sure you have all figured out by now, about my stay in the hospital. I collapsed out in the cemetery after I learned the truth. Then of course, I wanted to tell my kids and my sister Lucy, which was the real reason I went to Okinawa. Daniel went along to keep an eye on me and to make sure that I would be okay during the trip. He was a big help. I'm glad I could lean on him." She reached for Daniel's hand and smiled as their eyes met. In time, I know that the news is going to be all over town, but I would appreciate it if we could let it happen gradually. It doesn't need to be the talk of the day at the store. Okay, Charlie?" she asked.

There was an audible sigh throughout the room as everyone exhaled the breaths they had been holding while she had talked. Everyone agreed they would be discreet with her news, but it was certainly going to come out sooner or later.

Norm, then added, "I don't think we need to read your personal letter, I guess I can't stand in your way about the retreat house. It will be on your own property and Dorothy knew what you intended to do there. If she was okay with the idea, then I guess I should be, too. Can you tell us, what exactly your plans are?"

※ ※

April brought the first real signs of spring. The grass was taking on a fresh shade of green, crocus and tulip bulbs were blooming, the rose bushes and honeysuckle vines were sprouting new leaves. The community residents had talked Daniel into saying a Sunday service twice a month so they could keep the spirit of the original church alive. Of course, he could not tell them no. It was important to him too.

Norm Johnson had reluctantly accepted the way the town was changing. He even joked after one of the Sunday services. "Why, I remember about a year ago, we were looking for a part-time preacher for this church. And, as Patsy, God rest her soul, often said. 'God will provide!' She was right, He did provide a part-time preacher, but we also got a full- time wedding business, and a young lady full of ideas, too.

※ ※

Deborah began to draft sketches for the retreat house to be built on her land. She knew how she wanted it to sit on the property, so that the wide, wrap around porch would give views of sunrises and sunsets, depending on which side of the house you sat. Of course, there would be a porch swing hanging on both sides. An attached gazebo on the front corner, with rocking chairs and large ferns in hanging baskets. There would be a drive thru covered portico at the rear entrance, so that guests could unload their vehicles; no matter the weather. Depending on what group was meeting; ladies could be hauling in sewing machines, fabric and quilt batting. The painting groups would have their paints and supplies as well as books and computers.

The two main downstairs bedrooms would each have two twin-size beds each and the bathrooms would be handicap accessible. All downstairs halls and doorways would be wide enough to accommodate wheel chairs. The upstairs would have four large bedrooms, each with their own private bathroom within the room. Each room would accommodate four twin-size beds, lined up in a bunkhouse fashion. Each person would have their own night stand and reading light. Curtains could be drawn between the beds for personal privacy. The downstairs main meeting space would have floor to ceiling windows for lots of natural light for quilters or painters. A separate smaller house would be built off to the back for herself. That way she could turn the entire parsonage house into a bride's dressing space, with plenty of room for the attendants. The retreat house and her home would both be painted a pale buttercream yellow, with green shutters. Just like she had always dreamed.

❧ ☙

The first day of June arrived and *The Wedding Belle* was decorated and ready for Chelsea to walk down the aisle. She had wanted a simple and intimate wedding with just the family and a few select friends. She had not wanted an extravagant show off wedding like many of her friends were throwing. It was such a waste of money, she said. A simple punch and cake reception were all that was needed. However, Marsha insisted that she should at least have some ham and cheese sandwiches with a relish tray and chips. People would need to eat and the nearest restaurant was in Salem. Chelsea agreed to the sandwich idea, since it was simple. Marsha had baked a square three tired white cake accented with yellow and white frosting flowers, and a German Chocolate grooms cake. Chelsea's flowers were yellow and white pom-pom mums with yellow and white daisies. Yellow crepe paper streamers were placed down the center of each table with bud vases of matching daisies and mums.

At Daniel's house, he jokingly told Randy and his groomsmen that he may have to think about building a boarding house for the overnight groomsmen to stay in and save money on renting trailers. He teased Deborah about getting that retreat house completed and ready for guests before there were any more weddings. She reminded him, that he only rented trailers for immediate family. Other guests and wedding parties stayed in the other towns or with their own families. "Besides," she said, "with this wedding, our family members are all married. You shouldn't have to be renting anymore trailers! But yes, future wedding guests could stay at her place, if it wasn't booked for a group."

"Yeah, but from the other people we can collect rent! Think of the money we are losing out on!" replied Daniel.

Daniel stood at the front of the church ready and waiting to perform the nuptials. Randy stood nervously by his side, along with his best man and brother Davey.

Chelsea's dress was a classic column dress of white shiny silk dupioni with a mermaid hem that formed a self- falling train in the back. The hemline mirrored the back draped cowl from her shoulders. The simple lines accented her slim stature as she seemed to float down the aisle, on her father's arm.

The bright blue sky and the sparkling water on the lake made for perfect pictures after the ceremony. Deborah could not have been happier at seeing her youngest son and his new bride begin their new life together. She looked forward to them carrying on their love story, in the dream home that David had built for her so many years ago. Tears rolled down her face as she reminisced about those early days with David.

Daniel put his arm across the back of her shoulders and patted her arm. "It's okay to cry." Deborah rested her head on his chest and smiled.

The second most anticipated wedding that spring, was that of Sam and Beverly. They held the wedding outdoors on the covered deck at the lake. Beverly wore her mother's peasant style dress with the butterfly wing sleeves that were accented with bows and long ribbon streamers that fluttered in the breeze. She wore a wreath of flowers in her free-flowing hair and carried a simple bouquet of wildflowers cut especially for her by Sam, from the church grounds. As her father walked her across the grounds to a waiting Sam and Daniel, he told her she looked very much like the hippie bride that her mother had been forty years earlier. He kissed her cheek and gave her hand to Sam.

Marsha and her Bunco Bakers, as usual, prepared a great wedding feast for the guests. There was plenty of fried chicken, mostaccioli, mashed potatoes and gravy, cole slaw, green beans and corn.

Sam and Beverly had planned to live in Salem in her rent house in town. Sam would commute to work for Deborah and continue to maintain the grounds, as needed. He thought it would be easier for him to do the commuting. He did not want Beverly to drive the winter roads from out in the country to get to the Piggly Wiggly for her cashier job.

However, as a wedding gift, Deborah presented them with a deed for ten acres of her land, along with a sizeable check for them to build a home of their own. They tried to refuse the generous offer, but she insisted. It was the least she could do for the man who saved her life and who had worked tirelessly to help make her own dream come true with *The Wedding Belle*. They all knew a thing or two about what it meant to save a life. Sam and Beverly, reluctantly but graciously, accepted the gift and began to plan for their own dream home together. Deborah also said there would be a job for Beverly at the retreat house, if she wanted to help there, instead of driving to the Piggly Wiggly.

While Sam and Beverly both greatly appreciated Deborah's very generous gift, their most treasured one was delivered by Helen. It was a framed picture of Sam's children, Cooper now eleven years old and Abigail, seven. The note said: Dear Daddy; We love you and miss you. We are very happy that you are well now. Mommy says that we might be able to visit you soon. Love Cooper and Abigail.

"Yes, Son, I have been in constant contact with them and have been keeping Elizabeth informed of your progress. She is happy that you got the help you needed and that you found someone who could give you what she could not. She sends her very best wishes to both of you."

⁂

Annie was not at all happy when she heard about Deborah's wedding gift to Sam and Beverly. "Mother, how could you do that? You are giving everything away! Who did you consult before being so extravagant? It wasn't enough that you just sent Randy and Chelsea on a cruise for their honeymoon! But Sam and Beverly aren't even family!"

Deborah stood firm in her resolve, "Annie, you are forgetting that Sam saved my life! If it weren't for him, I wouldn't even be here today! I can never repay him for all the help he was to me when we were creating *The Wedding Belle*. This was the least I could do. Besides, I don't need all that land for myself and they will both be working at the retreat house when it is completed. I wanted to show them how much I appreciate their help."

Annie still feeling frustrated retorted, "You pay Sam a salary, don't you? And now you'll be paying Beverly a salary, too. Isn't that enough of a thank you?"

"What are you worried about Annie? Afraid there won't be enough money left for you?" Deborah questioned.

"Mother, I can't believe you just said that to me! I am worried about you. Afraid you aren't going to leave enough for yourself. Who is looking out for your best interest? Who is offering you financial advice? Do you discuss these matters with Randy, before you go giving it all away? Or, do you just sit down at your computer now, and transfer money around to everyone? Maybe daddy knew what he was doing, by not teaching you how to do all that on the computer."

"Annie, I am not worried. Besides, *The Wedding Belle* is doing very well on its own, and I don't see why the retreat house won't do the same. Don't worry sweetheart, there will be something for you and the boys too. And yes, I am quite proud of my new-found skills with the computer. I would like to think that your dad would be proud of me, too! Now, I do not want any more talk like this. Even if I were to spend every single cent in my account, it would be MY business, would it not?"

Annie recoiled. Hurt that her mother could not see the money issue from her point of view.

Daniel and his partners were spending endless days preparing for their first real year of working towards making a profit with the Christmas tree farm. They chose the name *Trinity Trees* and a logo with three pine trees grouped together inside a circle. The trunks of the trees were anchored to the bottom of the ring; while the various branches connected to the top and sides to represent their long-term bond as partners. Deborah of course, had a hand in some of their plans. She had Daniel design a modest sized log cabin at the entrance to the tree farm to serve as a gift shop. Local residents would be invited to sell their crafts and other handiworks in the shop on consignment. Jars of apple butter, local honey, and other preserves would fill the shelves on one wall. Homemade baked goods displayed on country cupboards, and holiday wood cut outs and floral arrangements in another area. Off to one side of the room would be a fireplace with a hot chocolate and warm cider bar nearby. Deborah suggested that next year they plant a pumpkin patch and have corn shucks for a complete fall to Christmas operation. Of course, wagon hay rides, bonfires, and sleigh rides in the snow were all activities to be enjoyed during a visit to Trinity Trees.

Daniel responded, "Your ideas never end, do they? Remember, I am also trying to re-build a house. I thought I retired and here you are with more ideas to keep me busy!"

Deborah just laughed and said, "Yeah, But, you love my ideas too!"

After his long days at the tree farm, Daniel spent late hours upgrading Aunt Millie's home to bring it up to code. He was having the home completely rewired and new plumbing installed. He was constantly asking Deborah for her input, on what other upgrades and remodeling should be done. A mudroom was a must, she said, for whenever he came in from the fields, his dirty boots and clothes could be left there. She didn't want dirt tracked all through the house. Even though Daniel had not officially proposed yet, but they both knew the relationship was heading in that direction.

~ ~

Daniel told Deborah to keep her calendar clear for July 25th. He told her he was making special dinner plans for the two of them. They went to a quaint little Italian place on the outskirts of Belleville. It was tucked away off a main road. The dim lights and soft background music were the perfect setting for his proposal. They were seated at an intimate corner table that was secluded by pillars and large planters filled with overgrown palms. Daniel told her that he had been trying to find the right time to do this. He wanted to make sure that everything was perfect. He told her, "I have only done this once before, and I really messed it up, big time. I don't want to mess it up again. I have waited most of my life to find you. I knew from the very beginning that it had to be you, but I also knew that we both needed time to figure out who we were in these new settings. These new lives that we both needed to build for ourselves, before we could merge them into one. I think we are at that point. I hope you agree with me. Today is the one hundredth anniversary of your third great grandfather's ordination as a minister at Grace Bible Church. I would like it to be the day that you agree to be my wife."

She could hardly contain her excitement as Daniel pulled a ring box out of his coat pocket.

Deborah shouted, "Yes, of course, I will marry you! I hope you understand how much this means to me. I never thought I would do this again. I thought I would never find love again after I lost David. I believe God sent you to me. And, I am sure that David would be happy for us, too."

As soon as she was composed and had the ring on her finger, they took turns calling their children and sharing the good news.

❧ ❧

Deborah decided that when the retreat house was finished it would be named *DK's Guest House*, in memory of David and the support he had always given her. No matter how wild and crazy her ideas were. The center would serve as a retreat location for quilters, painters, church groups and family reunions. Daniel and Deborah hoped that it would also serve as a much-needed B&B for guests and family members in town for weddings at *The Wedding Belle*, when not booked for retreats.

Beverly agreed to take care of the guests in the retreat house when it was completed. In the meantime, she would continue to work at the Piggly Wiggly. Sam was promoted to personal assistant to both Daniel and Deborah, helping in any capacity that was needed.

Deborah hired Harold Riley, one of the recently graduated high school boys to live in the basement and be the on-sight security person as well as her photography assistant. He had portrayed Joseph in the Christmas pageant and had been one of the first helpers to prepare the church to become the wedding studio that it is now. Harold had taken an intense interest in her camera work. From the very beginning she had taken him under her wing and had taught him all she knew about the art and he was turning into a very fine assistant.

Daniel and Deborah's wedding was planned to coincide with the October anniversary of the opening of *The Wedding Belle* as a tribute to the rebirth of Grace Bible Church and in memory of Aunt Patsy and her mock wedding to Norm Johnson. If it hadn't been for *The Wedding Belle*, Deborah and Daniel would never have met.

As Annie was helping Deborah get dressed for the ceremony she said, "I have something very special for you to wear today. It will take care of the 'something old' and the 'something borrowed' at the same time." From her bag, Annie pulled out the manila envelope that held the cameo pieces. "I hope you will wear these today. You know it would make your mother very proud if you did. Besides they go perfectly with your dress. Remember, you have always said that, God works in mysterious ways. Aunt Dorothy turning out to be your mother has been very mysterious to all of us, and look where that mystery has brought you. It brought you here to Orchardville and to Daniel."

Deborah cried as she shook her head in agreement and held her hair up, so Annie could clasp the necklace on her.

Phillip arrived to be Daniel's best man and Sam performed the ceremony. Harold recorded the memories using Deborah's cameras with her blessing on his first solo wedding shoot. Jeremy and Jacob served as ushers to greet the guests and show them to their seats. Deborah wore a cream-colored dress with a soft flowing long chiffon skirt that fell into a handkerchief hem. She carried a mixed bouquet of fall colored flowers, as her two sons escorted her down the aisle. Annie served as her mother's matron of honor. Marsha and her 'Bunco Bakers' of course, went above and beyond their normal scope of decorating and taking care of the food. The cake was a replica of the one she had made for Aunt Patsy's mock wedding for the grand opening of *The Wedding Belle*.

Everyone was there from both of their families and all their dear friends. Again, Davey's ex-wife Maria was present. Gary and Andrea could not be happier for them. Gary especially thanked Daniel. He said that David would be pleased with the man who had come along to take his place in taking care of Deborah. Aunt Millie beamed at watching her nephew marry the perfect woman for him. She never thought she would live long enough to witness this day, and she thanked God for letting her.

Norm and Charlie each made toasts to the happy couple and thanked them for what they were doing to preserve and enhance their community for future generations. Norm joked about how he had not wanted to go along with her idea in the beginning. How he could not have imagined people would come out to the middle of a corn field to get married. "That pretty, young lady over there set out to prove me wrong, and she did just that!"

As other toasts were being made, the happy couple received two very special and quite unexpected gifts. Missy announced to Daniel that he was going to be a grandpa and Randy announced to Deborah that she was going to be a grandma again.

Jeremy shouted, "Yeah, we will have two new cousins to take hunting and fishing in a couple of years!"

Jacob said, "And, you know what else Granny? Even though you got married to someone new, we can still call you our DK Granny!"

Deborah smiled at Jacob and looked up towards heaven and said, "Yes, you can. God does indeed work in mysterious ways, doesn't He? Your grandpa once told me that my initials would be DK forever. I guess he knew what he was talking about."

As special as those unexpected gifts were for Daniel and Deborah, the greatest gift, was that Lucy and Bill were both there to share the special day with them. Lucy said there was no way she would ever miss watching her sister get married. She told them their union was brought together by God and she had to be a part of it. Lucy complimented Deborah on how well the cameo jewelry went with her dress. "Annie told me she was going to loan it to you to wear today. Both of our Mother's would be proud of you, Sis. Everything is going to be fine, for all of us."

Deborah agreed with her sister.

୶ ୨ଡ଼

The skilled care facility in Salem called Daniel and told him that they were transporting Miss Millie to the hospital. They urged him to get to the hospital as quickly as he could. When

Deborah and Daniel arrived, Millie was awake and lucid, though her organs were beginning to shut down. They prayed together, talked about the good times and how proud Millie was of Daniel and his accomplishments. Millie spoke directly to Deborah, "I can rest in peace knowing that you will take care of my boy. He has worked his whole life to make sure that I was taken care of and now it is his turn to finally have someone to take care of him. He has not had an easy life, but together we have made it a good one. A part of me wishes I could live long enough to see him become a grandpa, but I am so very grateful that I could see you two get married. Never forget that God brought you two together. Have a good life, both of you!"

They sat with her through the night and as the morning sun broke through the darkness, a new angel was taken to heaven. Millie was buried in the church cemetery with the rest of her family.

❧ ☙

Randy's partner, Douglass Schaeffer, called Deborah and complimented her on the accomplishments of *The Wedding Belle*. He said that he and his wife were very impressed when they had attended Randy's wedding. He said he and his wife were preparing to celebrate their twentieth wedding anniversary in a few months and would like to do something very special.

Deborah said she would be happy to help him put something together. She also recommended that he should contact her friend Gary, at The Davie School Inn, for a romantic get-a-way. He has a beautifully decorated suite, called the Gold Room, complete with a spa tub and fireplace. Gary will also make arrangements for any extras you would like to surprise your wife with; such as chocolates, wine, candles or flowers.

Douglas said he would make those reservations and get back with her to set up the date for their renewal of vows. He said his wife was already looking forward to the anniversary celebration, and now he was looking forward to surprising her with the romantic stay at The Davie School Inn.

※ ※

Norm Johnson called Deborah and asked if she could arrange to have Marsha, Daniel, and Sam get together for meeting. He had some business he would like to discuss with them.

Deborah made the necessary phone calls and arrangements to meet at her house. Of course, Charlie showed up too, with food.

Norm started the conversation, "I'm sure all of you are wondering why I called you here today. Miss Deborah, you know I resisted your ideas when you first brought them to us, especially with you being so sneaky and not telling us it was you wanting to buy our church," he said with wink and a nod in Deborah's direction. "You know I was against a lot of change coming to our little town, and I must say you have respected our wishes. While we have seen some major changes that have brought many strangers here; we haven't had any problems. The ideas that you brought and shared with Sam, Marsha, and Daniel have also brought jobs to our townsfolk who wanted and needed them. You have taken some of our young people, like Harold Riley, under your wing and taught him a skill that he might never have realized if you had not come along. To quote your dear Aunt Patsy who always said, 'God will provide,' and he did when He brought you to us."

"Which brings me to the real reason, I asked all of you here. I am the oldest living member of this town. Some people like to say, I am older than dirt! Born and raised here. I've known everyone who has ever been through here. Miss Patsy and Dorothy and I were close knit friends ever since we were all knee-high to a grasshopper, and remained so, all our lives. Almost everyone is gone now, except me and Charlie, here. Except, he is a few years younger yet!" You know I thought very highly of your Aunt Patsy and for a few years, I was sweet on her and thought I would marry her, but instead she married your Uncle Floyd. That surprised all of us when they up and got married. I used to think I had a chance of making her my wife until Floyd Fitzgerald decided to join the Army and Patsy wanted him to know he had a reason to come back home. I went on and married my dear sweet Henrietta. We had good lives and all of us remained good friends. I must say though, that mock wedding you dreamed up for your opening of *The Wedding Belle*, was like a dream come true for me. I know it was all pretend, but I did get to finally marry my first special girl after all."

"I want to pass the torch for this town's well-being on to all of you sitting here at this table today. Deborah and Marsha, I don't know what your plans are for Patsy's house and land that she left to you two, and I know neither one of you needs the house to live in, so I'm sure at some point you will consider selling it. All I ask is that you do not sell it to some big box store or chain hotel. That is a prime piece of property sitting at the crossroads of highway 161 and highway 6. Two highly traveled roads. It will one day be an ideal spot for something big that would then forever change the dynamics of our town. I know I can't stop progress, and it is coming, I know it. But please do not be taken in by any of the big boys out there that will completely, and forever, alter our community."

Everyone sat in silence as Norm preached his wishes for the town. Then, almost simultaneously, everyone was talking at once. Coming up with ideas and suggestions. Of course, they wanted the same things that Norm had wanted from the very beginning.

Daniel was the first to suggest they consider a small boarding house or inn, so that wedding guests had a place to stay in town, instead of going somewhere else, like Salem, Cisne or Flora. Sam said they needed a country diner so that people had a place to eat too. "No offense to Charlie there, but you do have your hands full with the store, and townsfolk who will always stop into your place to meet up with friends. We need a real sit-down kind of restaurant for people visiting or passing through.

As they continued to discuss ideas it became clear what direction they would be heading with Patsy's property. Marsha suggested that since they had all of Aunt Patsy's cookbooks and hand written recipe cards, that they use them for *"Patsy's Kountry Kitchen",* or maybe *"Patsy's Place."* A small inn with only fifteen to twenty rooms would be sufficient to accommodate any wedding party that came to town.

Daniel said, "Also with having the inn and restaurant, when people came out to the tree farm they could make a full day of being in the country and spend the night at the inn, have a good hearty breakfast in the morning before heading home."

They all agreed that it sounded like a reasonable plan while protecting the integrity and history of their town. Norm was delighted that the next generation would be building a legacy for future generations of Orchardville and preserving its history as well.

Deborah reminded everyone that such an undertaking would require lots of help from people who were willing to work hard. She said that everyone sitting around this table were already stretched to the limits of what they could do themselves, they would have to look beyond this room for managers and other staffing needs.

Marsha added, "It is going to take quite a few people to run a restaurant and an inn. There should be jobs for anyone in town who wants or needs one."

Everyone agreed, that lots of help would be needed to manage and run *The Crossroads Inn*!

Your review of this story on AMAZON.com or Goodreads.com is greatly appreciated!
Thank you!
Carolyn

ABOUT THE AUTHOR

Searching for Something Special is the debut novel for the author. It is a fictional story based on a few childhood memories of her grandparents Southern Illinois farming community, combined with the struggles of grief and moving forward, following her mother's death in 2014. Her previous publication, *The Alzheimer's Roller Coaster; The Story of Our Ride,* (2013) was a personal journal account of the first ten years with her mother during their journey through Alzheimer's disease. The final two years and beyond will be written when the time is right. Mers' was also a contributing author for *Chicken Soup for Soul, 101 Stories of Living with Alzheimer's and Other Dementias (2013), and a short story in the anthology A Dark and Stormy Night.* She enjoyed this venture into fiction and is looking forward to writing more stories from the heart.

Made in the USA
Columbia, SC
21 November 2017